COLD CASE ON THE MOOR

A gripping Yorkshire murder mystery

RIC BRADY

THE BOOK FOLKS

Published by The Book Folks

London, 2024

This book is a work of fiction. Names, characters, businesses, organizations, places and events are either the product of the author's imagination or are used fictitiously. Any resemblance to actual persons, living or dead, events or locales is entirely coincidental. The spelling is British English.

ISBN 978-1-80462-187-5

www.thebookfolks.com

COLD CASE ON THE MOOR is the fifth standalone mystery in The Yorkshire detective mystery series by Ric Brady. The full list of titles, in order of publication, is as follows:

MURDER ON A YORKSHIRE MOOR
BUTCHER ON THE MOOR
MISSING ON ILKLEY MOOR
DETECTIVE ON THE MOOR
COLD CASE ON THE MOOR

More details can be found at the back of this book.

Chapter One

A dog walker found the body at 7.30 a.m. on Thursday morning. Former DCI Henry Ward didn't hear about it until the local news did a short segment at the end of the morning bulletin.

The announcement was short and only a few sentences. "Just coming in from Swinfeld Reservoir near Otley," the news anchor said, "there's news of a body being found. The reservoir up there has been in the news recently as people have been visiting its drowned village, currently visible during this long drought. We'll have more on that at lunchtime. Now, time for the weather, and what more can you tell us about this drought, Paul…"

Henry switched off the TV to think. The local news anchor had looked mildly excited as he spoke, as if he'd recently been to the drowned village with his kids and had fond memories of it. Or perhaps, Henry wondered, he was just excited about having a mysterious death to talk about. Journalists always liked tittle-tattle, especially when murder was involved.

However, Henry couldn't share the news anchor's apparent joy. He was sitting in his armchair in front of the television, cup of tea in hand, and Tessa, his wire fox terrier, was on the sofa opposite. She'd been slowly gearing herself up for another uneventful day. The living-room window was open, letting in the sounds and smells of the late summer and the fumes from the traffic on Main Street.

Henry placed his cup on the occasional table, next to the plate on which he'd eaten his toast. Crumbs still spread about it. He rubbed his unshaven chin and considered the news report.

"She's finally turned up," he said to Tessa, who replied with a bleary stare.

Henry had waited for this day to come for fifteen years, and now it'd arrived. It'd taken so long he'd almost forgotten about it. But his memory had been refreshed recently when the local news had shown images of the drowned village underneath Swinfeld.

Muddy stones and bits of drystone wall that looked like scenery from a low-budget dystopian horror. And calling it a drowned 'village' was a stretch. It was a small hamlet at best. A few farmhouses that dated back to before the Victorian era. Farmers who'd been booted off their land so their homes could be flooded to supply the people of Bradford and Leeds with fresh water.

Swinfeld Reservoir had been built after the war, using up a large swathe of land that stretched from the property lines of an old tycoon's estate to the forest on the other side of the valley. It was a nice walk if you took the paths around the water, and it came to about four miles in all. Fir trees and evergreens surrounded the embankments, which were made of old stone and weren't normally visible.

But they were today.

Maureen Villers, aged thirty-one, had decided to walk around that reservoir fifteen years ago and had been missing ever since. She'd taken her dog, Polly, which was found later that day. The dog's lead was still attached to her collar, and it appeared she'd spent most of her time looking for her owner.

It'd been mid-spring, and the weather was miserable. It had rained for weeks, and as Maureen wasn't known for hiking, her decision to go out and walk around the reservoir was considered an oddity. Especially when she'd taken time off work to do it.

It was 2008, before the worst of the financial crisis, though there had been a taster of what was to come when Northern Rock went belly up the year before. But at that time, people still had some hope about them. As Maureen went missing in suspicious circumstances, Henry was brought in as detective chief inspector to manage a small team working out of Otley police station. They were good; the detective sergeant he'd selected personally. It was going to be a difficult one.

First, they didn't have a body, so they lacked the most vital piece of evidence. Second, Maureen's husband was a police constable.

Tim Villers was a good cop and looked the part with his cleft chin, broad jaw, dark curly hair, and bright blue eyes. Resembling Clark Kent so much, his colleagues at Otley called him 'Kent'.

But this 'Kent', despite his heroic appearance, was a plausible suspect, given that he was the husband of the presumed deceased. However, with Tim's impeccable record and good reputation, he was never a serious suspect.

Henry's team thought someone else might have attacked Maureen and dumped her body in the reservoir while she was out walking. But random 'stranger' attacks in the area were so rare, they couldn't realistically consider it as an option.

And that was assuming she was dead. They didn't know that at the time, as her body had never been found and all the divers sent down into the dark depths of Swinfeld came up empty-handed. They claimed the drowned village and its ruins made a thorough search too treacherous.

There was also the receipt for an open-ended plane ticket for Canada, which had been paid for with cash and was in Maureen's name. Then, a few weeks after her disappearance, card payments on her credit card were made outside of Toronto.

So, the general view was that she ran off to live in Canada and start a new life, leaving her two young children and husband in Baildon, where they had a modest detached house. Henry's team was disbanded after a month of little to no results despite its large expenses. Those divers didn't come cheap, Henry recalled.

The files and case notes got boxed up and archived, and Henry was moved onto something else. He couldn't think what, as he sat in his chair. Possibly another murder inquiry.

But this case had stuck with him, as it didn't add up. Those card payments in Canada struck him as being odd. They'd only been a couple and then there were none ever since. All trace of Maureen had disappeared, but despite Henry's insistence her case be reopened, it was marked as a missing person's case and left on the pile, never to be touched again.

But the truth, just as Henry had always suspected, was that Maureen Villers had never left England, and had been in Swinfeld Reservoir the whole time.

And whoever murdered her had gotten away with it, until this dry spell had recently drained this normally wet county of its water. Then, when the walls of that drowned village emerged out of the mud, the body the killer hoped had been forgotten was exposed for all to see.

* * *

Henry didn't bother waiting, he got his phone and called Detective Inspector Kate Barnes. He wasn't expecting her to answer as he presumed she'd have been scrambled from police headquarters in Wakefield and would now be on the banks of Swinfeld with Forensics, trying to make sense of everything.

Come to think of it, Henry thought, attempting to get evidence from the bottom of an empty reservoir was going to be a bloody nightmare.

As he expected, Barnes didn't answer, and his call went to her voicemail. He didn't leave a message. Feeling energised, he strode up and down his small kitchen in his slippers and dressing gown.

He knew the cliché that there were 'some cases that never left you', but for him, the death of Maureen Villers really was one. There had been others throughout the years that had got to him, which had scarred him mentally, physically, or both. But this was the case he had thought about most often since retiring eleven years ago. Especially as this dry spell had got worse and worse.

The kitchen's back door was open, and the air was thick with heat and energy. It felt like a storm was needed later that day to clear it. The potted plants in his backyard were browning and distressed, but he wasn't allowed to water them due to the hosepipe ban.

Well, he had considered getting up at 5 a.m. and watering them discretely, but he reckoned his neighbour, Jean Whitehead, would still catch him red-handed. Most likely she'd be staring through her bedroom window with her phone out to film him. She'd enjoy dobbing in a retired police detective to the water company.

Henry stuck his head into the yard, hoping to hear if Jean was beyond the wall that separated his from hers, but he couldn't hear her. Mildly surprised she hadn't already come round to ask him about the body in the reservoir, he decided he'd best get showered and changed. And a quick shave wouldn't go amiss, he thought, scratching his chin.

He was halfway up the stairs when DI Barnes rang, and he answered without hesitation.

"I suppose you're at Swinfeld?" he asked.

"No. On my way," she replied.

It sounded like she was in a car moving at speed. He guessed she had the blue lights flashing.

"Who are you with?"

"On my own at the minute. They wanted a DI on scene to organise the uniforms. An MIT is being set up as we speak."

"Right. Will they keep you in the major inquiry team?"

"I presume so. Otherwise, I guess they would have sent someone else." She scoffed. "If they had anyone else. Saying that, have you heard?"

"Heard what?"

"They've made Hargreaves a Detective Sergeant."

Henry rolled his eyes in disdain. Hargreaves was Detective Superintendent Murphy's pet. Murphy, Henry's old partner turned rival, was the worst sort of copper. The backroom-dealing, quasi-corrupt kind, who would jump to indignation when the opportunity arose. Murphy's sort really did deserve the vitriol the force received. Though Henry didn't know who controlled whom in that relationship.

"Well, I'm glad she passed the sergeants' exam," Henry said. "I suppose she's only a few years away from claiming your job."

"Yeah, well. She can bloody have it."

Sensing the bitterness in her voice, which Henry thought was unlike Barnes, he moved the topic on. "So, what do you know about Maureen Villers?"

She sighed. "I know I don't have the mental capacity for a history lesson."

He heard her punch the horn and swear at someone on the road.

"Right," he said, sensing he was getting on her nerves as well. "Shall I leave you?"

"You can." Then she asked, "Do you really think it's her? This Villers?"

"Well." He paused. "It could be someone else, but I can't remember anyone else going missing around that area in recent years." He took a breath, trying to calm his frazzled nerves. "It could be a kid who drowned while swimming or a suicide, something like that."

"Nah, that's all been discounted. The body had been tied up and weighed down."

"Right. I guess that explains why they want a DI on scene."

"Yep, and that's not the worst of it. She's missing a leg."

"I beg your pardon?"

Barnes exhaled again as if trying to manage her anger. "You heard. Left leg missing."

"What the…" Henry couldn't start to comprehend what had happened there. "An animal? Fish? Something in the water?" He couldn't think what. West Yorkshire wasn't known for its alligators.

"I don't know." She beeped her horn again and swore loudly at another innocent road user. "Look, I'll have to go. There are too many dickheads on the road today."

She cut off the call.

Henry leant against the wall of his staircase, one foot on the higher step as if he'd been frozen climbing the stairs.

"Leg missing?" he asked himself. "What the hell does that mean?"

Chapter Two

Henry parked his Skoda Octavia in the car park near Swinfeld Reservoir. The area was meant for water company engineers but was mostly used by hikers. Marked police cars were already there, and Henry thought he spotted Barnes's black BMW among them. Taking the last available space, he got Tessa out of the back and attached the lead to her collar.

She was raring to go and pulled him towards the walking path, like a sniffer dog leading to a crime. But Henry knew full well that she was following the scent of a Labrador that'd just passed and neither of them would be allowed near the real crime scene.

Not that they weren't allowed to stand at a distance and watch.

The embankments of the reservoir were steep on one end and curved on the other. The dam was on the far end, with a small tower built into it, from which the water company's engineers could look out onto the expanse of water. Though, that water wasn't there today. Instead, they'd look out at a wide crater in the landscape.

Lumps of the buildings that had once formed the hamlet were visible, encrusted in sludge and drying algae. Dark pools of what was left of the water filled deep parts of the basin, but it wasn't enough to quench the thirst of the nearby cities.

Henry wondered when the rain would come back and fill in this mud-caked void.

Blue police tape shook in the breeze, and the path across the other side of the reservoir had been cordoned off. Figures stood around in a group too far away for Henry to make out. He led Tessa to a bench under the shade of some tall fir trees and took out his trusty binoculars.

He spotted SOCOs in white suits descending into the reservoir using ropes and pulleys. That lot were always ingenious at accessing difficult crime scenes, Henry thought.

He spotted Barnes on the path on the top of the embankment, wearing a light-blue blouse and dark trousers. The breeze failed to ruffle her short blonde hair. Her large designer sunglasses scanned the scene, taking in SOCO officers sliding around in the mud, before turning to a large man wearing a dark suit. Henry didn't recognise this detective. His shoulders were huge, almost weightlifter-size, and he looked to be older than Barnes.

Focusing his binoculars on the drowned village, Henry made out the forensic officers' white plastic suits moving between the mud-slicked relics. The walls had crumbled over the decades. From the look of it, the rotting brickwork didn't like being out in the fresh air. They had become accustomed to being submerged.

Tessa pulled at her lead beside him, giving him a look that suggested she'd signed up for a walk, not to sit around while he spied on crime scenes.

Ignoring her, he zoomed in on the drowned village again but couldn't see any sign of the body. He did however spot a white tent. SOCO must have erected it to preserve the scene. Knowing he wasn't going to see much else, he pocketed his binoculars and got up from the bench. Tessa was so happy she yapped.

As he walked Tessa along the path under the shade of nearby trees, he thought about the original inquiry. It'd gone well, all things considered. He had done his best, pursued every avenue that came up, kept an eye on the budget – though, he had to admit that back in 2008, budgets weren't as much of an issue. He doubted he'd get away with spending what he had then on finding a missing woman in the austerity years that followed. But luckily, he left the police before budgets were cut to the bone.

He kicked a pebble off the walking path and into the crater, and it skimmed off a stone sticking out of the silt.

So, she'd been here all this time, he thought. He'd guessed as much. Maureen Villers had either been in this reservoir or was dead and buried elsewhere. He'd always doubted the Canada thing was real. She had no links to the place.

As for Tim Villers, he never thought his wife was dead. He was adamant she was alive and believed she'd fled to Canada, despite not fully knowing why she'd run off there. He could never fully explain why he thought his wife had left him. Their marriage had been good, she enjoyed her job as the head of finance at a small cosmetics company in Leeds, and loved their two children – a son and a daughter. Henry guessed they would be in their late twenties now.

He remembered their sad, confused little faces and felt for them. They chose to believe their father's nonsense that their mother had abandoned them. Which was probably preferable to believing she'd been violently killed and dumped in a reservoir.

And to be fair, Henry couldn't blame them.

The groan of heavy machinery disturbed the calmness around the empty reservoir. Blackbirds fluttered off the higher branches of a fir tree.

Henry pulled out his binoculars to watch the activity at the far end. A large white vehicle reversed down the walking path, and the detectives and SOCO officers moved out of its way. The vehicle had a large yellow crane arm with a platform attached to its end.

"Looks like Barnes is about to go into the deep end," Henry said to Tessa, who gave him a confused glance – as if asking what business that was of theirs.

* * *

Henry waited a few minutes and watched the scene unfold across the empty void of the reservoir, until his phone buzzed in his pocket. He saw it was Barnes and answered.

"Aye?"

"Where are you?" she asked, sounding even more annoyed than she had earlier.

"Erm…" He paused. "Just out walking Tessa." Using his binoculars, he looked over in her direction and saw her large sunglasses glaring back.

"What the hell do you think you're doing?" she asked.

"I'm keeping an eye on things."

"Would you mind getting out of here?"

"Well, it's a free country."

"Listen," she said, lowering her voice. "You might think I'll be giving you titbits of information on this case and let you swan in and do whatever you like, but I won't. Not this time."

Henry had heard her say that before. "Right. I bet."

"It's true. I'm not on this MIT."

"You what?"

Henry felt the wind leave his sails. He couldn't believe it. Barnes hadn't been chosen for the major inquiry team? Watching her in his binoculars, he saw her give him a big wave and then leave in the direction of the car park.

"Where are you going?" he asked.

"I've been selected for another MIT in Leeds. A double murder that took place last night. Mother and child both killed. No suspect, apart from the boyfriend."

"Right," Henry said. He could see why Barnes's expertise might be better placed in that kind of investigation. And a new double-murder case took precedence over a fifteen-year-old one. "So, who's leading this investigation?" he asked, knowing that the investigative team had to be led by a detective inspector or detective chief inspector.

"The new guy. Hired from Manchester. You've probably seen him in your binoculars."

Henry focused in on the large man. He had short red hair, looked to be in his early forties, and his broad shoulders hung over his large body.

"What's he called?"

"Acton. He's a DCI."

Henry had never heard the name, but the fact he was a DCI was good news, as it meant Detective Superintendent Murphy was taking this seriously. If he weren't, Henry figured Murphy would have selected a DI to go through the motions and then close everything down after a week. Though he wouldn't put it past Murphy to do the same anyway.

"Is he any good?"

"I've not worked with him. But I've heard good things." She was nearly at the car park now, and Henry trained his binoculars at DCI Acton, who was talking to some SOCO officers.

"Shall I go introduce myself?" Henry asked.

"Do what you like. I'd be careful, though. He's a bit blunt."

"Blunt?"

"He is a Mancunian after all." Then she added, "I thought you Yorkshire folk didn't get on with the people over the Pennines."

"Aye, we don't normally. We've still not forgiven them for the War of the Roses."

"Who won that by the way?"

"We did… I think. Or that's what I tell people when they ask."

"But weren't the Tudors on the Lancastrian side?"

"Well, sort of. But they cheated at the end. I think… So technically we won. Anyway, we put our differences aside when dealing with southerners."

Barnes scoffed down the phone.

Henry knew she didn't like being reminded she came from London. He let her go after she started complaining about a wasted journey, and decided to head over to the police cordon to see who this Acton was.

He walked Tessa around the whole reservoir to reach the cordoned area. A uniformed officer eyed them up when they were twenty feet away and eventually spoke when they were within six.

"This is a crime scene. This area's off limits to the public."

That didn't stop Henry, and when he and Tessa reached the blue police tape, he asked, "Can I speak to DCI Acton, please?"

The young uniformed officer's face flushed with frustration. "Did you not just hear me? I said–"

"I heard you, so did the dog, but we chose to ignore you as I want to speak to DCI Acton."

The officer's head trembled, making Henry worry his helmet might wobble off. "Get back from here or I will push you back!" he said, turning nasty.

Henry looked down at the blue tape an inch away from his waist. "I'm not sure if you can tell, but you can only touch me should I cross this line. And as you can see, I've not crossed it."

The officer seemed ready to push him anyway, and Henry spotted DCI Acton over his shoulder and shouted his name.

Appearing confused, the large man halted and spun around to eyeball Henry. He approached, looking mildly pissed off.

"No press yet. We don't know what we've found," he said, in a breathless Mancunian drawl.

"I'm not a journalist." Henry held out his hand for Acton to shake. "I'm former DCI Henry Ward. I led the original investigation into Maureen Villers' disappearance."

Acton peered at Henry's hand before glaring at the uniformed officer, as if demanding to know why Henry was there. But after getting nothing from the officer, he gave Henry's hand a perfunctory shake.

"You probably shouldn't be here," he said, keeping his voice low. He patted his black suit jacket and produced a pack of cigarettes from his inside pocket. He offered Henry one, which was declined, and lit up.

His dark-red hair was cut short and greying in place. His jawline was wide, with his neck even wider. Frown lines around his eyes suggested he was perennially annoyed, and his pale skin was marked with red freckles that were the same colour as his hair. Despite looming over Henry, he had a calm and delicate energy about him.

Blowing out smoke, he gestured for the uniformed officer to get out of earshot. "Look, I'm not sure why you're here. You retired?" Acton asked.

"Eleven years."

He nodded his understanding. "And this was the case that you were always thinking about or some shit like that?"

Henry cleared his throat. "Well… not exactly."

Acton sucked in smoke. "Listen. I can't have you anywhere near this. Any evidence obtained could be ruled inadmissible if the defence learn you've been hanging around. Which I'm sure I don't need to tell you? Right?"

Henry nodded.

"So, I ask myself again. Why are you here? 'cause all you'll do is mess up my case. And I don't want it messed up, thank you very much."

"I suppose you'll want to talk to me," Henry said, his voice suddenly weak. "To learn what I know about the original inquiry?"

"I'll find most of that out when I read your case notes, if you left good ones – which, to be fair, I think you did, as I've heard good things about you." He sniffed. "I've also heard some bad, but I think that's mostly bullshit. I find it unlikely a detective who's done good his whole career suddenly turns rotten at the end. And as I always say, people only get battle scars if they go into battle, am I right?" He grinned, showing tar-marked teeth.

Henry smiled as he agreed, but really he wondered which battles this Acton had been scarred by.

"Anyway. You'd best skedaddle with your mutt while I try to figure out who killed this lass." He bent his large frame over to pat Tessa on the head, who seemed to welcome it.

"You think it could be her, then? You think it's Maureen Villers?"

Acton looked in the direction of the mud-filled basin. "Right now, I know as much as you do. But if you don't mind," he said, lobbing his spent cigarette over the police line so it landed next to Henry's shoe, "I'd best find this killer. And no thanks to you, he's had a fifteen-year head start."

Looking over his huge shoulder, he gave Henry a knowing wink, as if he was just joshing.

But behind Acton's cheeky smile, Henry didn't sense much humour.

Chapter Three

Addingham Main Street had plenty of parking spots available. It was mid-August. Summer holiday season. Henry suspected a few of the cottages next to his own would be empty while their owners were away, sunning it up in the South of France or wherever. Pulling up in front of his cottage, he looked at next door but one and suspected it was unoccupied. He hadn't seen the middle-aged couple who lived in it for over a week.

Saying that, Henry knew that August meant the holiday-let properties would be full, and there were more and more of them in Addingham these days. He feared that in the future, the village would just be full of holiday cottages. A few crusty pensioners, too stubborn to move, would hang on until the very end – possibly including him, if he made it that long. In the winters, the whole place would be a ghost town. He hoped that wouldn't be the case. Villages like Addingham had to be lived in and not become a holiday resort.

Henry got Tessa out of the back of his Skoda and led her through his front gate. He'd been mulling over what DCI Acton had said to him on his drive back from the reservoir. While he couldn't blame him for sending him away, Henry had hoped to be involved in the inquiry a little bit. He had managed the original one, after all.

He wanted to needle Barnes for information, but she'd been put on another investigation. He then realised that move had probably been intentional. Murphy would have known Henry would be interested in Maureen Villers' case and tap Barnes for info, so he had probably put a stop to it before it could begin.

Oh well. "Them's the breaks." He sighed, wondering which well-known idiot had recently used that phrase.

Glancing over at his neighbour's home, he couldn't tell if Jean was in. He hadn't seen her that day, and come to think of it, he last saw her the previous morning. That wasn't like her, he thought. Getting slightly concerned, he ushered Tessa through his front door and then headed over to Jean's.

It took three knocks before she answered, and she poked her head through a two-inch gap. A surgical mask covered her lower face, her eyes were bleary and red. And, to Henry's surprise, she wasn't wearing make-up. He didn't think he'd ever seen her like that. Her hair wasn't done, and she was in her dressing gown at 11 a.m.

"Alright?" he asked, stepping up to the door to get a better look through the gap.

"I've got COVID," she whispered with a hoarse voice. "Tested positive last night."

"How?" Henry said, instinctively taking a step back.

"Grandchildren."

Henry recalled she'd looked after her second son's kids earlier in the week.

"Want me to fetch you some shopping or anything?"

She shook her head while coughing, covering her mouth despite her face mask. "I'll be fine."

"Don't be silly. Text me what you want, and I'll get–"

"No, Henry! You've got really bad asthma. I don't want you getting it."

Henry rolled his eyes. She's always playing the martyr, he thought. But, while his asthma wasn't that bad, he had done his best to avoid the virus so far. "The offer's there if you need it."

She nodded her thanks. "I'll give you a bell tomorrow or something."

"Aye, and if you need anything–"

"I won't be calling you!"

"No," Henry said, chuckling. "Call your bloody son. It's his fault you caught it."

* * *

Back in his cottage, he went up to his spare bedroom where he kept his ageing Apple computer. He had to move a few cardboard boxes to get into the room and tossed them onto the single bed that was never used. Taking a pile of clothes in need of ironing out of the desk chair, he placed them next to the boxes so he could sit down.

Hoping the computer would show signs of life, he turned it on. He hadn't used it for a few months and hoped it still worked. Its large silver screen flickered to life, and he was set.

Logging onto his profile, he went to the documents folder. When wrapping up the original investigation into Maureen Villers' disappearance, he'd asked one of his detective constables, DC Emsley, to get him a copy of all the case files.

Henry didn't make a habit of taking confidential information from the police, but he knew this case might raise its ugly head in the future. And while taking information home was frowned upon, holding onto it shouldn't get him into too much bother. Anyway, he'd been right that Maureen would turn up at some point, hadn't he?

DC Emsley did what Henry had asked without question, always an obedient officer, and while Henry was expecting ring binders full of case notes, photos, statements, and transcripts, what he got was a thin USB stick. Henry hadn't been happy with that at the time, but now, as he removed it from the drawer in his antique desk, he could see the benefit of it. If only for it saving on storage space.

Sticking the flash drive into his computer, he opened its files and started reading. He had reviewed these files once since he left the force, only to arrange them better. They contained interview transcripts, photos, statements, task lists, and everything else he'd need to solve this case. Some CCTV footage of the area around Swinfeld Reservoir existed, as the reservoir was near one of the water company's processing sites. However, Henry had no idea where that VHS tape was. Probably inside one of the many archive buildings West Yorkshire Police had around the county.

The first thing he did was click on the photos folder and select the image used on the missing-person poster. Maureen Villers had long, curly brown hair that reached her shoulders. She was tall, slim, and had a handsome face. Smiling at the camera, her bright brown eyes sparkled. In the background, there were pink rainforest plants. Her husband had explained the photo was taken at the botanical gardens in Leeds. She appeared happy, comfortable, and content with her lot.

Henry clicked on the personal notes about the case that he had kept when he was the lead investigator. He took a notepad and pen from the desk and started scribbling down things that stood out to him.

Maureen's husband, Tim Villers, had been questioned twice, first on his own and then with a Police Federation rep by his side. Tim hadn't been under caution at any point but was worried he might get blamed for his wife's disappearance, as he had an inkling as to how police investigations worked. It was normally assumed that the partner or a family member was involved, only because, in the vast majority of cases, they were.

There hadn't been many other suspects. Her work colleagues had been questioned. The company where Maureen had worked – Leeds Luxe Cosmetics – had folded in the financial crisis that overwhelmed the economy later in

2008. It ended up having more debt than clients; a sorry state of affairs that afflicted many companies that year.

Henry had been interested in its managing director, Shelley Peters, and her husband, Arnold. She ran the company, while he was a major shareholder. His income came from gambling on the stock markets, and Henry doubted he'd fared well in the recession.

Maureen had a strong working relationship with Shelley, however. The two spoke to each other all day, every day, and Shelley had been devastated by Maureen's disappearance.

Looking through his case notes, Henry couldn't see any more suspects. As the case was never confirmed as a murder, due to them not finding the body, the focus had shifted onto Canada. Despite Henry thinking it wasn't a very realistic possibility.

The receipt for the open-ended plane ticket to Toronto showed it had been purchased on 8 April 2008. Two days before Maureen went missing.

DC Emsley had tracked down the small travel agency in Bradford where the ticket had been purchased. Long since closed down, the agency said a woman had bought it with five hundred pounds in cash. They couldn't give much detail, only saying a woman who roughly matched Maureen's description came in to reserve the flight. They didn't have CCTV inside or outside, so there was no footage of her.

After hitting that dead end, having spent a considerable amount of public money on several detectives and three dives into the reservoir, the investigation was wound up.

Henry's notes ended with his short summary, written in 2008.

> *Not sure if this will end well. My money is on Maureen being at the bottom of Swinfeld, but only time will tell if she rises back up.*

"How right I'd been," he said to Tessa, who'd stuck her head through the door to see why he was using the computer.

His phone vibrated in his pocket, and he pulled it out. The number came up as Tim Villers. Henry had kept his number all these years and hadn't changed his own. Hesitating, he wondered why the hell Tim was ringing, before answering to find out.

"Ward?" Tim said, sounding tense.

"Mr Villers. How are you?"

"You've heard?"

"Aye. I have."

"I didn't do it. You know that?"

Henry leaned back in his chair, scanning what he'd scribbled down on his notepad and seeing a thick circle around Tim Villers' name. "I'm not investigating this anymore. I'm retired."

"Aye. I heard. But I need your help."

"What…?" Henry shook his head. "Listen, Villers. Seriously, what do you need me for?"

"They'll be coming after me. Like you nearly did."

"I never came after you. I just had to eliminate you from the inquiry. You know what it's like."

"Aye, I do. But you, I could trust you – just about. This Acton… Well, I've heard stuff."

"What stuff?" Henry asked, not bothering to pretend he didn't know who Acton was.

"He likes easy results. Doesn't push things past the obvious, like you did. He's an 'if the shoe fits' kind of bloke, and he'll try to fit it on me." He went quiet a moment, as if he didn't have full privacy. "Look. Can we meet?"

"I…" Henry didn't know what to say. He'd already been bollocked for trying to stick his nose into the investigation. Meeting with a possible suspect would only make things worse. "I don't think that's such a good idea."

"I didn't kill her, Ward. And I can prove it."

"Right. And how can you do that?"

"I know why she went to the reservoir that day."

"How?"

"Meet me. Ilkley Park. In one hour."

"How do–?" The phone line went dead.

He looked at Tessa, who was sitting by his desk chair, looking up at him.

"Well, that was unexpected." He placed the phone on his desk and raised an eyebrow at the dog, who seemed to have sensed another walk was on the cards. "In your dreams," he said. "The last thing I need when meeting a possible murder suspect is you dragging me about."

Tessa cocked an eyebrow back at him, sensing he hadn't said no.

Chapter Four

Of course Henry had to bring the dog. He wouldn't have heard the end of it otherwise. Tessa ran towards the grass, pulling Henry along behind her as he didn't want her off her lead. They headed to Ilkley Park, following the path that cut through the central lawn. The River Wharfe was on one side, with a few bathers braving the possible sewage in the water, and the centre of Ilkley was on the other.

The sun shone down, and Henry squinted at it as he pulled at the collar of his blue and white chequered shirt. It was going to be another hot day, he thought. He considered getting lunch at the riverside café near the car park after meeting Villers. He might even venture out and get an ice cream. It was definitely the weather for it.

He spotted a lone figure sitting on a bench under a cherry blossom tree.

As Tessa yanked him closer, he recognised the lonesome figure as Tim Villers.

Tim stared blankly into the distance with a lit cigarette held close to his lips. He wasn't smoking it. Instead, he just held it between his fingers as its smoke wafted into his face. He hadn't aged much over the years, he'd done better than Henry, and could still pass for a Clark Kent. Though possibly a more mature one, Henry had to admit. Tim's curly hair was still there, with locks hanging lazily over his forehead. Grey tinted his sideburns and was peppered throughout the rest of his curls.

He glanced at Henry and tossed the unsmoked cigarette onto the walking path, stamping it out with his boot. He wore dark jeans that covered the tops of his leather boots and a dark-red T-shirt. While he wasn't as in shape as he'd been fifteen years ago, he didn't look bad for a man in his late forties. His beer gut was hardly noticeable.

"Thanks for coming," he said, huffing. He appeared to be in pain, wearing a disdainful expression, like he'd eaten something rotten.

"No bother," Henry said, guiding Tessa towards the bench so he could sit down. She sniffed at the half-burnt cigarette, and Henry tugged her away.

"So, how are you doing?" Henry asked.

Tim's pained grimace didn't lift. "How do you think?"

Henry couldn't begin to imagine, so he instead asked, "And the kids?"

"Fine. Well, I've not told them yet. I've got to do that later today so they can announce Maureen's name in the press."

"Ah," Henry said, not envying him. "How are they getting on?"

"Not bad," Tim said, cheering up slightly. "Paul went to uni, now he's an IT fella in Leeds. Siobhan is doing a master's in Cambridge."

"Cambridge?" Henry repeated, impressed.

"Aye." Fatherly pride briefly replaced his suffering. "She got into Durham for her degree, missing out at Oxford, but Cambridge took her in for her master's. Mathematics, if you can believe it. Just like her mum. Always had a head for numbers." His blank stare returned, as did his grimace.

"So, you'll be expecting them back in Baildon?"

He shook his head. "I moved seven years ago. Live here now."

"In Ilkley?"

He nodded. "Remarried seven years ago." He cleared his throat, as if he still wasn't comfortable admitting he'd moved on from Maureen. "Listen. I know this Acton will be on at me."

"Have you heard from him?"

"Not yet. But it's a matter of time. I'm the desk sergeant at Otley station now. I know there've been uniforms all over the reservoir. I was organising it this morning, until I was told to get lost and take a personal day." He huffed. "God knows if they'll let me in tomorrow. This is just the beginning of it."

"Hang about, Villers. You know they can't let you be anywhere near the investigation. We both know Acton will want to talk to you. You were her husband."

"I know," he said, sounding as though he wished otherwise. "It's just… I thought all that was over."

"Well, it's not."

Tessa barked at Henry, wondering why they were sitting in the park when she wanted to run off and play. Giving in, he undid her lead and let her wander around while keeping an eye on her.

"So, what's this proof you have?" Henry asked, getting to the point of their meeting.

"Proof?" Tim asked.

"You said you knew why Maureen went to Swinfeld that day."

He nodded. "Aye." He inhaled, filling his big chest. "I came across them when I was moving from Baildon."

"Come across what?"

"Letters. Love letters."

Henry felt his eyebrow rise. "To whom?"

"Her. Maureen."

"From whom?"

He exhaled and patted his pockets, producing his cigarettes, a fresh packet with only one missing. The plastic casing still covered the lower half.

"Gave up, did you?" Henry asked, nodding at the cigs.

Tim caught himself opening the packet and then put it on the bench. "Aye. Four years ago. Karen doesn't like me smoking. I thought they'd help with the stress, but…"

"Who were they from?" Henry asked. "These love letters?"

"I don't know," he said. "They were just signed 'yours always'."

"Great," Henry couldn't help saying under his breath. "Where are they now?"

Tim patted a supermarket carrier bag next to him.

Henry fought the urge to grab it and read them there and then. "Where were they?"

"Under her beside cabinet. Taped under the bottom drawer. Karen spotted them when I picked them up." His hand clutched the bag, scrunching the plastic. "I felt sick at first."

"You'd no idea she'd been unfaithful?"

He shook his head. "None. I was too busy thinking about myself."

"What do you mean?"

"Well, I've had my share of women wanting me to break my vows – and once or twice I did." He bit his lower lip as if he regretted doing so. "I was just worried she'd find out about my indiscretions. I never thought she had her own to hide."

Henry didn't comment. His own marriage had collapsed after years of silent misery, so he wasn't one to judge. Glancing out at the park in front of them, he saw Tessa getting too close to a Labrador and whistled her over.

When she'd strolled towards him, he said, "I'm not sure why you rang me about this."

"I want you to help."

"How? What can I do? I'm out of the game. Retired. All I'm good for now is watching test cricket and walking the dog."

Tim turned to him for the first time, locking his blue eyes onto Henry's. "Bollocks. I've heard all about some geriatric PI pissing off the top brass. And I'm stationed at Otley, remember. Who do you think sent out uniforms to that shoot-out on the Chevin? All I could hear on the radio was people cursing your name."

Henry covered his mouth and faked a cough to hide his awkwardness.

"I want you to do your own thing on the side and find out who really killed Maureen."

"Hang on. We don't know it's actually her they've found yet," Henry said, trying to bring in some perspective.

"Then why did they send me home?" He looked out towards the river. "It's her."

"But I've been warned off already…"

"How?"

"I went to Swinfeld this morning and had a tête-à-tête with Acton."

"What do you make of him?"

Henry shrugged. "I don't know. I'm undecided."

"I've heard some shit about him, believe me."

"Aye, well. I'm not sure I'm going to be dipping my toes into this."

"Don't bullshit me," Tim said, raising his voice slightly. "I know you'll have the case files at your house already. You'll have spent the morning going through them."

Henry wore his best poker face. "You know, retired detectives have better things to do than read up on old cases."

"Aye, other detectives. But not you. Not The Bloodhound."

Henry bristled as he heard his old nickname. He thought it'd died along with his police career all those years ago.

Tim leant forward. "I need help. I can't do time for this. I've been a cop twenty-five years. If I go to prison – Armley or somewhere – I won't last my sentence. They're animals in there, and they'll kill me eventually. And what about my kids? What about them? Maureen's legacy?"

Henry sensed the immense pressure Tim was putting himself under. The man's big shoulders struggled under the weight of it all. Henry felt like patting his arm and telling him it'd be okay, only he wasn't satisfied that Tim wasn't involved somehow. Mystery love letters or not.

He decided to be frank. "Look, I'm not sure what I can do. To be honest with you, and just between you and me, I normally have a detective on the inquiry who tells me what's what. But I don't have that this time. She's not on the MIT."

"I know someone who's involved," Tim said, turning to him. His blue eyes had reddened, and tears had collected in the corners.

"Right?"

"She's just been promoted and is working under Acton. She's said she'll keep an eye on things for me. I know she'll help you."

Henry winced in anticipation. "What's she called, this detective?" But he knew the name before Tim said it.

"She's called Hargreaves, and she's now a detective sergeant."

Chapter Five

It wasn't that Henry had anything personal against DS Hargreaves. It was just that they hadn't got on well in the last few investigations Henry had been involved in. Not only was Hargreaves' general demeanour caustic, but

Henry just didn't like the woman. Plus, she was Detective Superintendent Murphy's pet, and Henry had an even greater dislike for Murphy than he did for her. Though, Henry doubted Murphy was as in control of Hargreaves as he thought he was.

Henry cleared his throat and realised that a few moments had passed since Tim had said Hargreaves' name. "Aye, I know her."

"She's a good cop, is Ellie," Tim said, sensing he had to prove it to Henry.

Ellie? Henry wondered. He'd never heard Hargreaves' first name before.

Tim turned to look at him, his blue eyes full of sincerity. "She is a good copper – one of the best."

Henry nodded as if he knew this, but he didn't. He thought Hargreaves was sharp and perceptive. But she was also lazy and arrogant, and seemed too eager to please those upstairs.

Henry attached Tessa's lead to her collar before she could run off and have it out with a white mongrel she'd been eyeing up.

"How do you know Hargreaves?" Henry asked, sounding as casual as he could.

"I worked with Ellie when she was a PC. I was partnered up with her, taught her the ropes, and then she rose through the ranks, leaving me behind."

"I heard she was a detective sergeant. Only a stone's throw away from becoming a DI."

"She's bright. I wouldn't put much past her."

"So she's your contact in the MIT?"

He nodded. "She'll give me whatever I ask for. She's sure I'm not involved and says she'll steer the investigation away from me if needed."

Henry thought that was curious. Only two minutes ago, Tim was worried he was the only suspect; now he admitted to having someone on the inside trying to influence the MIT.

"Right. And Ellie's happy for me to talk to her?" Henry asked.

Tim looked at him. "Well, I was thinking you could talk to her through me."

Ah, Henry thought. That would be a problem.

"Listen," Henry said, masking his annoyance by sounding as polite and considerate as he could. "I don't think that would work. Me doing my own investigation outside of the murder inquiry might just pass muster. Letting you be the conduit between me and the major inquiry team is something else."

Henry couldn't tell whether the emotion behind Tim's eyes was frustration or fear. Tim took out a cigarette from his new pack and tapped its filter against his lips with no intention of lighting it. "I can ask if Ellie can talk to you?" he said, speaking slowly, as if he wasn't sure he liked the idea.

"It's that or nothing," Henry said, standing up.

Tessa was sitting next to Tim as if she'd sensed he was sad and needed cheering up with her presence.

Henry tugged her lead.

Tim nodded as if agreeing with himself. "Right. I'll speak to Ellie. But you'll investigate this your end?"

Henry took a deep breath. He knew he was going to investigate it either way, he just didn't want Tim to think Henry was doing it for him. Once this case got started, it could lead anywhere. "Don't get me wrong. I think you're a good copper and that you've done well with your kids."

Tim peered up at him, waiting for the 'but'.

"If I look into this, and I will, I won't be doing it for you. Your two kids, mostly, but I'll also be doing it for Maureen. Because it looks like someone killed her while she was walking around Swinfeld Reservoir fifteen years ago and weighed down her body so that she'd never be found."

Hostility radiated off Tim Villers, but he eventually rubbed his eyes with his free hand and nodded. "I know.

I'm trying to bloody control everything. Be the centre of things. Force of habit."

He stuck the unsmoked cigarette in his mouth and lit it. Taking in a drag, he pulled a disgusted face and exhaled the smoke. "Disgusting things," he said, looking down at the cig.

"Aye. Maybe you should remain a non-smoker?"

"Maybe you're right," he said, sadly.

Then a mobile phone rang, and it wasn't Henry's.

Tim took it out of his pocket and looked at the screen. His big shoulders slumped, and he tossed the cigarette away. Tessa tried to chase after it, and Henry pulled her to heel.

"It's Siobhan," Tim said. "I'll talk to Ellie and get her to liaise with you. You're right. I'll stay out of it." His weary blue eyes locked onto Henry's. "I didn't do it, though. I didn't kill my wife."

Henry nodded. "I hope you didn't. I'd hate to see a good man like you get put away for the rest of his life."

* * *

Henry got back inside his cottage and let Tessa off her lead. She pounded the carpet as she hurtled towards the kitchen to her bowl of water. The day was turning hot, and Henry opened the windows of his stuffy living room, letting some air in.

He made a cup of Yorkshire Tea and went upstairs to his spare room. The computer was still on, and as he sat down, he looked at the notes he'd scribbled earlier.

Sipping his tea, he clicked on the transcripts of the interviews carried out in 2008. He found two with Tim Villers.

The first had been conducted by two DCs – Emsley and another detective Henry couldn't remember. The second, which was more serious than the first and had the Police Federation rep present, had been handled by Henry and DI Simon Chambers, who'd since retired from the service.

Gulping more tea, Henry wondered what had happened to DC Emsley and his colleague, and if they were still on the force.

He opened the folder that contained the two interview transcripts, both typed up by administration staff based on the audio recordings of the original interviews. He scanned through them and immediately got a sense of how anxious Tim had been at the time. Henry could tell from his choice of words.

Tim had spoken in stilted, half-finished sentences. Repeated himself. Circled back to what he'd said earlier to clarify, as if his brain had picked up on something that needed to be corrected. It wasn't surprising, seeing as Tim was in the frame for his wife's disappearance. If Maureen's body had turned up at the time, they would have looked more closely at him and probably interviewed him under caution.

There was little evidence suggesting Tim was involved. He'd been working the day Maureen had gone missing. However, there were three hours when he wasn't seen at the station. That emerged in the second interview, with Henry asking Tim where he'd been from 10 a.m. to 1 p.m. on the day Maureen disappeared.

Tim's explanation was that he had a bad tooth that caused him to leave work in a hurry. Henry had followed it up and had spoken to his dentist who confirmed Tim had kept to an appointment. However, this was at 10.30 a.m. Factoring in his travel time, this only accounted for one of the three hours he'd been missing. Where had he been for the other two?

He sipped more tea and scribbled down 'missing from 11 a.m. to 1 p.m.' on his notepad. That could put Tim in the area of Swinfeld Reservoir. And these love letters he had found seven years ago, Henry realised, could give him a motive.

One of the oldest ones in the book, in fact: jealousy.

What if Tim had found these letters back in 2008, lost the plot, and planned to meet his wife at Swinfeld? What if he did away with her and dumped her body in the water? Henry wasn't sure it was *the* explanation, but it was definitely one.

He then scribbled down 'love letters' on his pad and drained his cup. Whoever sent these letters could also be a suspect, he realised. Finding out who had sent them, and who Maureen was having an affair with, was crucial.

And then – he mused, plonking his cup on the desk – there was the third possibility.

That neither her husband nor her secret lover killed Maureen Villers, and it was someone else entirely.

Chapter Six

Henry was halfway through his ham and tomato sandwich when he heard a knock on the door. Placing the bap on his plate, he turned down BBC Radio 4 and toddled into his living room to answer. He swallowed his mouthful of brown bread and opened the door with a smile.

But his grin quickly scarpered when he saw DS Ellie Hargreaves on his doorstep. She didn't look much happier to be calling in on him. Despite the warm summer's day, she was wearing a long black dress as if on her way to a goth bar. A red and black chequered jacket hung over her shoulders, and her hands gripped a bright-pink phone. Her large black sunglasses peered at him. They were too thick for him to see through to her eyes.

"Want to come in?" he asked, opening the door for her.

He could tell she didn't want to accept his invitation but reluctantly stamped over the threshold.

Bringing her into his living room, he pointed to the sofa. "Want a seat?" he asked.

She gave a curt shake of her head, causing her large silver earrings to tinkle. "I'll stand."

"Are you sure?" Henry said, seating himself in his armchair opposite.

"The last time I sat there, I had white dog hair on my arse all day," she said, but then gave in and perched on the arm of the sofa.

"So," Henry said, interrupting the guarded silence that passed between them. "Tim Villers has been in touch?"

"He's a good cop. A good father. A good bloke."

"I know."

She glared at him before looking down at her phone as it buzzed with a notification. "They're in the process of pulling her out."

"Right. So, you're okay keeping me informed about what's going on?"

"Am I bollocks," she snapped. "I told Tim to kick you into touch. But he insisted. Said you're 'The Bloodhound' or something. Said you'd get to the bottom of it." She shook her head, as if she thought Tim had lost his mind and was annoyed she couldn't talk sense into him.

"Well, hopefully you and DCI Acton will get to the bottom of Maureen's death. I'll just be fannying around on the sides, or whatever you think it is I do."

She huffed, already exasperated by something. "We're planning on bringing Tim in later today."

"Why?"

"Acton's sure it's him," she said, and then used a deep idiotic voice to quote her superior. "'It's always the husband.'"

"You're not impressed with Acton?"

Her pout answered his question.

"So, what is it you're thinking? I'm happy to do my own thing, drive about, ask questions, look through the case files."

She shook her head. "Don't do any of that." Then, she added, "Do that if you need to, just don't tell me what you're doing. I only want to hear from you if you find anything. And don't let Acton get wind of it. If anyone finds out, I've never heard of you."

"Right." He frowned. He realised Hargreaves had decided to speak to him in person so there would be no records of her contacting him. She was planning to accept no blame should Henry get caught doing a side investigation. "Aren't you a bit concerned Tim could be our man?" he asked.

She shook her head without thought. "Never. That man's a hero. And I shan't go into any more detail, but let's just say, that man would never harm a fly – unless that fly needed a kicking."

Henry gazed at her, wondering if this was just loyalty talking.

"Well, if that's the case," Henry said, "he should be able to explain where he was the day Maureen went missing."

Hargreaves frowned, as if Henry had just insulted her. "You what? He was working the whole day."

Henry shook his head. "Read the case files. He went missing between 10 a.m. and 1 p.m. I asked him about it in the second interview, and we never got to the bottom of it. Probably too late to do that now, but if Acton gets wind of it…"

She waved her hand over her throat to silence him. "I'll handle that."

"Has he told you about these love letters?" Henry asked, keeping his eyes trained on her to see how she reacted.

She lowered her eyes to look at her pink phone. "Aye. He's showed me them."

"And?"

She shrugged. "Bloody OTT if you ask me. Sounds like whoever wrote them fancied himself as a writer. A bloody shit one."

"Can I get copies?"

"He didn't give you them?" she asked, looking at him with interest.

"Would I have asked you for them if he did?"

She nodded slowly, as if coming to realise something. Something she didn't plan to share. "I'll pass them along. Or at least scans. He says he's going to hand them to Acton later."

Henry leant back in his armchair, feeling the cushion on the back of his head. "You don't think Tim could have written them?"

She jumped up off the sofa. "Here! Listen up, as I'll only bloody say this once: you're supposed to be helping me keep Tim away from this."

"Oi! I'm not helping anyone steer this thing in any direction. If this ends up incriminating Villers, then that's that. I'm following the evidence and seeing where it takes me." His voice quavered as he had mental images of Tim in the dock for murder. "Even if that does pain me."

She blew a raspberry. "Get off your high horse, Sir Bloody Nobody." She pointed a black and red striped fingernail at him. "If you see anything that leads you to Villers, you tell me first."

"Why? So, you can cover it up?"

Her pale face flushed red. "I beg your pardon?"

The icy feeling that descended Henry's spine suggested he'd overstepped the mark. Holding up his hands in surrender, he said, "Alright. I'll take that back. If too much damning evidence starts painting a picture like that, I'll forewarn you."

She nodded but wasn't completely satisfied. "You'd bloody better."

Her phone pinged again, and she looked down at it.

"Any idea of the cause of death?" Henry asked after she'd finished reading the message.

She shook her head. "Dr Anderson's had a look, but there's too much damage on the corpse. He needs to get her to the lab."

"And I heard about her leg," Henry said, stepping delicately, as he didn't want to give away how much he knew.

Hargreaves glared at him. "How did you hear about that?" Then she realised. "DI Barnes was there this morning." She shook her head. "Bloody hell! Am I turning into Barnes now?"

I bloody hope not, Henry thought, not daring to say it.

Hargreaves continued. "Aye. She's missing a leg. But don't worry, there isn't a great white shark in Swinfeld. Seems like she had a knee replacement that broke down in the water."

Henry wasn't aware Maureen had her knee operated on. "When did she have that done?"

Another notification grabbed Hargreaves' attention, and she looked at her pink phone. "Right. I've been summoned."

"You're heading to Swinfeld?"

She shook her head. "Leeds District Station. They've called Tim in."

Henry stood up and followed her to the front door. "Is MIT based there?" he asked.

"We are. So don't bother popping in for a cup of tea. You won't be welcome."

"I wasn't thinking of it. I've got better tea here."

While on the doorstep, she spun around to stare at him. "It's not Tim." Her eyes peered into Henry's. "I swear on my mum's grave."

Henry was taken aback by her frankness. He also hadn't known her mother had passed away. He reckoned Hargreaves must be in her early thirties at the oldest, so if she was swearing on her mother's memory, it must be worth a hell of a lot to her.

"And, if you want my advice," she continued, squinting at the sun until she put on her sunglasses, "look up this secret lover. Tim thinks it could be someone at her work or her club."

"What club?" Henry asked.

Opening the front gate, Hargreaves said, "Tennis. She played semi-professional."

Without any further explanation, she closed the gate behind her and walked down the street.

Chapter Seven

Henry went back upstairs to his desk in the spare room, forgetting his half-eaten sandwich and cup of tea on the kitchen table. Sitting down at his computer, he scribbled the key things Hargreaves had told him in his notepad while they were still fresh in his mind. Then he used a trick he'd learnt from an IT technician years ago and searched all the documents related to the Villers case for the word 'tennis'. His computer took a while to think about it and came up with two files.

Clicking on the text file, Henry saw that it was a document that contained background information on Maureen Villers' life. Her daily habits, routines, contact details for her friends and her work address. The name of the detective who'd compiled the information was typed in the footer: DC Emsley.

Henry skimmed the notes and quickly came across: 'Tuesday afternoons – Tennis Practice at Heaton Tennis Club. 6 p.m. till 8 p.m.'

Henry leant forward, wondering if DC Emsley had ever questioned the coaches at the tennis club to see who'd trained Maureen and if she had ever participated in any tournaments. From what Hargreaves had said, Maureen seemed to be a regular player.

Henry read to the end of the document and, finding nothing else, clicked on the second file. It was a scanned image of a tennis tournament flyer, found in Maureen's house.

The advertisement publicised 'The Ilkley Tennis Cup', which Henry had never heard of. He was aware of the large tennis club in the town and knew a few people who were members. The Tennis Cup on the flyer was dated June 2008, two months after Maureen died.

Had she been preparing to participate in it? His eyes searched the flyer, and there was no clue to suggest Maureen was going to.

He then noticed the document had two pages, the front and back. Looking at the back, he found a handwritten message:

M, you should reconsider. I bet you'll win this time.

There was no signature nor name.

Henry leant back in his chair, wondering if the handwriting in those love letters Tim had found would match that in this message. If it did, it would mean her secret lover was at the tennis club and not at work.

That didn't mean the man she was having an affair with was the one who killed her. But it might help him find out who did, Henry thought, as he rose out of his chair to head downstairs and fetch a fresh mug of tea.

* * *

Chucking his uneaten ham sandwich in the bin, Henry cleared the rest of the kitchen table and took out a large sheet of A3 paper from the dresser in the living room. He'd forked out for a ream of paper at the stationary shop in Ilkley, as he kept using them for these cases he worked on.

Come to think of it, he thought, as he laid the sheet over his tablecloth, the first few cases he'd looked at over the past two years had come about through happenstance. But these latest ones were coming about through his own design.

He was seeking them out, wasn't he? Which was something he hadn't fully realised until now.

He had tried to return to the police, having applied for their out-of-retirement programme. But his CV and cover letter had been rejected by Detective Superintendent Murphy. To say the two didn't get along would downplay the utter contempt they held each other in, as Henry was sure the feeling was mutual.

Which was odd, as they'd been partners back in the day.

He remembered Hargreaves and Tim Villers had also been partners, but their relationship was completely different. Henry had never seen Hargreaves like that before. He'd never thought loyalty came easily to her unless it was self-serving. Hargreaves did what Murphy instructed, but Henry sensed that was more because Hargreaves was astute enough to know which way the wind blew.

But Hargreaves was close to Tim Villers. Something had gone on there, Henry felt, for her to feel that way towards him. There must be a reason why she's so adamant that Tim didn't murder his wife.

Parking that thought for now, Henry started writing on the sheet of paper. The nib of his new pen squeaked as it ran over the page. He drew three large circles around the words 'husband', 'work', and 'tennis'.

He then filled in what information he had from the scribbles in his notepad, and quickly realised he had more information on Maureen's marriage and work than tennis – for which he hardly had anything.

"It looks like I know where I need to start digging," he said to Tessa, who'd been dozing on the paving stone outside the open back door, minding her own business.

She didn't bother opening her eyes, as if she didn't want to encourage a conversation.

"Right, then," Henry continued, finishing his cup of tea, which was slightly too hot to drink quickly. "Let's go pay these tennis people a visit."

* * *

The tennis club in Heaton was a large building made of corrugated iron and looked like a warehouse. If it wasn't for the tennis courts and greens near the car park, Henry could have been forgiven for thinking it was a distribution centre for a supermarket, like the other buildings in the area.

He was in the outskirts of Bradford, a city in West Yorkshire that had its heyday back in the late nineteenth century when it helped power the Industrial Revolution. It had been downhill ever since, and parts of the city were now amongst the most deprived areas in the United Kingdom.

He found a spot in the car park, noticing some of the vehicles parked around him looked to be more expensive than he'd expected, and spotted games going on in the netted tennis courts at the side of the building.

Getting out of his car, Henry heard a man shout, and, glancing over at one of the tennis greens, saw a middle-aged coach in a grey hoodie giving a young woman a bollocking. The exact words didn't travel in the wind, but Henry wondered if this was the style of coaching they used here.

He approached the front desk, where two teenagers were busy hiring a squash court. Henry recalled playing the game back in the nineties. He thought he must have played it three times and didn't enjoy any of them, finding the loud thwack the ball made as it hit the wall more stressful than pleasurable.

The receptionist looked used to speaking to hundreds of people all day. She was middle-aged, wore a white polo shirt, and had hair dyed copper red. As the teenagers left, she quickly checked her computer screen, as if needing a moment's respite, before smiling at Henry and going again.

"Can I help?" she asked.

"Aye," Henry said, before going into his pre-planned speech about being a former detective chief inspector who was looking into the death of a woman that'd been a member.

"When would this have been?" asked the receptionist.

Her name tag said 'Wendy', so Henry used it, in an attempt to get her on side. "2008. You wouldn't have been working around that time, Wendy? You seem too young."

She batted a hand in his direction and chuckled. "Get away with you, I was there back then. Been here nearly twenty years. What was the woman's name again?"

"Maureen Villers," Henry said.

She appeared nonplussed. "Never heard of her. Sorry."

Henry put on a disappointed expression. "Ah, shame."

She waited a moment, before asking, "What happened to her?"

Henry leant on the counter. No one was waiting behind him, so he knew he could take his time. "Well, just between you and me, Wendy, she was murdered."

Her eyes widened. "Really?"

Henry nodded and looked around again, as if he shouldn't have divulged the information in a public place.

"And you think she came here?"

Henry nodded. "One of my detectives at the time found out she was a member, but it was never followed up."

Wendy frowned. A slither of doubt entered her eyes. "If she was murdered in 2008, why are you following it up now?"

"Well, just between you and me again, Maureen's body has only just been found. At the time, we thought she'd gone missing."

She covered her mouth. "Bloody hell."

"So, would you have records of your members back then?"

She shook her head. "We changed computer systems back in…" – she pulled a face as she remembered the year – "2012. And everything before then was on the older one, which I think we got rid of eventually."

"No other records?"

She shook her head. "We keep stuff for six years and then delete it. Unless they're still members."

Henry had suspected as much. "Any staff who might have known her, apart from yourself?"

"Well, I was there in 2008. But I don't remember her name."

Henry pulled the photo of Maureen that he'd printed off from his computer. He slid it across the counter towards Wendy, who picked it up and squinted at it.

"Come to think of it, she does look familiar." Her eyes rested on the photo. "And you say she was murdered?" Shaking her head, she asked, "Married with kids?"

Henry nodded. "Aye. Two."

"Such a shame," she said, still looking at Maureen's picture.

"What's a shame?" asked a gruff voice to the side of them. The middle-aged coach in the grey hoodie whom Henry had seen outside stood by the counter, looking at Wendy. He seemed less angry than he'd been earlier.

Wendy spun her chair to look at him. "Oh, Gary, you might know."

"Know what?" he asked, looking suspiciously at Henry.

"You were with us in 2008?" Wendy asked.

"Aye," Gary said, sounding more wary.

"Do you know her? I remember the face, but that's all."

Henry noted the briefest of glances the man made at the picture of Maureen.

Shaking his head, Gary said, "No. Can't remember her. What's this about?"

"Maureen Villers. Does the name ring a bell?" Henry asked.

The man shook his head like it meant nothing to him.

"I'm investigating her murder," Henry said, keeping his eyes squarely on Gary. "Would you have a few moments to have a chat?"

Chapter Eight

Gary was around fifty and had let himself go. A large gut, covered by a white T-shirt, stuck out through his unzipped grey hoodie, and his pecks had turned to man boobs – not that Henry could judge, as he wasn't in perfect shape himself.

Gary's hair was shaved short, and grey stubble encrusted his jawline. Henry guessed he might have been good-looking back in 2008, but now looked tired and washed out.

"Been here long?" Henry asked him, leaning against the counter.

Wendy was looking at the two men, as if sensing trouble was brewing.

"That's my business," Gary said, broadening his shoulders.

"Aye, but I'd like to know, because, as mentioned, I'm investigating a murder."

Gary's dissatisfied expression remained.

"So, how long have you been working here?" Henry repeated.

"Who are you?" Gary said, avoiding Henry's question with an angry barb.

"He's the police," Wendy said.

"Former police," Henry corrected Wendy. "I was a detective chief inspector."

Gary raised his chin in a slow nod. "Right. I was a former tennis champion. Doesn't mean much these days."

Henry looked Gary up and down, wondering how far this former champion had got. "Well, there is a slight difference, in that I'm investigating someone's murder."

"Where are the real police?" Gary asked, glancing around the reception area. "I can't see them."

Henry sighed. "I can get them here if you'd like? They're very busy though. So, they won't be happy when they arrive."

Gary shrugged. "I don't care if they're happy or not. Ring 'em. Get them down."

"Are you sure you want me to do that?" Henry said, stepping towards Gary, who tensed up with each step.

"Yeah," Gary said. "I won't hang about to chat with them, like. So, it'll be a wasted journey for them."

"Alright. Then off you go, *Gary*." Henry said his name as menacingly as he could. Then, he pulled the image of Maureen away from him, letting it slide over the countertop.

Looking at Maureen's picture, Henry said, "She was a pretty woman, wouldn't you say?"

Gary had made no effort to leave. He shrugged a response.

Henry spun the image around and held it up for Gary to see. "She was good-looking. Played tennis a lot, so must have been in shape. She was also planning to do the Ilkley Cup."

Gary's eyebrow made the tiniest of movements while the rest of his face remained frozen in a repulsed expression.

"Somebody told her that she was going to win it this time, but unfortunately, she was killed two months before the tournament. You wouldn't happen to know anything about that?"

Gary scrunched his face up into a snarl and said, "Get the fuck out of my face." Spinning around, he stormed off down the corridor. His trainers squeaking on the vinyl floor.

Wendy huffed as the atmosphere died down. "Blimey. That was tense. I thought you two were going to end up in a fight."

Henry gave the image of Maureen one last glance before folding it up. "You wouldn't happen to have his records, would you?"

"Gary's?" she asked, glancing down the corridor the tennis coach had just stormed down.

"Aye, you wouldn't be able to see who he's been coaching?" Henry asked.

She considered it and nodded, but her turned-down mouth suggested she didn't want to. "I'm not sure if I should tell you, though. Seeing as you're not the real police."

Henry understood her concerns. "Aye, you're right to think that. But what you can do is have a look for Maureen Villers, and if her name comes up, just say yes. You don't need to tell me anything else."

She seemed unwilling to try and glanced at the main doors hoping some customers would come in so she could serve them. But none did.

She typed at her computer, biting her lower lip as she did. After telling Henry she was doing the search, she shook her head. "No. It's not come up with that woman's name." She sounded relieved.

Henry thought it was worth the shot. "Thank you, Wendy. And that Gary, what's his second name?"

"Steele."

"And was he really a tennis champion?"

She nodded and pointed at the far wall.

Henry turned to see a framed photograph of a man on a tennis court. The man was thin, wore whites, and was celebrating winning a game with his racket still in hand. The signature in the lower right-hand side said, 'Gary Steele'. Under it was printed: 'Winner of the Queen's Club Championships, London, 1998'.

"Ever made it to Wimbledon?" Henry asked Wendy.

"No. Got as far as Queen's then he went into coaching. He could've done, though – but he packed it in."

"Do you know why?"

She shook her head. "You'd have to ask him."

* * *

Henry returned to his car, and he could still hear the sounds of tennis balls being hit and players grunting after closing his door. Looking at the netted courts around the side of the large warehouse, he searched for Gary Steele but couldn't find him anywhere.

This Gary was definitely a person of interest, Henry thought. If he could be linked to Maureen, Henry could hand him over to the police inquiry – keeping them clear of Tim Villers.

That was assuming Tim didn't kill his wife. Just because Gary might not have coached Maureen, didn't mean he hadn't killed her. But if it was all innocent between the two, why wouldn't Gary talk to Henry?

Checking his mobile for messages, Henry found one from a number he didn't recognise:

What's your email address?

The message had come in twenty minutes earlier while his phone had been on silent so he wouldn't be distracted in the tennis club. He sent his email address to the mystery number, hoping it wasn't a hacker, and then after a few moments, he got another message.

Check it.

Henry checked his emails on his phone and found a new one that had just come in from an odd-looking address. Clicking on it, he found an image file along with some text.

It wasn't just her who was unfaithful.

There was no signature. No name.

Henry was about to click on the image but stopped, wondering if this was some kind of phishing attack. But how did this would-be hacker know details of the case, he asked himself.

He tapped on the image and hoped for the best. It was a grainy black-and-white photo of a car's windscreen. Henry suspected it had been taken at night with night-vision equipment, producing a low-quality picture.

Two people were in the vehicle, embracing, and Henry recognised the first one. It looked like Tim Villers, but it wasn't a recent photograph.

Next to him, was a young woman with dark hair.

"Oh God," Henry said, as he realised who the young woman with short jet-black hair was.

He sent a message back to the mysterious texter.

Who are you?

No reply came, which was what Henry expected. "But if you don't ask, and all that," he said to himself.

He returned to the image of Tim and Hargreaves embracing in the front seats of a car on his phone. He now realised why she was so keen to make sure Tim wasn't suspected of killing his wife.

She'd been in love with him herself – and maybe still was.

Chapter Nine

Henry arrived back at his cottage and managed to find a parking spot just outside Jean's front gate. Getting out of his car, he decided to pay his neighbour a visit to see how she was coping with COVID.

He knocked on her door and waited for her to open, but she didn't. After his third knock, he decided she must be asleep and to check on her later on. He craned his neck to look at her bedroom window, which faced the front. The window was open, and the white curtains were pulled back. He sent her a text message saying he'd knocked on and would call back later.

Back in his cottage, he trudged up the steps to his spare room and sat down at his computer. He transferred the image he'd taken of Gary Steele's framed picture to his desktop, and put it in a folder he named 'Tennis'.

He then downloaded the image that had been sent to his email from the mysterious texter. Squinting at his screen, he zoomed in on the two people embracing in the front seats of the car.

On this bigger screen, it was even clearer it was Hargreaves and Villers. Henry realised the photo couldn't have been taken in 2008, however, as Hargreaves would have been doing her A levels then.

This photo, he reckoned, must be less than ten years old.

He right-clicked the mouse on the image and selected 'Get Info'. He knew that almost every digital image had a timestamp, unless it had been scraped, and not many people went through the hassle of doing that.

The date and time popped up: 18 July 2015. Seven years after Maureen had disappeared.

And while a young police constable having an affair with her training officer was most definitely frowned upon, it was nothing illegal – unless they'd changed the regulations since his day.

But it did make Henry question Hargreaves' assurance that Tim was innocent. She was biased, and definitely shouldn't be on the MIT investigating the murder of her former lover's wife.

The main question was, however, who had taken this photo and why the bloody hell had they sent it to Henry?

Was this mysterious texter hoping Henry would do something with the knowledge?

He had no idea.

Closing the image down, he put it in a new folder, which he labelled, 'Lord Knows What'.

He then clicked on the image he'd taken of Gary Steele's framed picture.

There he was, centre court, celebrating a win. The other player was out of shot. Gary was in his white tennis outfit with green smudges on his shorts and a white headband over his long black hair. The stands were crowded around the court, all applauding him.

Henry opened his internet browser and searched 'Gary Steele Tennis 1998'. Some results came up, all linked to the Queen's Club.

Looking through them, Henry learnt Gary had come second and third in previous tournaments, and then won the championship in 1998. After that, he'd pretty much disappeared. He played at Wimbledon before winning the Queen's Club but hadn't fared well and got kicked out early each time. It seemed he stopped competing at a national level after his win in 1998. Henry wondered what made him pack it in.

Leaning back in his chair, he pondered ways to get Gary to talk. He'd probably need some evidence that would pin him down so that he'd stop being so defensive. This defensiveness was a sure sign that Gary knew more than he'd let on. Had he been in a relationship with Maureen? Possibly, Henry felt, going by Gary's reactions.

But Henry would need more than gut instincts to prove anything.

His phone started ringing. Picking it up, he inspected the number, hoping it was the mysterious texter calling to identify themself and their motives, but it wasn't.

It was Hargreaves.

He answered. "Aye?"

"Meet me in Otley."

"Otley?" Henry asked, he checked the time and saw it was mid-afternoon.

"It's just between me and you," Hargreaves said.

"Aye. Alright. When?"

"Twenty minutes." She hung up before explaining where in Otley she'd meet him.

As he pulled himself out of his desk chair, he wondered if it was worth telling her about the image he'd received. But he thought he'd keep it up his sleeve for the time being. Hargreaves was beginning to trust him and showing her the image would only destroy that. Although, keeping it under wraps might make things worse in the long run.

Well, Henry thought, trundling down the steps, he had twenty minutes to decide what to do.

* * *

Hargreaves texted Henry the name of a pub, which he assumed was the place she wanted to meet. He found a spot for his Skoda in a supermarket car park in the centre of Otley; an old market town that was nestled in under rolling hills on one side and the River Wharfe on the other. He hoped parking near a food store would remind him to get some more milk and bits for dinner when he came to collect his car.

As he walked along the busy street towards the pub, he recalled he'd always thought Otley had too many cars. The street at his side was filled with a constant stream of traffic despite the town having a bypass. The old stone buildings, most dating back to the Victorian era, were blackened by a century's worth of exhaust fumes.

The pub was in the market square, tucked in at the side. It looked older than the other buildings, and Henry thought it probably had been here as long as Otley. Scraps of plastic sheeting and cardboard boxes littered the square, suggesting a market had been held there earlier but cleared up for the day. A few people were seated outside the pub on wooden tables, enjoying the sun that peeked through fluffy white clouds.

Henry walked past the young drinkers, wondering why they were out on a Thursday afternoon, drinking pint after pint. Either the Jobcentre had given up hope or they were students enjoying what was left of their summer. By the sight of them, Henry couldn't tell.

He found Hargreaves at the bar, sipping a sparkling water through a pink straw that matched the colour of her huge phone, which lay face down on the bar. Henry wondered if she'd brought the straw with her as another accessory.

She gestured to the barman, who was serving some of the young people outside, and Henry shook his head at her offer of a drink. The yeasty smell of beer was making his mouth water, and he didn't want to let temptation anywhere near him. Not today. He watched a young lad in a Manchester United top take a fresh pint of lager from the barman, drops of condensation sliding down his glass. Henry looked away and pointed at a small nook in the far corner.

The wood-panelled walls had seen better days, and the smell of stale soot came from a nearby fireplace. They took seats at a round table, its surface sticky, and Hargreaves sent off a text message on her phone while sipping Perrier.

"So, what is it you wanted?" Henry asked.

Her eyes went back to the phone's screen for an instant, and then back to Henry. "They've got Tim in for questioning."

"Right. What are they questioning him about? They've only just found Maureen."

"It's a preliminary," she said. Her eyes rested on him a moment. "It's Acton and another DS in with him."

"Who's the DS?"

"Emsley," she said, pulling a repulsed expression.

Henry repeated the name to her. "Emsley? Is he in his fifties?"

She shrugged. "He's oldish. Not as old as you. Near pensionable age, no doubt. Tim doesn't like him. Says he's wet lettuce and does whatever his superior says."

She went back to tapping a message on her phone. "He's got a nasty nickname for him, which I won't share with you." She noticed Henry was staring off into the distance. "What is it? Do you know him?"

"I might just… aye. There was a young DC who was on the first case called Emsley. It's an unusual enough name."

Hargreaves flicked through photos on her phone. Turning its large screen to face Henry, she showed him an image of a man's face. If Henry ignored the marionette lines and the thinning brown hair, he could just about make out the young DC Emsley he'd known fifteen years earlier.

"Aye, that's him," Henry said.

"He always wears this thick tweed jacket the whole time. Even in summer. He reeks of sweat."

"Who else is on the MIT?"

She went through the other headshots, naming some administration staff whom Henry didn't recognise.

"Where did you get these photos from?" he asked.

"Their internal profiles."

"*How* did you see them?"

She shrugged, as if it wasn't important, though he knew only officers of inspector rank and above could access internal profiles.

"So, this Emsley was on the original case?" she asked, sensing the need to change topic.

"Aye. He was alright… Well, a bit of a lightweight, to be fair. I'm not surprised he didn't get higher than DS."

"Why?" she asked.

Henry guessed she was more concerned about avoiding the same fate.

"Well," Henry continued, "he was dependable, good with admin, but he wasn't brilliant and wasn't a leader. You need both of those attributes to have any hope of getting ahead."

Henry could see her making a mental note and wondered if she had either of those qualities or if it even mattered. He reckoned she'd get ahead with or without them.

"What was Emsley's opinion of Tim?" she asked after a pause.

"I'm not sure, to be honest. Emsley never really shared his thoughts with anyone. He was quiet. Diligent. Very good with his seniors. In fact, too good. It used to grate on me."

"Ah, you were his DCI, though, weren't you? I doubt you gave a shit what a little DC like him thought."

"Now now, I cared about what all my team thought. I asked them regularly."

"You just can't remember what this Emsley believed?"

Henry couldn't answer. He surely must have asked Emsley for his opinion and made a note of it somewhere. Maybe it was in the computer files typed down on a document. He then looked at Hargreaves. "You're worried Emsley thought Tim killed Maureen?"

She shrugged. "Why is he on the team if Acton hadn't picked him for that reason?"

"Why are *you* on the team?" Henry countered. "Because Acton must surely know you have history with Villers."

She gave him a slightly wounded look, and for an instant, her impenetrable bravado looked fragile. "What are you getting at?"

Henry felt pressure to reveal his hand regarding the grainy, compromising image he had received. This was surely the best time to tell her, he thought, but he didn't.

Instead, he said, "That Tim trained you. That you were both partners."

The flicker of unsatisfied suspicion rested in her eyes for a moment before fizzling out.

"So, how did you get onto the MIT, despite your history?" Henry asked again. "Was it Murphy?"

She scoffed. "Bloody hell. He's only a detective superintendent. He doesn't run the police force."

Henry felt like chuckling. "Have you realised he can't pull all the strings?"

She leant her black designer jacket sleeve on the sticky round table. "Listen, if people do favours for me, it's because I'm a good copper and I do favours for them. It's not for any other bloody reason."

"So someone did you a good turn. That's how you ended up on the MIT?"

She sucked the last of the sparkling water through her straw in an attempt to avoid the question.

But Henry's silence got the better of her, and she huffed. "What does it bloody matter how I got on it? I'm on the MIT, I'm a DS with Emsley. And they seem none the wiser about my history. Besides, so what if I worked with Tim? Half the coppers around here have."

Aye, Henry thought, but how many of them have been in a relationship with him? He didn't say that, of course; instead, he asked benignly, "No inspectors on the team?"

She shook her head. "They're tied up with that double homicide in Leeds."

"Right," he said. So that made it just DCI Acton and his two detective sergeants, which, as major inquiry teams went, wasn't very big. "So, what is it you wanted to talk to me about?" he asked.

She placed her black leather handbag on the table and pulled out a crumpled sheet of paper. "Here's the love letter."

Henry took the sheet. It was a short message, only a few lines, written curtly, but the admiration for Maureen was clear.

'You mean everything to me' and 'I can't wait for us to be together for longer' stood out to Henry. He also noted the phrase, 'your undeserving husband'.

Reading it, Henry got a sense it came from a man unacquainted with expressing his emotions, which unfortunately was a common trait in Yorkshiremen.

Henry raised an eyebrow at Hargreaves. "I thought there were more?"

"There are, but I could only get this one. It's the last one that was sent to her."

Henry opened it up and skimmed the handwritten note. There was no date, but the cursive was similar to that found on the flyer for the Ilkley Cup.

"I'm not a handwriting expert, but this love letter could have been from whoever wrote on that tennis flyer."

Hargreaves tilted her head like she'd missed something. "What flyer?"

"Keep up, DS Hargreaves. You'll never make it to inspector rank at this rate," Henry said, half-smiling.

Chapter Ten

Hargreaves moved closer to Henry, and he got a whiff of her strong citrusy perfume. The stench of stale soot from the fireplace and the spilt beer from the table couldn't match its potency.

Her eyes had narrowed as she glared at him. "What bloody flyer?"

"The tennis flyer from the original inquiry."

She leant back in her wooden seat, nodding as if it all made sense. "Right. I thought you'd have all the evidence from the first case stashed away somewhere. How many boxes of files have you nicked?"

Henry ignored her question. "Listen. There's a flyer that we didn't pick up on back then. It was for the Ilkley Tennis Cup."

"Ilkley? They play tennis over there?" At Henry's nod, Hargreaves rolled her eyes. "I suppose it's a toff's game."

Henry batted aside her reverse snobbery. "Anyway. There's a tennis cup every year in June. And on the back of this particular flyer was a handwritten note, addressed to *M*."

Henry then glanced at the love letter in his hand, but Hargreaves beat him to it and pointed at the name of the addressee, written in ballpoint pen: *M.*

"So, you think it's the same person?" Hargreaves asked, leaning forwards to study the love letter which was now in the middle of the sticky table.

Henry glanced at her as he made sure the paper hadn't become filthy. "This isn't the original, is it?"

She rolled her eyes. "Do you really think I'd be walking around with evidence?" Her frustration got the better of her, and she struggled to speak through it. "Do you really think I'm that thick?"

"No, no," Henry said, defensively.

She huffed and carried on looking at the letter. "So, we have this flyer that could be tied to these love letters."

"Aye. And Maureen went to Heaton Tennis Club."

Hargreaves frowned at him. "How do you know that?"

"We actually knew it back in 2008, but we didn't follow it up."

"Why?"

"Well, it was Emsley who was meant to…" Henry's voice trailed off as he realised why Emsley hadn't investigated these tennis links. "Ah. Maybe it is clear what this DS thought back in the day."

"Emsley was supposed to look into this but didn't? Meaning he was pretty damn sure it was Tim who killed his wife?"

Henry nodded. "I didn't even know there was a tennis link until you told me. I was too busy looking in other directions."

"You mean at Tim?"

"And that flight to Canada."

Hargreaves raised her head as if she'd forgotten about that. "Right. The feigned trip to Toronto. Well, that turned out to be nonsense, didn't it?"

Henry agreed with her. "But you have to remember, we didn't have a body and we didn't know Maureen was actually dead." He shrugged, feeling as if he didn't have more to add. "It's not much of an excuse, but it's all I have."

Hargreaves didn't seem interested in his excuses. "So, this flight. Who organised it? Was it the killer? Was it someone else?"

"Was it Tim?" Henry asked, to gauge her reaction.

She shook her head. "No. It was a woman who booked it, wasn't it? That's what I read in the notes."

"Glad you've been doing your homework," Henry said. "It was a woman with dark hair if my memory serves me well."

"Maybe she did it herself? Maybe Maureen was planning to make a run for it?" Hargreaves pointed at the copy of the love letter on the table. "She had a fella on the side, but the affair went south. She'd had enough of Tim and the kids, and thought 'sod this' and decided to start a new life over there – on her own."

Henry shook his head. "A mother abandoning her two kids?"

He considered his own question but wasn't convinced. Maureen had been the responsible type and was the head of finance at her firm. The idea of her skipping the country to get away from it all didn't seem to fit the bill. But then again, she can't have been that responsible if she was having an affair, which these love letters suggested she was.

Looking down at the letter on the table, he read some of it with more interest. There was longing in the words, not just lust, but longing to be together. A couple against the world. Whatever they'd had, appeared to have been real.

"There is another option. That she and this secret lover were planning on going to Canada together."

"She booked only one ticket, though, didn't she?" Hargreaves asked.

"Aye. But he could've booked one himself. Maybe on a different flight."

Hargreaves tilted her head as she thought about it. The sun broke out of the clouds and shone through a nearby window illuminating her face. It made her look even paler than she was, and she squinted at it.

"I like that," she said. "I bet they were planning on starting a new life over there. Maybe he had contacts. Any ideas who this secret tennis lover could be?"

"Gary Steele. A coach over at Heaton Tennis Club."

She put a hand over her eyes to protect them from the sun. "That's a bit specific. How do you know it's him?"

"I spoke to him this morning, but he wouldn't say a thing."

"At this tennis club?"

Henry nodded. "Aye. He was defensive enough to make me suspicious."

Hargreaves snatched up the love letter from the table and stuffed it into her handbag. "Right. Let's go see what this coach has to say for himself."

Henry wasn't sure if he'd heard her right. "With me?"

She nodded, shaking her short black hair. "Who else is going to point him out to me?"

Henry thought she could find out by herself but thought it was worth going, just to see Gary Steele's face when Hargreaves laid into him. "Right. I'll follow your car. I'll have to pick mine up, mind."

She shook her head as she stared at her phone. "No time." She held up a message to him, which he couldn't read as it was too far away. "Tim's just text me. He's been let out of questioning. They've found out Maureen's cause of death, and Acton and Emsley are gunning for him."

* * *

Hargreaves had changed her vehicle since the last time Henry had shared a ride with her. She had a new silver Audi that still had the new-car smell. The sun shone down over the moorside as they drove from Otley towards Bradford.

Hargreaves called Tim over and over again, and his dial tone thundered through the car's top of the range speakers. Her call was ignored, and Tim's cheery voicemail message came up for the fifth time.

"Bastard!" Hargreaves said, cancelling the call and then putting her hands back on the steering wheel. "He must be with his solicitor."

"Already?" Henry asked. There hadn't been any formal proceedings made against Tim Villers, who hadn't even been arrested. The need for him to have a lawyer at this point wasn't clear. "Why don't you call Acton or Emsley? Ask them what they think?"

She shook her head and then checked the blind spot before merging into the second lane of a dual carriageway. "No. Not with you in the car."

When they arrived at Heaton Tennis Club, it was nearly 5 p.m. The sun had started to die off, casting a red glow over the thin cloud cover. Games were still being played in the netted courts at the side of the corrugated-iron warehouse, and Hargreaves watched them as if looking at an alien species.

"I never got tennis," she said.

"Yeah. It's not been my go-to sport, either."

"What's yours?" she asked, turning to him.

"Cricket, probably."

She guffawed. "Bloody boring! Rugby for me. Bradford Bulls. I like to see a real man in shorts..." She stared at two men playing tennis in the nearest court. "Not these pansies."

Wendy was still at reception, sitting behind the off-white counter. Henry wondered when the poor woman could leave for the day. A queue of people wanting tennis courts congregated around her, and Henry guessed it was the post-work crowd. Their trainers squeaked on the vinyl flooring, which was cream-coloured and meant to look like marble but didn't. He couldn't blame people for wanting to play while it was still slightly hot outside and neither cold nor raining – as the rest of the year was likely to be.

When the crowd had been dealt with, Wendy clocked them. Her frozen smile cracked into a frown. "Yes?" she asked nervously, eyeing Hargreaves, as if sensing trouble. And Henry couldn't argue with her on that.

He stepped forwards to take the lead. "Hello again, Wendy. I'm here with Detective Sergeant Hargreaves–"

Hargreaves flashed her warrant card and then butted in. "Is Gary Steele here?" she asked, looking over Wendy's head at a corridor that lead to the changing rooms.

Henry glanced around as well, trying to see if Gary was there and finding he wasn't.

"He's stepped out," Wendy said.

"When will he be back?" Henry asked, trying to sound positive.

"I don't know. He left an hour ago."

Hargreaves tapped the countertop with a nail to get Wendy's attention. "His home address and contact details," she ordered.

"Erm… I'm not sure if I can just give them…"

Hargreaves waved her warrant card in the air again. "Please, don't waste my time, love. I'm investigating the murder of a woman, so just hand it over."

"What… you think Gary killed someone?" Wendy looked at Hargreaves and then gave Henry a wounded look. "You never said you thought Gary murdered a woman."

Henry held up his hands. "We're just doing a preliminary investigation. We'd like to rule out Gary's possible involvement. So, there's nothing to worry about."

Wendy wasn't convinced. "Yeah. That's what they said to my Josh, and he ended up with three months for–"

"Listen, love!" Hargreaves said. "I'm not too fussed about what your Josh did or didn't do. I'd just like those details, please."

Wendy attempted a staring match with Hargreaves but quickly lost. "I'll go print them off."

After she stood up from the desk and went to a printer a few feet away, Henry sidled up to Hargreaves. "Would being nice kill you?"

"I've got more important things to do than be 'nice'. I'm investigating a murder."

"Aye. I know. But surprisingly, people don't like being bullied and harassed. If you're more careful with them, they'll let you into their confidences and tell you stuff that could very well be helpful."

She considered his point but then shook her head, as if it was nonsense. However, when Wendy handed her the details, Hargreaves attempted a smile that looked as real as the vinyl marble flooring. "Thanks for your help."

Wendy didn't bother acknowledging her and sat back in her chair.

"Thanks," Henry said as they went, but Wendy didn't look up.

Outside, Hargreaves glanced at the sheet Wendy had given her. There was a faint breeze that shook the paper as she read it. "Right. We've got a phone number, email, and home address. He lives in Shipley."

"I suppose we ring him first. I doubt he'll be at home."

"He probably won't answer us if we ring."

"Well, what do you suggest?" Henry asked.

She opened the front door of her Audi. "A little stakeout might be in order. He'll have to turn up at home eventually."

Henry wasn't sure he wanted to spend an unknown number of hours locked in a car with Hargreaves, but recalled his own Skoda was parked in Otley – nearly twenty miles away.

"Are you sure?" he asked.

"You really think I want to spend my evening sitting with you? But what else can we do?"

Henry forced his brain to come up with a better solution, but none were forthcoming. "Right. I suppose we should stop off somewhere beforehand to pick up some dinner."

She rolled her eyes. "Fine. Come on, then."

Chapter Eleven

Henry leant back in the leather passenger seat, kicking the supermarket bag-for-life next to his feet. They'd stopped for sandwiches and Scotch eggs before arriving at Gary Steele's house. The sun had gone over the horizon, leaving an inky blue sky dotted with clouds. The dome light in the car was off, as they didn't want to bring attention to themselves.

They were outside the centre of Shipley, a run-down town in the outskirts of Bradford with a train station and a couple of curry houses to its name. Gary Steele's house wasn't what Henry had imagined a former tennis champion to live in. It was a former council flat on the top of a three-storey pebbledash building. Two other identical buildings were close by, and the three of them were known collectively as White Rose Court. The elegant name didn't match the reality. Gary's flat was in the first building, which was close to a main road where they'd parked.

Hargreaves' silver Audi sat among a row of cars on the other side of the cast-iron fence, and they kept an eye on Gary's building while listening to local radio. Henry checked the time. It was nearly 8 p.m. He worried about his own vehicle in the supermarket car park in Otley, wondering if it'd been towed away for being left after closing time.

Hargreaves scrolled through social media, looking up from her phone to glance at Gary's building every now and then. Not much conversation passed between them, and they relied on the radio to fill the silence.

A red Ford pulled into a parking spot further down the road. Henry spotted it and guessed it was well over a decade old, much older than his own Skoda. He kept his eye on it, as it seemed strangely familiar. After a few minutes, the driver got out and rushed down the pavement towards White Rose Court. His grey hoodie flashed under the amber glows of the street lights.

Henry recognised Gary. "It's him."

Hargreaves lowered her phone. "Are you sure?"

"Aye." Henry was out of the car in a flash, not even checking for traffic on the road. He ran to the pavement, getting to the gate before Gary.

"Now then…" he said, trying to sound as confident as he could, despite feeling winded from his brief exertion. He hadn't moved for nearly two hours.

Gary slowed his pace as he approached Henry. His face scrunched up into a snarl. "Not you again. What do you want?"

"I'd like to talk," Henry said.

"Me too," Hargreaves added, stepping onto the pavement and eyeing up Gary.

"Who the hell are you?" he asked.

"DS Hargreaves." She flashed her warrant card. "I'd like a few words–"

Gary spun around and legged it, moving fast for a man in his fifties.

Hargreaves gasped and ran after him, with Henry following suit.

Gary had slammed his car door shut by the time they arrived.

Hargreaves banged her fists on the driver's window, yelling at Gary to stay and talk. She tried the old door handle, which failed to open, as he was pulling it shut from the other side.

Henry was less concerned and strode around the other side of Gary's parked vehicle. He tried the passenger door, which was open. Stooping inside, he sat on some tracksuit bottoms and a gym bag left on the passenger seat.

Gary turned to him in confusion. "What the bloody hell are you doing?!"

"Now," Henry said, putting on the seatbelt. "Wherever you go, I'll be right beside you." He smiled at Gary, unsure if the man would punch him.

Hargreaves had given up banging on the window and remained on the pavement, her arms crossed.

"So," Henry said. "Shall we go and have that chat?"

* * *

The interior of Gary's flat matched the outside, in that they both hadn't changed much since their construction in the 1970s and neither had aged well. The living room had white walls that had turned a cream colour from years of nicotine. Henry seated himself on an old grey sofa next to Hargreaves. Not seeing any ashtrays, he assumed the previous tenants had caused the smoke damage.

The only window was single-pane, and mould grew around the corners of its frame. The Caesar blind that covered it was broken and stuck in an odd arrangement with one side bunched up. A single light bulb hung precariously from a wire in the ceiling, casting the whole untidy room in an intensely bright light.

Gary hadn't offered them tea and took a wooden chair from the table that had files and papers on it piled up two-feet-high. Henry looked around the room for signs of Gary's past glory but didn't find any. Old cardboard boxes with crisps logos on them were lined along the wall, and above them were marks where pictures had once been mounted, but none remained.

Gary slumped on the chair in front of them with an aura of shame hanging around him. He stared at the thick brown carpet, which Henry guessed could be as old as the flat, as some places had got so threadbare, he could see the underlay.

"What is it you want?" Gary asked, sounding defeated.

Henry glanced at Hargreaves next to him, who seemed as comfortable in the room as Henry did. "We want answers to some of our questions," he said.

"Like what?" Gary didn't look up.

Hargreaves gestured for Henry to speak, as if she wasn't sure what to say and was still sussing the situation out.

Henry took a moment. "Maureen Villers," he said eventually. "You coached her, didn't you?"

Gary's face didn't change. He still appeared despondent, and just stared at the carpet.

"You know she's been found?"

Even that didn't get a reaction.

"You were a tennis player, weren't you?" Henry asked, trying a new tack.

"Still am."

"You won the Queen's Club in 1998?"

"So you've seen the photo in reception. Well done."

"Did you ever have a relationship with Maureen Villers?"

He didn't respond.

Hargreaves lost what little patience she had. "Listen, we're investigating Maureen's murder. She was a wife, a mother, and had a good job. She was an upstanding type of person. And she was violently killed. Now, some of the evidence we've come across has led us to you. You wouldn't know why that is, would you?"

Gary shook his head. "I'm just trying to get on with my life. I coach players, play when I can." He looked up at them and opened his arms wide. "Look at this shithole I'm living in. Look at it! I used to be someone. A winner. I had a nice home, a wife, a family."

"Yeah?" Henry asked. "What happened to them?"

Gary didn't say. He bit a well-chewed thumbnail.

Henry continued. "Go on. When did you lose your wife? It didn't by any chance happen around 2008?"

Gary met his eyes. "I didn't do anything to Maureen."

"So, you knew her?"

Gary spat out a chunk of fingernail onto the carpet. His thumb bled, and he sucked at it. "She was someone I coached."

Finally, Henry thought. He looked at Hargreaves who shared the relief. Henry continued asking the questions. "How close were you?"

"We were… close. She was a good player. She'd played a lot as a kid. At Heaton. Never gave it up, even when she was working and had kids."

"Could she have gone far?" he asked.

Gary thought about it and nodded. "Possibly. She would have had to quit work and train full-time. Plus, she was getting old and had a few injuries. Her knee gave her gyp. She would have only had a year or two left in her, like… But yeah, she could've gone on and won a few tournaments. Regional, maybe national."

"Like you had done?"

Gary's eyes hardened. "Yeah. Like me. I suppose."

"You won in 1998?"

Gary didn't nod.

"And then the year after you all but disappeared from the scene," said Hargreaves, making it sound like a question.

Gary shrugged. "What's your point?"

"Why did you quit?"

Gary scrunched up his lips. "Is that relevant?"

"It might be," Henry said.

He swallowed loudly and looked down at his hands. The blood on his thumb was still there. "I had issues."

"Physical? Mental? Drugs?" Henry asked, his voice raising with each one.

Gary shook his head and sucked at his thumb. "I had a thing for…"

"Women?" Henry asked.

Gary shook his head. "No. Nothing like that." He exhaled. "It was gambling. I got into gambling."

"In tennis?" Hargreaves asked, sounding dumbfounded.

Gary nodded. "Courtsiding. It was big back then; still is now. A few–" he cleared his throat "–some people ran it on the side. A syndicate. I even bet on myself a few times."

Henry wondered what this meant, and then realised. "You didn't happen to bet on yourself losing, and then, just by chance, went and lost the match?"

Gary didn't confirm, but his expression admitted as much. "I didn't place the bets, but it was my money. I had others do it for me. I used my winnings and cash from training people, whatever I could get my hands on, to make more bets. And it worked out pretty well. Until it didn't."

"The police caught you?" Henry asked.

Gary shook his head.

"Ah. The fellas who ran the gambling schemes," Hargreaves said. "Did you piss them off by getting them to bet against you?"

Gary met her eyes and then looked down at the carpet. "Something like that. I was forced to stop playing."

"Hence you became a full-time tennis coach," Henry said. "And within ten years you were in a relationship with Maureen Villers."

Gary's head shot up. "What? No. Never."

"Come on, don't mess us about," Henry said. "You've said you trained her, that you were close to her."

Gary raised his hands in the air. "Seriously. Maybe there was just that one time, but there was no relationship."

"So you made a move once?" Hargreaves said.

Gary nodded. "We were drunk. She'd just won a game, and it was a good one. She'd played fantastically. Won straight sets. And I tried kissing her in the bar later, but she pushed me away." His flabby cheeks reddened at the memory – the shame of rejection still clearly fresh.

Henry looked to Hargreaves to gauge what she was thinking. She turned to him, not looking convinced. Henry glanced over at the dining table covered in papers and files.

"Well," he said, as he stood up, "we can quickly clear this up."

Gary watched him cross the room. "What are you doing?"

Henry pulled out a handwritten document from a lopsided pile. He scanned the shoddy penmanship, which looked as though it'd been scrawled by a drunk, and felt uneasiness fill his gut. It was nothing like the love letter's. "Is this your handwriting?"

Gary appeared perplexed by the question. As he couldn't see the document, he got up from the wooden chair and went over to look. "Aye. It's mine." He snatched the sheet away from Henry as if its contents were private.

Henry had already figured it was the plans of some tennis technique written for the benefit of a student. "Well, I think that settles it," Henry said.

"You what?" Gary looked at him and then Hargreaves. "You're not going to do anything about the gambling or anything?"

"There's no point," Hargreaves said, getting off the couch. "It happened outside of West Yorkshire twenty-five years ago. I don't give a toss." She grabbed the sheet out of Gary's hands and quickly glanced at it. "Henry's right. We'll leave you be."

They went to the door while Gary remained near the table, looking at the sheet of paper in his hand. He was trying to divine what it had meant to the two detectives.

Before Henry stepped out of the door, he asked, "What happened to your wife and kids?"

Gary gave up on the sheet of paper. "She wasn't happy about my change in fortunes, and she also found out about me being unfaithful."

"I suppose Maureen wasn't the only one?"

Gary gave the slightest of nods.

Henry was about to follow Hargreaves into the hallway when he turned back to Gary. "How did your wife find out?"

"About Maureen and the others?" He shrugged. "I never did work that out."

Chapter Twelve

Hargreaves gave Henry a ride back to his car in Otley. They both discussed what Gary had told them. The secrets and shame he'd revealed about his past and how he ended up in such a manky flat. Luckily for Gary, as his scrappy handwriting discounted him from being Maureen's secret lover, he wouldn't have the eyes of several homicide detectives on him. That didn't discount him completely, however. He had some involvement in Maureen's life and could still be worth talking to later.

Hargreaves pulled into the empty supermarket car park after 10 p.m. The place was dead, lit only by a few street lights. Her phone rang, and she answered it by pressing the large screen on the dashboard.

Tim's voice boomed through the speakers. "How's it going?" he asked.

"I'm here with Henry," Hargreaves said, pulling her car up beside his Skoda, the only vehicle left in the dark.

"Even better. I need a word with both of you. Where are you?"

"Otley," Hargreaves answered, keeping her engine turning.

"Meet me…" Tim paused as he tried to think of a place. "Ilkley Moor, near the hotel. Do you know it?"

"Aye," Henry said, looking at Hargreaves. They'd both spent a lot of time there on an investigation recently, looking for a lost girl. Though, on that occasion, he and Hargreaves had been at loggerheads.

"See you there in fifteen minutes." Tim hung up.

Henry opened the passenger door. "I'll take my own car then."

"Too right. I'm not bringing you back here after," Hargreaves replied, checking her rear-view mirror. "I'm not a bloody taxi service. I've got better things to be doing." With that, she sped off through the empty car park.

Henry got into his Skoda. Looking at the closed supermarket with its shutters down and spots lighting up its logos, he remembered he needed to buy milk and some food. Tutting, he got in and followed Hargreaves' Audi, which was now far down the street.

He caught up with her and then followed her car along pitch-black roads, unsure of how he felt about meeting a potential murder suspect at the dead of night.

Henry had to agree with Acton's hypothesis, that it was most likely the husband who killed her.

What if Tim had found the love letters sent to Maureen, went into a rage, and killed her? He might even have come across the receipt for the airplane ticket to Canada. Maybe he confronted her and didn't like what she'd said?

As a police officer, Tim would've known how best to get rid of her body and clear up after himself.

Hargreaves' car sped through some traffic lights after they'd turned red, leaving Henry waiting. He also didn't know what to think of his new partner. Hargreaves was way too biased and couldn't be relied upon.

He was half-tempted to let her meet Tim on her own. He could even go to Acton with what he knew about her, which was always an option. If the likelihood was that Tim had killed his wife and Hargreaves was doing her best to protect him, either believing him or not, then Henry didn't want anything to do with them.

But, unfortunately, he'd found himself smack bang in the middle.

He chewed his lower lip, waiting for the red light to turn green. He'd had his suspicions of Tim all along but had always thought that was the easy solution – a cop-out.

If Maureen's body had turned up at the time, Henry could have pushed his team to come up with charges against Tim Villers. But he hadn't as he felt sure there was something else going on. Whether it was tennis or Maureen's family life, he didn't know.

His phone vibrated and he saw it was Hargreaves. She was probably wondering why he wasn't directly behind her. Clearly unaware that she drove like a maniac.

He didn't answer, and when the light turned green, he trundled off to Ilkley Moor to find out what Tim had to say for himself.

* * *

From one empty car park to another, Henry pulled his Skoda into the one opposite the Cow and Calf Hotel. There were no street lights up here on the tops. Apart from the sea of orange and yellow dots in the valley below, there was just wild untamed darkness.

Henry's Skoda bumped along the gravel, falling into deep potholes and rising out of them, until he parked on the opposite side of a dark-blue estate, now sandwiched in between his car and Hargreaves' Audi. They all turned their headlights off.

Winding down his window, Henry smelt the grass and musty dirt from the moors, and then some other kind of herbs being smoked.

Tim clicked on his interior bulb and nodded at Henry as a greeting. His dark curly hair looked glossy so close to the light. "Just waiting for them to sod off," he said pointing into the car park.

Henry spotted a car in the far corner. Its lights off, the only sign of life the fiery ends of lit joints being smoked.

After a few minutes, the mystery people got the message and drove towards the exit. Henry saw the driver and his friend were only just driving age.

"They come up here to smoke weed," Tim said, as if Henry hadn't already sussed that out.

"So, what is it you wanted to say?" Henry asked, speaking loudly so that Hargreaves could hear him on the other side. "It's nearly half-eleven, and some of us have got a lot on tomorrow."

Tim glanced down at his steering wheel. "They were coming for me today."

"Why's that?" Henry asked, keeping his voice neutral.

"Forensics have an idea of what killed her."

"And that implicates you?"

Tim didn't nod. Instead he looked at Henry. "How good is Dr Anderson?"

"The Home Office pathologist? He's been on the job as long as I've been," Henry said, as if he'd forgotten he'd been officially retired for eleven years.

"Is he likely to mess things up? Or, you know, make things look worse than they really are? Has he a thing against cops?"

Henry had put up with a lot that day. He wasn't going to sit there and listen to someone question the competence of the best pathologist he'd ever worked with.

"Here! If Anderson says it's so, it's bloody so!" Henry enunciated by pointing his finger as he spoke.

Tim looked downcast.

"Why? What is it?" Hargreaves asked from the other side of Tim's car.

"They say…" Tim huffed. "She had injuries to her head."

"Right?" Hargreaves asked. "And?"

"She…" Tim stopped. "They said she'd been hit over the back of the skull several times… with a blunt instrument."

"Like what?" Hargreaves asked, but Henry knew the answer.

"A police baton?" he suggested.

The whites of Tim's eyes lit up under his dome light as he stared at Henry. "Did they tell you?"

"No. Just bloody good guesswork. So, was it yours?"

"Mine?" Tim asked, sounding confused. "It couldn't have been. I mean… I had one at the time, obviously, but I didn't kill her." Tim sounded stressed and worried.

Henry had flashbacks of the interrogation he'd done fifteen years previously, when Tim couldn't finish a sentence and kept on repeating himself.

"Do you still have the baton from back then?" Henry asked.

"I replaced it years ago when they released the new ones."

"So, you don't have it now?"

Tim shook his head.

Henry thought it through. Without the murder weapon, Acton couldn't tie Tim to the murder. But if he could get enough circumstantial evidence together, he might charge him. Even if the case later fell apart at trial, which wasn't a given, Tim's police career would be left in tatters, which Acton still might take as a win. But that was all guesswork on Henry's part.

"Henry," Tim said, looking at him. "What are you thinking?"

"It wasn't you?"

Tim shook his head.

"Well. I don't know. It could have been someone who had access to a police baton."

Hargreaves piped up. "How do they even know it was a baton? Hadn't she been in the water for years?"

Discussing his late wife's demise was starting to get to Tim Villers. Either that, Henry thought, or he was feeling the pressure.

Tim wiped his tearless eyes. "They don't know, exactly. But the marks left on her skull match those left from something the size of a baton. And that's what Acton's going on."

Tim stared into the dark moors.

"Have they cautioned you?" Henry asked.

Tim shook his head. "Not yet. I've told the kids." He heaved a sigh. "Which was shit, to tell the truth. I also had to ring her parents, who already hate me. Her name's being released tomorrow morning to the press."

"They'll probably see if that stirs up any new info," Hargreaves said, trying to sound reassuring, but Henry wondered what new clues that would bring.

"Could someone have accessed your baton?" Henry asked.

Tim had the blank expression of a man with too much on his mind. "I… no. It was locked up at work. I never took it home."

"So it would have to be another copper?" Hargreaves asked.

Henry looked at Tim, who slouched behind his steering wheel.

"Aye, another copper," Henry said, answering for him but not quite believing it.

Could another copper have killed Tim's wife – or was Henry speaking to her killer right now?

Chapter Thirteen

Henry got up early the next morning to catch the first local news bulletin on TV. He made toast and pulled the crust off to chuck at Tessa, who was sitting on his kitchen tiles looking up at him. He heard the music start for the local news in his living room and dashed inside with his toast half-buttered and a cup of tea in hand.

He sat in his armchair just as the news anchor announced Maureen's name. Her image from the original poster from 2008 came up in the background. Henry slurped his tea, which still had the bag bobbing around in it. Well, he thought, the word was out there.

There wasn't much for the local news to go on. After a few shots of Swinfeld Reservoir, and the footage of people walking around the muddy ruins of the drowned village, the news anchor moved onto something else.

Henry sat and stared at the television screen while he finished off his toast. He thought about the previous night and Tim's revelation about the police baton.

Back then, Tim would have been issued with a black metal ASP one. They were expandable and made an aggressive noise when whipped out to full length. Detectives and plain-clothes officers weren't issued with them.

Henry himself hadn't had a baton since he walked the beats around the terraced houses in Bradford after he joined the force. Back then, he'd carried a thick wooden truncheon that could knock someone out. He even recalled seeing his own inspector at the time snapping a lead truncheon in a riot, pummelling someone senseless.

Henry had always felt uneasy with his weapon and was happy to give it up when he joined CID. He felt it was a slippery slope. Other countries had guns, with most detectives having to carry one, but Henry thought guns and truncheons only bred trouble – if my enemy has a weapon, so must I.

The fact that Tim's baton had been replaced with a new one wasn't surprising. The regulations had changed several times since 2008. Now they even had batons with torches at the end. If Tim had used his to kill his wife, it would be long gone now, probably in some landfill.

Henry heard his mobile phone ring and wondered where he'd left it. Getting up and heading into the kitchen, he saw it on the table next to the A3 sheet of paper with all his notes on. It was Jean calling, his next-door neighbour. He put down his empty plate by the sink and answered.

"How are you feeling?"

She coughed down the phone. "This woman at Swinfeld. That's why you've been scurrying about, isn't it?"

"Well, what if it is?"

She coughed again, but this time made an attempt to cover the phone. "What do you know about it?"

"I investigated it the first time round."

"What? Back in 2007 or whenever it was?"

"2008," he corrected. "And how are you feeling?"

"Better. I was out of it yesterday. Slept all day. I saw your text message, thanks. I'm alright for shopping. Chris sent Avocado round this morning. I'd no idea what he was on about? I was looking out for a bright green van. Or black. What colour are avocados, anyway?" She coughed again and spoke in short breaths as if her lungs lacked the capacity for long sentences. "It was pricey, I think. Well, it must've been. It all comes from Waitrose."

"So, you're alright then?"

"I'll be fine tomorrow; still probably positive, mind."

"How did you know I've been scurrying about if you were asleep all day?"

"Well, not all day. I pottered about a bit then noticed your car was missing. I also heard you get back near midnight." She wheezed and cleared her throat. "Plus, Tessa barks when you're not there. I can hear her through the wall."

"Ah, does she?" he asked, looking at his dog who was sitting by his back door, waiting for it to be opened. "I'll have to get her a walk in soon, as I'll be out for most of the day."

"She's fine when you're not there, I think. She just pines after you. So, what's this missing woman about?"

"Dead woman."

"Right. Drowned in Swinfeld, did she?"

"She was murdered."

"Right. Who by?" she asked.

Henry happened to glance at the A3 sheet of paper on his kitchen table and the big circle he scribbled around Tim's name. "That's something I'm not sure about yet."

* * *

Henry took Tessa for a walk before his day was taken over by Maureen Villers' case. His dog came willingly, and he walked her down Main Street, nodding at a few people he recognised. The day was cooler than the one before, which he took as a sign that summer was coming to an end. Maybe that would mean the rain would come, filling up the depleted reservoirs and rivers that were struggling to provide the county with water.

He looked in on Jean's yard as he walked by. The white curtains at her bedroom window were drawn, so too were the ones in her living room. She really must be ill, he thought. She must have called him from her bed.

He took the dog to the park around the side of his house. The playing fields had a steep incline, with a football pitch at the top and a children's play area painted in primary colours at the bottom. He surveyed the football pitch for other dogs before letting Tessa off her lead. She'd been bitten by a Dalmatian that lived in the village, and since then he'd been wary about letting her run free around here.

He walked along the white boundary lines of the pitch, kicking at the dew-covered grass. It was slightly chilly, with the cool moist air getting through his grey fleece.

Recalling the information Tim had shared the previous night again, he realised what it was that had bothered him about it. Since he'd heard it, he felt as if a splint had got stuck in his mind that he was unable to pull out. It was the specificity of it, the police baton. An odd thing to say for Dr Anderson, a man Henry had worked with for twenty years. Through all that time, Anderson had been as specific as he could while remaining completely vague. "Possibly this, but also possibly that," was how Dr Anderson would normally put it.

He'd never said anything as specific as this.

Had Anderson changed? Was he getting less cautious in his twilight years? Or perhaps Tim had heard the news second-hand, and it was Acton who had been so specific?

Henry knew there was only one way to find out, and he called Anderson's mobile, hoping the doctor had kept his number as long as Henry had kept his own.

Stopping his stroll, he found himself at the halfway line on the opposite side of the pitch from where he'd started. Tessa was running up and down it, chasing imagined sticks.

Henry heard Anderson pick up and pressed his mobile closer to his ear. "Morning, Doctor."

"What are you doing ringing me so early?" Dr Anderson said, his voice bellowing down the speaker. "I thought the retired slept till noon. That's what I'll be doing when they eventually let me go."

"Always a pleasure to speak to you, good sir," Henry said, layering his charm on thick, as he knew it grated on Dr Anderson.

"What is it? Ah! Don't tell me. The wet woman."

Henry chuckled. "You've figured me out quickly."

"My mind's sharper in the mornings. So, what is it? You know I can't break confidences and all that. It's a live case, and as I recall, you're no longer a serving officer and haven't been for years." Dr Anderson took a breath. "You know, I have a grandson born after you left the force. He's heading into year six next month, one year off grammar school! Can you believe it?"

Henry didn't like the idea of comparing his misspent retirement to the whole life of a child.

Dr Anderson continued, "If an oak tree had been planted after you left, it'd be fifteen feet by now–"

"Alright, pack it in," Henry said, losing his charm.

Dr Anderson chuckled loudly, finding pleasure in winding up Henry. Clearly, he'd won this round.

"I know about the head injuries," Henry said.

Dr Anderson stopped laughing. "Right. How did you come across that?"

"I heard it from an acquaintance."

"They must have been well-informed." Dr Anderson sounded more intrigued than annoyed.

"Aye. I heard you've said it was a police baton that'd killed her, which I thought was odd."

"Not just odd, but incorrect. I think your acquaintance needs to clean their ears out. Cerumen impaction is a common complaint and can be easily remedied."

"I'll pass on the medical advice. So, it's not true?"

"Erm…" Dr Anderson thought about it and went silent.

Henry glanced around the field, as he'd lost track of Tessa, and saw her in the distance sniffing some tree saplings the council were trying to grow. Henry whistled her over, not wanting her to cause any damage.

"So?" he asked Anderson, pressing him for an answer.

"Well, it could have been a police baton, I suppose. I recall suggesting that as a possibility."

"Why is that?"

Dr Anderson exhaled, realising he'd already crossed the line of breaking confidences. "Don't go passing this on, but there was a single wound made by a large, blunt object. About an inch thick; could be less."

"Not a hammer then?"

"No. This left long lines; hammers leave rounder impacts."

"So, a spanner or a wrench or something?"

"Possibly. Held sidewards," Dr Anderson said, sticking to his standard evasive style.

"Did the head injuries break the skull?"

"Well, seeing we're getting into the nitty-gritty, can I ask if you're looking into this in an amateur capacity?"

"What do you think?"

"Thought as much. I did hear you tried to rejoin the..." Dr Anderson left his point hanging. "Which was a shame, as you were a good one."

"Was she dead when she went into the water?" Henry asked.

Dr Anderson huffed. "You know, I'm not a fan of being harassed for details when I'm halfway through my muesli. And she'd been in there a long time. It's hard to be certain of anything."

"Doctor, be straight with me. It'd mean a lot."

"Well, there wasn't much left of her. Mostly skeletal. But the hairline fractures on the back of her skull were clear to see. No evidence of defensive marks, but that's hard to be certain about, as the fish in the reservoir had eaten most of her.

"But what I can say, if I was forced to hypothesise, is that she might have been killed by the blow – or was at least knocked unconscious by it – when the killer weighed her down and rolled her into the water."

Henry imagined it. What if Maureen had turned away from her murderer – someone she trusted, explaining the lack of defensive wounds – and was hit on the back of the head? Then tied up, weighted down, and chucked in the water still breathing.

"What was she tied up with?"

"Some hessian tarpaulin wrapped around her, head to toe, and ropes around her ankles, waist, and shoulders. They did a good job. The knots were still mostly intact. Plus some weights, lots of them. Of the kind found in gyms."

"Dumb-bells?"

"No. Those round ones that go on the end of whatever it is they lift... I don't know. I haven't stepped in such a place for years."

All that equipment must have been arranged beforehand, Henry thought, suggesting premeditation. Someone had lured Maureen to Swinfeld Reservoir to kill her.

"Is that all, Ward?" Dr Anderson said. "Only, I've got to finish my breakfast and get a shower before heading to the office. You know, not all of us have the life of Riley."

"Just one more question, Doctor, and I really do appreciate this: could it have been a tennis racket that struck her?"

"A tennis…" Dr Anderson shut up as he thought about it. "With enough strength, and if the edge of the racket was reinforced, it might have knocked her out, yes. Giving the killer time to tie her up. I suppose, in that case, she'd have woken up while in the water."

The thought of it made Henry feel even chillier.

Chapter Fourteen

Henry got back to his cottage after looking in again at his next-door neighbour's house. He let Tessa through his front door, who seemed to have enjoyed running around, and she tottered towards the sofa that she'd claimed years earlier. She jumped up onto it and curled up in the corner next to the arm rest, glancing at Henry as if asking when he was going to leave.

He rolled his eyes at her and went into the kitchen where he'd left his notes on the table. Studying his notes, he read the words he'd circled the previous day: 'husband', 'work', and 'tennis'.

He picked up one of the black marker pens and added a new circle – 'cause of death' – jotting down everything Dr Anderson had told him.

He clicked on the kettle to start a boil and pulled out the chair at the table, scraping its legs on the floor tiles. What did the cause of death change, he thought as he sat down. It kept the tennis line of inquiry open for a start and also the possibility that Tim or someone else in the police murdered Maureen.

He skimmed his notes again, and the 'work' circle stood out to him. He'd not done anything about that yet. Maybe it wasn't relevant, he wondered, getting up to make some tea. Though, he had looked into Maureen's boss and her husband back in 2008. There'd been something iffy going on there, he thought, and he'd never got to the bottom of it.

Slumping back in the chair with a fresh cup of tea, he took a slurp and smacked his lips. Something he wouldn't do if he was with company as they'd probably find it egregious. Then the sudden feeling of being watched crept over him, and he glanced through the kitchen windows at his walled backyard.

But there was nobody there.

It couldn't be possible for someone to spy on him from his own yard, unless it was Jean's grandson who had a collection of drones. He'd flown one over Henry's wall once before. But Robbie was at his home miles away, preparing to start his first semester at university.

Ignoring the odd sensation of being spied on, he picked up the black marker and scribbled 'Mysterious Texter' on the paper.

He'd almost forgotten about the email and SMS that he'd received the day before. Who'd sent that to him? he pondered, sipping more tea, being conscious not to smack his lips. They must have been following him. Who'd want to do that, he wondered, other than the killer?

He chewed his lower lip and put his mug down. Did that mean the killer knew where he lived? Not that it was a problem if they did. He'd come after dozens of murderers and serious criminals in his time. They all knew where he worked, and his home address wouldn't have been impossible to find.

But this felt different. He was doing this off his own bat. It was a personal investigation, and he didn't have the strength and power of the police behind him. A murderer is hardly going to attack a police station, as normally it'd be the last place they'd want to go near. But a cosy little cottage on Addingham Main Street? That was different.

He was halfway through rethinking his home's security, which already was more advanced than anyone else's in the village, when his phone rang. He wasn't surprised to see Hargreaves' name, but he had expected her to call before now. It was almost 9 a.m.

"I'm outside," she said after he answered, then she hung up.

Henry looked around him. Did that mean he had to go with her? Did she want to come in? Shaking his head, he patted his pockets to check his car keys and wallet were in them, picked up his phone, and left his half-finished mug of tea on the table.

* * *

"Get in," Hargreaves said through her car window. Her silver Audi was parked outside Henry's front gate, squeezed into a spot in front of his Skoda.

He got into the passenger seat, and she'd merged into traffic before he'd put on his seatbelt. She manoeuvred the long executive coupe with ease, sliding between traffic to overtake cars on the road to Ilkley.

Hargreaves didn't speak. The local radio was on, playing an old song from the nineties that Henry was about to comment on, before thinking better of it. He watched the hills go by on one side, and the tall elms and oaks on the other, before stretches of farmland opened up that rolled down to the river, which was lower than normal. The drought was still with them.

"Any news?" Henry asked, wondering when she was going to reveal their destination.

"Aye," she said, her eyes on the road, and one hand gripping the steering wheel. Her short jet-black hair had been styled into a bob.

"Well?" he asked.

She looked at him and then back to the road. "How much can I trust you?"

"You what?"

She didn't reply and cast another doubtful glance at him.

"Where's this coming from?" Henry asked.

"I want to know if you're on our side?"

"As I said to you yesterday, I'm on no one's side. I'm on my own. Listen, I'm here to find out what happened to Maureen, as the question's been weighing on me for fifteen years. If it looks like Tim did it, then I'll see that justice is done." This provoked a nasty expression from Hargreaves, but he carried on. "If it turns out it's someone else, from her work or from the tennis club, then I'm fine with that, too." He paused for effect. "I just want the truth, Detective Sergeant. What do *you* want?"

She bit her lip, which was glossed in purple. "I want what's best for Tim."

"But what about this police baton business?"

She kept her eyes ahead. "It could have been someone else."

"So, another officer at Otley station killed Tim's wife?" Henry blew air out of his lips. "That's a pretty big leap."

"Yeah, well. Look what the officers have been getting away with down south?"

Henry had been following the crimes that officers in the Metropolitan Police had been accused of with a mixture of anger and shame.

"But murdering a colleague's wife?" He shook his head, unable to think of it.

"Well, we've got to think of something quick, or DCI Acton and DS Emsley will charge Tim."

"Charge him with what? They've got no evidence."

"They've got the baton."

"Have they found his one from fifteen years ago?"

She gave him a confused look. "No. But they could prove he had one by checking the police records. Then they could use the love letters as a motive. Say Tim found them back in 2008 and went into a rage. That's motive, means, and then I found Maureen's phone records from back then–"

"Hang on. From fifteen years ago?"

She nodded. "We requested the case boxes out from storage, and they arrived yesterday. I went through them and found the original phone records. They were missing a few pages, but they clearly show Tim's mobile number attempting to reach Maureen multiple times on the day she died."

That intrigued Henry. He couldn't remember seeing Maureen's phone records among the documents on his home computer. However, thinking about it, he knew they had been requested back then as due course.

Making a mental note to find them on his computer when he got home, he said, "Well, that doesn't look good for Tim now, does it?"

"No," Hargreaves said through a clenched jaw, "and it gives Acton motive, means, and opportunity. He'll say Tim tried calling Maureen that morning, and then he went missing for that hour or so at work."

As much as Henry didn't like it, he could see how all this circumstantial evidence might paint an unflattering picture of Tim.

"So these phone records you found, they were in these boxes?"

Hargreaves nodded. "I went through them all last night after I left you and Tim."

He regarded her with mild respect before wondering if she'd got any sleep and if she should be driving. Though, she did look spritely for someone who'd been wading through dusty boxes all night.

"What else did you find?"

Stifling a yawn, she said, "I found Maureen's phone records and an old dusty VHS tape."

"Ah," Henry said, suddenly interested. "That'll be the CCTV footage from around the reservoir."

"I thought it might be. I found it right at the bottom of a box. I can't say much for the data handling back in 2008."

"Aye, things were different then."

"I've sent it off to IT for it to be digitised. They said it'll be on the system in a day or two."

"Well, I'd be careful what you wish for. You might find Tim's car on those country lanes the day Maureen died."

"I might… but shouldn't you know what's on it?" She eyed him. "Didn't you look at the footage back then?"

"Well… I must've done," Henry said, attempting to mask his uncertainty. "But that footage would've come in after the receipt for the plane ticket was found. By then, we'd stopped combing through all the evidence."

Hargreaves grunted, her dissatisfaction evident.

Henry let his mind wander as he stared out his window at the yellowy green countryside behind the grey drystone walls.

"Tell me this," Henry said carefully. "Do you agree with Acton?"

"That Tim killed Maureen?" she asked, sounding like Henry had struck a live wire. "No." She shook her black bob. "Well… There's a picture they could paint, isn't there?"

"Whatever they tried to paint can't possibly get past the Crown Prosecution Service. There's no hard evidence, only circumstantial." Henry then remembered what he thought Acton would do. Get enough rumours together and pin them on Tim Villers. Then force a flimsy case into the courts so that its failure rested with the Crown Prosecution and not him.

"He's a clever swine this Acton, and not in a good way," Henry said.

"But it can't be him," Hargreaves said, not listening. "Tim couldn't have killed his wife. He's not that kind of person."

As Henry watched her, he felt the pressure to reveal his hand again. To tell her about the photo he'd been sent by the mysterious texter. But, while he was debating what to do, she said, "We're heading over to Leeds."

"Why?" he asked, forgetting what he was thinking about.

"I've traced down Shelley Peters."

"Maureen's old boss?"

She nodded. "I thought it'd be worth us having a word."

"Together?" Henry asked. "You do know questioning someone with a retired detective in tow is generally not welcomed by police command?"

She gave him a displeased look. "Don't remind me." Then, with her eyes back on the road, she let out a sigh that suggested she'd resigned herself to her fate. "I could have done this by myself. I know I could." She sounded oddly fragile, as if her bullish mask had slipped. "But it'd be easier and quicker with a walking encyclopaedia of the case at my side. Even if he does smell of old man and dog."

Henry guffawed and looked out the window. He didn't know if that was an insult or a compliment, but took it as the latter. As compliments went, it was probably the best he'd get from DS Hargreaves.

Chapter Fifteen

Henry recalled all he could remember about Shelley Peters before they arrived in Leeds. Back in 2008, Shelley had been the owner and managing director of a small-scale make-up business, Leeds Luxe Cosmetics. She ran it out of a shiny glass office block in the centre of town, not too far from Harvey Nichols and the other luxury stores the company supplied.

Leeds Luxe was well known from what Henry could remember and did a lot of business. But, as he'd never been an expert in cosmetics, he'd relied upon the opinions of a handful of female detectives and the wives of members on his team. Apparently, Leeds Luxe hadn't been a bad brand, and survived on its local origins in a market dominated by international corporations.

But Shelley Peters' company had borrowed too much and went bust in those scary days of 2008, when sales had dropped and the banks grabbed all the cash they could get their hands on – needing it to fend off bankruptcy themselves.

Henry had no idea what Shelley had done since, or her husband Arnold, who had been the main investor in her business and had probably lost a lot in its demise.

Henry looked over at Hargreaves, who hadn't said anything since admitting she needed Henry around. Her face suggested she was either mortified about it or sulking. He couldn't work out which.

"So, what's she up to now?" Henry asked when they were nearing Leeds city centre. They passed the new curved-glass university buildings that had been funded by overpriced fees.

"Shelley Peters?" Hargreaves asked, stirring herself out of her funk. "She's a managing director."

"For another make-up company?"

She shook her head. "Some sports thing."

"Sports?" Henry asked. "It wouldn't have anything to do with tennis, would it?"

"I'll guess we'll find out when we get there," Hargreaves said abruptly, clearly wishing to go back to her sulk rather than make conversation.

They pulled into a multistorey car park near the docks. Some of the buildings around them were renovated red-brick warehouses from the Victorian era, which had once stored wool but were now home to fancy cafés and shops. The rest of the buildings were a mixture of apartment blocks built at the turn of the last century – which already looked tired and out of style – and glass corporate office towers that gleamed in the sun.

Henry saw a sign for the Royal Armouries Museum when they stepped out of the car park's pedestrian entrance. If he had any sense, he'd walk in to look around its exhibitions. He'd done it years ago and enjoyed himself. But instead he hurried after Hargreaves, who was walking at pace.

They made a beeline for one of the glass towers next to the stone banks of the River Aire. Colourful barges were moored to its side, and Henry wondered if people lived in them to avoid paying the city's silly rents.

The glass tower's lobby was cold from being too air-conditioned, and its interior designer had been too keen on the glossy granite and silver furnishings, which didn't add any warmth. A large desk took up the centre, and after Hargreaves introduced herself, they were told to take the lift to the third floor.

Looking at the row of buttons in the elevator, Henry worked out Sports Entertainment Content Ltd took up three of the building's eight floors, being by far the biggest company in the place.

"What is it they do?" he asked Hargreaves, who shrugged in response. He hadn't seen any clues since he'd entered, and its name sounded dull and corporate.

When the lift doors opened on the third floor, he got an answer. There was a life-sized cardboard cut-out of a football player, with a well-known league name underneath. Next to it on a frosted glass wall was a poster for an international tennis tournament.

"Well, they do something with sport, that's for sure," he said to Hargreaves.

They walked down the white corridor with sheets of frosted glass on one side, which, combined with the cool air, made him feel like they were walking next to a glacier. The air was fresh mint and processed cold.

Henry thought he recognised Shelley standing near a reception desk by a window that looked out over the river outside. Taller buildings were on the opposite side, looking more upmarket.

Shelley hadn't changed much in the intervening years. Her hair was still blonde, cut short, and she wore a powder-blue suit jacket and some cream chinos. A brilliant white shirt contrasted with her tanned skin. The only signs that she was in her fifties were the faint lines around her forehead and eyes. She was slender, as if she exercised daily, and shorter than average. But the vibrant energy emanating from her made her seem taller.

She watched Henry and Hargreaves approach, her eyes narrowing as she tried to figure out who they were. Then she appeared to recognise Henry. "Oh. Who are you?" Her brilliant blue eyes almost matched the colour of her jacket.

"I'm the detective who called earlier," Hargreaves said, offering her hand.

Shelley shook it and smiled, showing brilliant white teeth. "Oh. Yes." She said something to the young receptionist behind her, and then went to shake Henry's hand.

As she held it, she narrowed her eyes and asked, "Do I know you?"

"I'm Henry Ward," he said. "I investigated the original inquiry into Maureen Villers' disappearance."

She nodded as she withdrew her hand from his. "Yes, I remember you. I think we spoke several times." Her expression was light and good-humoured, but a well of darkness remained behind her eyes.

"Yes," Henry said. "I believe we did speak back then."

"Mr Ward is here as a consultant, offering some expert advice," Hargreaves said, robotically. "He'll be sitting in on our discussion if that's okay?"

"That's fine. Why wouldn't it be?" Shelley asked, looking confused.

Hargreaves didn't elaborate. "Good."

* * *

Shelley opened a glass door and led them into a boardroom. Colourful life-size graphics of smiling sports personalities covered its walls. Henry spotted football and rugby players, cricketers, and tennis champions gazing down at him.

As they took their seats opposite each other at the long white table, he asked, "So, what is it you actually do here?"

Shelley leant forwards in her seat, resting her elbows on the glass table. She kept her blue jacket on, despite it being warmer in here than in the corridor. Her eyes then danced around the personalities mounted on the wall.

"It's quite simple, really," she said. "We align sports personalities with brands to leverage their star power and social media followers, which boosts the brand's recognition."

Henry had no idea what she'd just said. "Right. And what does that mean in plain English?"

Shelley took it as a joke and laughed. "It means, we match brands to sports stars so that they can work together."

"How do brands and sports stars 'work together'?"

She looked bashful. "Well, it's quite easy really."

"Can you give me an example?" Henry asked.

"Well…" Her eyes ran along the celebrities on the wall behind him again until an idea struck her. "Take Guillaume Dupont up there. Major international football player. Plays on the French national team, and he's also in one of the UK's biggest teams. That makes him valuable for brands in France and Europe and the UK. We made a deal with him, so we represent him and his agent in any cross-branding negotiations, and we search for appropriate companies that he can do business with. Sports brands, aftershaves, watches, luxury brands. You know the kind."

Henry wasn't much wiser and looked at Hargreaves, who appeared to have got it. "They're a middleman between sports stars and companies," she said bluntly. "The sports stars say they like these trainers or whatever on social media, and Shelley gets a cut."

"Ah," Henry said. "You're into advertising?"

Shelley's head tilted. "I prefer content curation and brand alignment."

"Well, call it what you want. I'll think of it as that." Henry leant back in the comfy leather chair he was sitting in. Whatever it was they were doing, it was making them enough money to afford these offices. Unless, of course, the whole place was built on debt like Shelley's last business. "It makes a change from make-up."

Shelley's tanned cheeks reddened slightly. "Ah. Leeds Luxe. That company will always have a place in my heart. But we were outmatched. Outgunned. The other brands were just stronger, and while we had a good local reputation, we were never able to compete." She tapped the tabletop. "Lesson learnt."

"Maureen was with you at Leeds Luxe," Henry said.

"Yes, she was." Shelley's eyes went glassy. "She worked with me for years. If it hadn't been for her, I think we'd have gone under earlier." She brought herself back into the room and gave a curt nod. "She was a good head of finance."

Hargreaves leant her elbows on the table. "What can you remember about Maureen?"

"Well, she was a reliable employee, a very loyal friend."

"Were you close?" Hargreaves asked.

"Yes. As I said to Detective Ward at the time. We were close and chatted every day. A managing director needs her head of finance."

"Are you aware," Hargreaves asked delicately, "that Maureen has been found?"

The question dampened the energy buzzing around Shelley. "Yes. I heard it this morning."

"And what did you think?" Henry asked.

"I thought it was awful. For her and her family."

Henry kept his eyes trained on Shelley, letting Hargreaves continue the questioning.

"Would you have any records from back then? Any company emails or employee details we could look at?"

"We have a duty to keep records for six years, which we did, and then we deleted everything and sold the servers." Shelley shrugged. "It was a cost, and seeing how the company collapsed so spectacularly, we simply couldn't afford to keep everything running."

Henry took over. "You lost a lot of money when Leeds Luxe went under?"

Shelley nodded. "And I lost my job and my confidence."

"And your ex-husband?" Henry asked. He'd noted a wedding ring was no longer on her finger, and had suspected Arnold Peters was out of the picture.

Shelley exhaled. "Yes. He also lost a lot."

"If we wanted to talk to Arnold, where would we find him?"

"He's in investment banking and flies all over the place. He can normally be found in Dubai. I think he still has a house nearby, but he's never there."

"Keep in touch much?"

She shook her head. "We separated shortly after Leeds Luxe went under."

"When did you last see him?"

"Except for bumping into him at a few business conventions, I've not seen him for" – she raised her head – "four or five years."

"Do you think he had much contact with Maureen?"

She shrugged. "I don't know. I mean, they must have spoken to each other every now and then; she being the head of finance and him our lead investor. But I couldn't say they were in touch daily."

"Not like you and Maureen?" Hargreaves asked.

Shelley considered the question and nodded. There was a tap on the glass door, and the receptionist opened it and gestured something to Shelley, who nodded her understanding.

"Well," Shelley said, when the receptionist went, "I'm afraid that's all the time I can spare."

"Right," Henry said, looking at Hargreaves, who didn't look ready to leave. Henry, however, thought they'd reached their limit for now. He really wanted to press Shelley on the rumours of her husband's womanising and if he'd tried it on with Maureen, but Shelley wasn't the type to offer up embarrassing personal information unwillingly.

"Shall we go?" Henry asked Hargreaves, his tone suggesting they should.

Hargreaves picked up on it and nodded. "Right, Ms Peters. Thanks for your time. We would appreciate it if you could look for any employee details from that time."

Shelley rose from the board table. "I really think that's doubtful, as I know everything's been wiped. But I will ask someone to double-check."

As Shelley walked down the other side of the long table, Henry spotted a well-known tennis player on the wall behind her. "Oh, you've got him on your books?"

She looked up at the picture and nodded. "He said he'd only join us if I could beat him in a game."

"What's that?" Henry asked.

She flashed her white teeth, going back into brand management mode. "Yes. We played on the Wimbledon courts, not while the tournament was on, obviously; and I managed to win one game through a technicality. He didn't try to weasel out of the deal, though, and signed up straight away. He said he appreciated me actually facing him."

"Blimey. You must be a good player if you could beat one of the world's best?"

She beamed at them, and with forced modesty said, "I'm not that good. I only won due to the technicality and luck – not skill. But I do like playing."

"Funny story," Henry said, chuckling. "Ever play tennis with Maureen?"

Shelley's smile slid off her face. "What?"

"Maureen was a keen player as well. I just wondered if you ever played together?"

Her eyelashes fluttered as if she'd received bad news. Shaking her head, she said, "No. I don't think we ever did."

"Shame," Henry said, opening the glass door. "By all accounts, she was a good player, too."

Chapter Sixteen

Henry decided it was best to fill Hargreaves in on the discussion he'd had with Dr Anderson that morning. The traffic was lighter getting out of Leeds, and thanks to Hargreaves' smooth driving, they were making quick progress. Which Henry thought was good, as the air-conditioning inside the car was almost as bad as Shelley's office building. He wrapped his arms around his chest to keep warm.

"So, you withheld the information Dr Anderson gave you because…?" Hargreaves asked, glaring at him before refocusing on the traffic ahead.

"Well, I didn't know what it meant. It could have been a police baton, a tennis racket, or something else like a wrench. Anyway, I always thought something had gone on at that Leeds Luxe, something to do with Maureen and

Shelley's ex-husband. I always thought he could be implicated somehow."

"The investment banker? Yeah, I noticed you were interested in him. Why didn't you go into that more?"

"I'm not sure a woman like Shelley Peters would sit there and let us ask questions about her ex-husband's affairs? We could try tracking down the husband and getting the information from him?"

"I doubt we have the budget for a trip to Dubai. Although, it does sound like a nice idea." Hargreaves' eyes narrowed as the sun shone through the windscreen into them.

Henry spotted her designer sunglasses in the cup holder beside him, picked them up, and passed them to her.

She put them on after giving him a nod as thanks. "So, are we back looking into this tennis lead or not?" she asked. "Seeing as the murder weapon could now be a police baton or a racket, or whatever the killer found in his garage."

"It could be tennis or her work, or something else," Henry said.

"Well, that's helpful."

"Either one is more likely than a copper at Otley station killing Tim's wife."

Hargreaves turned up her nose at Henry's dismissal of her idea. "Well… I was mostly grasping at straws with that one, to be honest."

"Then there's the revelation that Shelley played tennis. What did you think of that?"

Hargreaves shrugged while keeping both hands on the steering wheel.

Henry continued, "And did you see her face drop when I asked if she'd ever played tennis with Maureen? I've never seen a smile vanish so quickly."

"This bloody case…" she said. She shook her head, wobbling her black bob, and got lost in her thoughts.

Henry considered asking her to turn down the air conditioning, as he felt like he was being blasted by a blizzard. But before he could, Hargreaves said, "It doesn't mean Shelley did it, though. If she did play tennis with Maureen. I mean… Or am I missing something?"

"No. I suppose not. So, where does that leave us?" he asked.

Hargreaves' phone rang, and she silenced him with a glare. She answered the call, and Acton's voice came through the speakers. Henry held his breath so that he couldn't be heard on the other end.

"Now then, Hargreaves," Acton said. "Where are you?"

"Just coming back from following up that lead I told you about," she said innocently.

"The former boss?"

"Aye. That's the one."

"Get anything?"

She glanced at Henry. "Not quite. There might be something with the husband. She confirmed that Maureen could have had a relationship with him."

"The boss's husband?"

Henry raised an eyebrow at Hargreaves. He hadn't heard Shelley confirm anything like that. All she had said was that it was possible Maureen and Arnold had spoken, not slept together.

Hargreaves continued, keeping her eyes stuck on the road so she wouldn't meet Henry's stare. "Yeah. I asked the former boss about it after going through the case notes. The original lead investigator thought the ex-husband was a possible suspect."

"Right. And where is this ex-husband?"

Hargreaves said unwillingly, "Dubai."

"Dubai? Well, sod that for starters. Listen, forget what Father Time thought fifteen years ago, and remember that I want you to eliminate all other possibilities before we press charges," Acton said.

Hargreaves' voice wavered. "Against Tim Villers?"

"Aye."

"Have we got anything else on him?"

"Not yet. Emsley is going through the old evidence to see what we can find. We can almost tie the police baton to Villers, and these love letters, but we need a couple of more things."

"Right," Hargreaves said. She cleared the emotion out of her throat. "Does that give us enough to charge him?"

"Let's see what the CPS say. If they want more, we'll have to find it."

"Okay." Hargreaves sounded downbeat.

"Listen, I know he's a local copper and that people around here respect him, but he's the most likely suspect, isn't he?"

"Aye," Hargreaves said, through a pained expression. "I suppose he is."

"And it's a cold case. Fifteen years old. Unless we nail him now, we'll never get answers. We have to strike while the iron is hot."

Hargreaves murmured a half-arsed agreement.

"Right," Acton said, sounding satisfied that his talk had got through to her. "When are you getting to MIT?"

"On my way."

"Good. Speak soon."

She hung up his call and said, "Shit."

Henry waited a few moments until he thought it was safe enough for him to speak. "So, it's only a matter of time until they find Tim's phone records and see he tried calling Maureen several times that day."

Hargreaves clenched her jaw, clearly not needing Henry to vocalise her thoughts. "We just need something else. Some red meat to slap down in front of them."

"I see you tried to give Acton Shelley's ex-husband."

"Yeah… Well, that didn't work, did it?"

Henry let her stew on her thoughts and looked out the passenger window. They were approaching the centre of Otley, driving between its two-storey Yorkshire stone buildings blackened by decades of pollution.

The look on Shelley's face when he asked if she'd played tennis with Maureen came back to him. And how quickly her smile had slid off it. Maybe it was worth checking his files when he got home to see if he had anything with Shelley's handwriting on, as it might be worth seeing if it matched those love letters.

* * *

Hargreaves couldn't give him a ride back to Addingham, as she had to zoom back to MIT and show her face. She dropped Henry off at Otley bus station, where he called a taxi after seeing the next bus to Addingham was in forty minutes' time.

When his taxi arrived, the driver asked him to sit in the back, which Henry didn't like doing as he didn't want to feel like he was being chauffeured around. But the driver insisted. Something about health and safety.

While they travelled through Ilkley, Henry spotted the tennis club in the valley beyond the road, next to the winding River Wharfe. The three-storey white building glimmered in the late-morning sun. The usually lush fields around it were yellow and showed signs of drought stress, but the tennis club's courts were a glaring green. Henry wondered if the club was breaking the hosepipe ban or if they used artificial grass. He decided he'd go find out and asked the driver to drop him off there.

Henry walked up the front steps of the club building; its walls were made of Yorkshire stone brick on one side and glass on the other. A big difference to the rusting corrugated-iron warehouse of the tennis club in Bradford. Most of the courts around the building were taken by players, which Henry found surprising for a Friday morning.

Inside, there was that strong detergent smell found in swimming pools, but added to it was the fresh aroma of cut grass from the lawns outside. A young fair-haired man in tennis whites was seated behind the desk, talking to two older men dressed to play. The men carried expensive black gym bags and had brand-new-looking kit. When they'd walked off to the courts, the young man looked up at Henry and smiled.

"How can I help?"

Henry glanced at his chest, looking for a name tag, but only found the brand name of his kit. "Now then. Are you still doing the Tennis Cup here?"

The young man must have thought it was an odd question, as he scrunched up his eyes for an instant. "Erm. Yeah. We just had one."

"In June?"

"Yeah."

"You wouldn't happen to have records of all the players who've participated in it, would you?"

"Erm…" The young man looked around his desk, at his computer, and then his notepad that had a few doodles scrawled on it. "I've nothing here…"

Henry didn't think the young man was taking the mickey. He was just easily bamboozled.

"I'll tell you why I want to know," Henry said, taking a step closer to the desk so he could talk conspiratorially. "I'm investigating the murder of a woman who might have played in the cup. I have a suspicion that her killer might have played with her."

The young man's blonde eyebrows nearly reached his fringe. "She was murdered here at the club?" Then he looked doubtful, showing the suspicion of someone who knew they could be easily deceived. "I never heard about that."

"No, lad. She was murdered later on, elsewhere. Have you heard about that body found up at Swinfeld Reservoir?"

Some recognition clouded the young man's brown eyes. "Yeah, I think I did. On the news? Didn't she die a long time ago?"

"Aye. 2008. I'd like to know who participated in the cups around that year."

The young man nodded slowly. "2008?" he repeated, almost as if it was ancient history.

"Would it be possible to find that out somewhere? I've looked online and got nowhere."

"Erm…" The lad looked around the reception area, until his eyes alighted on a closed door. "Hang on. I'll go check."

Henry watched him jump off his seat and rush through the closed door. He didn't know what the young man was going to do – if he was going to ask someone or he'd just decided to hide in a cupboard until Henry gave up and left.

While waiting, Henry looked through the open doors at the green courts outside and the players knocking balls around. He still couldn't work out from this distance if the grass was real or not. It smelt real, but then again, the scent could be artificial.

The door opened slightly, and the young lad poked his head out of the gap. "My manager is dealing with it. Do you want it printed or via email?"

Henry didn't want to cause the young man more stress by asking what it was he was offering to print. So, he said, "Printed is fine."

The young man nodded and disappeared back behind the door. Ten minutes later, with a queue of disgruntled tennis players forming behind Henry, the lad returned looking flustered and carrying a wad of paper, two inches thick.

He slammed it on the desk in front of Henry. "That's all the participants from 2000 to 2010."

Henry sheafed through the sheets, which were still warm from the printer. There were four columns of names on each page, printed on both sides. He guesstimated there would be around eighty names per page, and around four hundred pages. He didn't know if he'd been given a gift or a curse.

"Right, thanks very much."

The young man nodded. "Always happy to help the police."

Henry shuddered and was about to explain he wasn't with the police but thought it would take more time than it was worth. He apologised to the queue behind him and left with the papers.

As he walked up the hill to the main road, he flicked through them to see if any names jumped out. None did, but he wondered if he'd find Maureen Villers' name among them, and that of her secret lover.

Chapter Seventeen

There are four bus stops on Addingham Main Street, and Henry got off the bus at the one outside the pub near his cottage. He stepped off the double-decker to Skipton and glanced at the wooden tables outside the pub, most of which were under the canopy that had been erected the previous year. A few tables were occupied by diners. Henry recognised some of his neighbours eating salads and gave them a wave.

He carried the wad of paper under his arm, wondering how the hell was he going to read it all. He'd round up his estimation of the number of pages to five hundred, with eighty names on each side. It'd take him the best part of the day to get through them. He could pass them to Hargreaves, but doubted Acton would allow a detective to leaf through them when he was only looking for evidence against Tim Villers.

Henry recognised a fellow dog walker he usually bumped into in the mornings. He stirred himself out of his thoughts to have a quick chat about the late-summer weather and how their respective dogs were doing. As he continued down Main Street, Henry walked past Jean's house and suddenly thought he had a solution to his problem.

Would Jean be well enough to read these papers?

Standing by her front gate, he pulled out his mobile and called her. The white curtains in her bedroom window upstairs had been drawn back, but her front ones were still closed.

She didn't answer his call and, quickly giving up on the idea, he walked to his own gate barely two metres away.

His phone buzzed in his hand, and he answered it.

"What do you want?" Jean asked, talking through a cough.

Henry waited until she'd stopped spluttering. "How are you doing?"

"Feeling better, thanks. Still coughing, as you can hear. But I'm alright." Then, after a moment, she asked, "What's under your arm?"

Henry looked up at her bedroom window but couldn't see her. She wasn't in the spare-bedroom window either. He then found her peering at him through a gap in the living-room curtains, phone pressed to her ear.

"Are you spying on me?" Henry asked, chuckling.

"I thought I heard someone at my gate. Thought it might be those Avocado people again. Though, I've not ordered anything." She stifled a cough. "So?"

"It's this case I'm on. I've got a lot of reading to do and wondered if you'd be interested in helping out?" Henry knew Jean couldn't normally resist an offer to help him. In all his recent cases, she'd managed to involve herself one way or another.

She covered the phone to cough, and came back on to say, "Hang on."

Her front door opened, and she stuck her head out. Her blonde hair, usually coiffed, was dishevelled, and she squinted at the sun as if she'd not looked at it for days. A blue surgical mask covered the lower part of her face.

"Bring it here," she said, holding out gloved hands. She wore a pink fleece top and some grey tracksuit bottoms as if she didn't know it was warm.

Henry laughed to himself and walked into her front yard. "How many pages can you read?"

"How many are there?" she asked, withdrawing her hands until she got an answer.

"Five hundred."

"Blimey. And what is it?" She opened the door further and remained behind its threshold like a prisoner.

"It's a list of players for the Ilkley Tennis Cup."

"Tennis?" she asked, sounding less interested in helping.

"Aye. I think the murder victim might have played at the cup, and her killer could have done as well."

"Right? So, you want me to look through to see if the victim played tennis?"

"Aye. And I'll give you a couple of other names of people who could have killed her."

That intrigued Jean. The idea of being the one to link the murder victim with her possible killer was too much for her to resist. "Go on then. I've nothing better to do. I've turned the telly off because daytime TV was getting on my nerves."

Henry stepped towards her and passed her the papers, which she handled with her plastic gloves. She flicked through them. "Christ! How many names are there?!"

Henry cleared his throat. "A lot. You don't have to do it if you're not up to it."

"No, no. I'm alright. I'll make a cup of tea and start reading."

"They gave me all the tournaments between 2000 and 2010, but you just need to look at 2008 and possibly the year before." Henry remembered what the note on the flyer for the Ilkley Tennis Cup had said: 'I bet you'll win this time'. "Maybe look at the two or three years before 2008, in fact. I think you should find her name."

"Right," Jean said, looking at the papers with dying enthusiasm. "I'll give it a go. Any news on this case?"

Henry shook his head. "Do you think I'd be asking you to do this if I had news?"

"Probably not."

Henry glanced around her front yard, and then turned to face Main Street to see if anyone was around. "They think the husband did it."

"Oh, right. And you don't?" She narrowed her eyes at him, quickly reading his thoughts.

"No… Well, I'm not sure. It's a possibility, but…" He shrugged. "You know when the solution to a problem is staring you right in the face, but you just can't bloody see it?"

She nodded.

"I've got that feeling. The problem is, I've had that feeling for fifteen years. I'm missing something obvious. It's like a crossword puzzle when you're sure you know the answer, but just can't articulate it."

"Well, you know what I do with crosswords when I can't answer the bloody things? I chuck the newspaper onto the coffee table and do something else for a bit. Then, when I come back to it, the answer is as clear as day."

"Aye. But I thought the fifteen-year gap would have done the trick."

She tilted her head and looked at him sympathetically. "Or you could come at it from another angle."

"I thought I've done that with the tennis."

Jean glanced at the wad of papers. "The answer still might lie in here, but it could be somewhere else." She thought for a second, as if trying to find a solution for him. "She had kids, didn't she?"

Henry nodded. "Two."

"Have you looked into them?"

"The kids? Murdering their mother? They were eleven and eight."

She shook her head. "I don't mean the kids killed her, but the school, their clubs. The mum would have driven them to places, picked them up, and probably spoke to other parents. That might be something to look at. She might have met someone that way? Or it could just have been a random stranger who killed her?"

"No. I don't think it was a stranger who did it." He furrowed his brow while considering Jean's other point. He'd not thought about Maureen meeting someone at one of her children's after-school activities before. He glanced at Jean and realised it was a typical thing for her to say, considering she'd been a teacher herself before a long career as a school inspector. "Aye. It could be worth looking into."

She nodded, clearly happy to have helped, and tapped the pile of papers under her arm. "You look into that while I read these papers, and you can let me know what you find out later."

Henry agreed cheerfully. It wasn't until he got to his own front yard that he realised he'd let Jean take over his investigation.

* * *

Henry took a seat at his computer desk with a fresh cup of tea in hand. He'd eaten a hastily made cheese and pickle sandwich for lunch while Tessa barked at the back door. He eventually let her into the backyard, and she was still out there, perched under the shade offered by a potted fern.

He'd texted Jean the list of names of people he wanted her to look out for in the register of Ilkley Tennis Cup players. The list had three names: Shelley Peters, Arnold Peters, and Gary Steele. He wondered if any of them would turn up or if he was just wasting Jean's time. Well, she didn't have much better to do, he thought.

Bringing his computer to life, Henry clicked on the folder for Maureen Villers' case. Jean's idea of looking into any links with the children's after-school activities had made an impression on him.

He searched all the case files for the son's name, Paul, and it came up with a dozen text documents. He clicked on each and saw they were interview transcripts with Tim Villers, where Paul's name had been mentioned. After checking all of them, Henry was satisfied there weren't any mention of after-school clubs in the files. His search for Siobhan's name got the same results.

He slurped some tea and stared at the white wall behind his computer screen. There was nothing in the case files that could help, so the next thing to do would be to ask Tim directly or speak to his children. That would be risky, however. He didn't want Tim to think Henry suspected his children of being involved, which he didn't. The man was already under a lot of suspicion. Enough to make a sane man paranoid and delusional. But if Maureen had had a secret lover, which it seemed she did, she must have met him or her at work, at tennis, or through her children's after-school clubs.

Unless Maureen had other hobbies that she kept private from everyone, which Henry doubted. From what he recalled, the couple didn't socialise much and rarely went to the local pubs.

That settled it, he thought. He'd have to go speak to Tim and his children to find out what after-school clubs they'd been in.

It was just past 12.30 p.m., and he felt there was no time better than the present. He left his barely touched tea on his desk and got out of his chair.

He'd have to get Tessa back in from outside, he realised as he headed down the steps, and he'd also have to find out where Tim lived these days.

Chapter Eighteen

Henry finally got Tessa to come inside by bribing her with dog treats. Three, in fact. He was locking the back door when his phone buzzed. It was Hargreaves. He'd texted her earlier asking for Tim's new address and hadn't received a reply.

Tessa was yapping for more treats, as if the three she'd had weren't enough compensation for giving up her spot outside. He answered the phone while dropping two more treats on the floor tiles.

"Why do you need Tim's address?" Hargreaves asked when he answered. She sounded defensive – almost outraged.

"I wanted to talk to him," Henry said, giving Tessa one more treat to stop her barking.

"He's busy. The kids are there, and he wants to be left alone."

"Aye, right. I understand that," he said. "Does he want my help or not?"

Hargreaves didn't answer. Henry imagined her flaring her nostrils and snarling at her pink phone.

She came back on and asked, "Why do you need to talk to Tim? Have you found out summat?"

"Not yet. I want to check something."

"What's that?"

Henry realised he wasn't going to get Tim's address until he spilt the beans to her. "I want to know what after-school clubs and activities his kids did back in the day."

"The kids? Why?"

"Because, I've had it pointed out to me that Maureen could have met her killer at one of them. Assuming she was the one who collected the children, seeing as Tim was in the police and worked shifts."

"Right." Her tone had changed. She now sounded intrigued.

"Listen. I want to talk to Villers, and maybe the kids if that's possible. You know what it's like. Sometimes the tiniest little detail can open up a new line of inquiry."

Hargreaves didn't answer, but Henry suspected he'd got through to her.

"I'll text you his address," she said, before hanging up.

And two minutes later, she did, and Henry set off for Ilkley.

* * *

Henry pulled up outside a detached house on the outskirts of Ilkley in an area he would have called Ben Rhydding, but the boundaries separating the two towns seemed to have blurred over the years. Ilkley was a spa town nestled between the banks of the River Wharfe and the steep inclines of craggy moorlands, with the Cow and Calf, its most famous rock formation. Ben Rhydding, by contrast, was smaller and mostly residential, with a mixture of Edwardian terraces and 1960s council houses.

Tim Villers' house looked to have been built in this century and had red brick rather than the usual Yorkshire stone. There was a blue Ford estate in the drive with a smaller French car parked behind it, which Henry guessed belonged to one of the kids. The grass in the front lawn had dried to yellow and brown, and the flowers in the boxes underneath the bay window were decaying. It looked like the police sergeant was following the water company's hosepipe ban to a tee.

Tim answered the door and ushered Henry down a hallway as if he was expected. Hargreaves must have called ahead and warned him, Henry realised.

"This way. We're all in the living room," Tim said.

As Henry followed, he spotted three pictures hanging on the wall at the foot of the staircase. All had Tim embracing his new partner, a woman with brown shoulder-length hair. They were in different holiday destinations: Greece, a ski resort, and the third looked to be Egypt. The children and Maureen didn't feature in any of them.

Tim stood outside an entrance to a room and gestured for Henry to step inside. He walked down the carpeted hallway, getting a strong smell of coffee as he neared the kitchen.

Entering the living room, he saw two young people he didn't recognise, and immediately realised they were Tim and Maureen's children. Siobhan was curled up in an armchair by the bay window, with sunlight streaming over her. A black-and-white pillow covered her lap. Paul slouched on the end of the sofa, as near to his sister as possible, staring at the phone in his hand.

Siobhan looked at Henry as he entered, while Paul didn't. The TV wasn't on, and they were sitting in silence. The room smelt of cats, and Henry guessed Tim kept some. Then the black-and-white pillow on Siobhan's lap stirred to life and cast green feline eyes at Henry.

"Take a seat," Tim said, sounding both excited and nervous.

Henry thanked him and took an armchair near the door, giving him an angle where he could observe both Paul and Siobhan with ease.

The cat curled back up on Siobhan's lap and went back to sleep.

"So," Tim said, remaining near the door. "Ellie told me you had something to tell us."

Ellie? Henry wondered, and then realised he meant Hargreaves. He'd almost forgotten her first name. "Well…" Henry said.

He looked at Paul and Siobhan, who were both staring back at him. They appeared dismayed and depressed. Their father had recently confirmed the obvious truth they'd hoped wasn't true, and they both seemed crushed by it. Which led Henry to wonder again if believing your mother had abandoned you for a new life in Canada, as they might have thought, was better than knowing she'd been murdered and dumped in a reservoir. Going by their broken-down spirits, Henry suspected he was correct. At least thinking your mother was in another country gave you hope she was still alive.

"So, you had something to tell us?" Tim asked again. He ran his fingers through his greying curls and scratched his scalp.

"Well," Henry said again, unsure what to say. Hoping something would pop into his mind. "Investigations are ongoing."

"Are you with the police?" Paul asked, sounding sceptical.

"Detective Ward here is one of the best," Tim answered. "We knew him as The Bloodhound. No matter how hard the case, he'd put his nose to the ground and find out the truth."

"Aye, well…" Henry said, his cheeks reddening as Tim slapped his shoulder. "I did my best, but I didn't always get the truth."

"Nonsense," Tim said. "You got to the bottom of loads of cases."

Henry wasn't sure if Tim was saying this for his own benefit or his children's. When Henry glanced at them, Siobhan looked half-interested while Paul had gone back to staring at his phone.

"Well, thanks for the introduction," Henry said, hoping to change the subject. "Looking at what's happened since the investigation started, I've been tracking down a few leads."

"Ellie's been keeping me informed," Tim said. He pointed at his children. "But maybe explain it to them."

"Well, I've looked down two routes. There's the possibility that the… person who did this to your mother–"

"The murderer," Paul said with venom, looking up from his phone.

Henry nodded. "Aye. Well, the murderer could be linked to your mother's tennis hobby."

"Tennis?" Siobhan asked, sounding confused. "What about her work?"

"I've looked at her work and have spoken to her former boss," Henry said, suddenly feeling the need to defend his actions. "And that's the second avenue I've been looking down."

"Do you actually know who killed her?" Paul asked.

"Not yet. But we'll get there."

"Right, 'cause if you don't find out who did it, people will think my dad killed my mum. And he didn't."

Henry held up his hands in submission. "I know the score. As far as I can tell, there's little evidence linking your father to anything."

"That doesn't matter," Paul said. He held up his phone's screen, but from the distance between them, Henry couldn't see what was on it. "It's all over social media that Dad murdered my mum," he said.

"Stop," Siobhan said, breathlessly. She lowered her head and wiped an eye. As if sensing her distress, the cat woke up and nuzzled his head into her arm, provoking a stroke from Siobhan.

"Let's just..." Tim started, but he couldn't finish his sentence.

He stared at the grey carpet, powerless over what to do. He was being accused of a crime that came with a guaranteed life sentence, and was watching his children try to comprehend they might lose him after just learning their mother was dead.

When Tim couldn't answer, Henry took charge. "First, lad, get off that social media nonsense. If you listen to the ramblings of hare-brained simpletons, you'll lose what little sense you have left. Secondly, there's no hard evidence that ties your dad to anything. So, people can say what they like, but if they can't prove it, they're opening themselves up for a libel charge. Is that clear?"

Paul didn't seem okay with it, but he locked his phone's screen and placed it on the sofa beside him.

Henry continued, "Now, there's something I've come here to do. I'd like to ask you both some questions if your dad's alright with that?" Henry looked at Tim, who'd crossed his arms over his large chest and was slouching against the wall.

Tim noticed Henry looking up at him and nodded.

"Good. And perhaps it's better I talk to you individually," Henry said, looking between brother and sister. He didn't want one dominating the discussion, preventing the other from voicing something that could be of interest.

"What's this? An interrogation?" Paul asked, looking at his dad.

Tim stepped off the wall. "It's nothing like that, is it, Ward? It's just a chat. I'll be here, don't worry."

"Actually," Henry said, peering up at him. "It might be best I speak to them individually and alone."

Tim looked nervous but tried to hide it with a grin. "Are you sure? They might not answer you if I'm not here."

Henry glanced at Paul and Siobhan. He'd managed to get tougher-looking characters to talk before, and could handle two overgrown teenagers. "I'll be fine," he said.

Tim nodded an understanding that he'd lost the argument. "Well, I'll go make some more coffee."

Henry asked for one, and then his eyes aligned on Siobhan, who'd made no effort to move. The cat now lay on its back across her lap. "Maybe we could talk first?"

She shrugged, and Paul jumped up off the sofa. "This is stupid. I'm not talking to anyone."

Tim nearly lost his rag and pointed at him. "You'll talk to him if I have to bloody hold you down."

His anger upset Siobhan. "Dad. Calm down. You'll just make everything worse," she said.

Tim nodded his understanding and took deep breaths. His face had reddened, and he looked close to having heart complaints.

Henry noticed his clenched fists were shaking. "Villers, why don't you go make that coffee?"

Tim seemed to take offence at being bossed around in his own home. But when his eyes locked on Henry's, his shoulders slumped, and he nodded. "I'll be in the kitchen."

When he left, Paul slipped out after him. Henry heard his footsteps go upstairs and then a door slam. He realised the children must still have rooms in the house, despite having moved out.

Henry looked across the room at Siobhan in her chair, stroking the cat. "Alright, Siobhan. I have some questions for you, please try to answer them as accurately as you can."

Chapter Nineteen

Henry kept his questions to Siobhan vague and general until Tim returned with cups of coffee. When Tim stepped out, he closed the living room door behind him, but left it open an inch. Henry ignored it and sipped his coffee, which was rich and strong.

Siobhan drank hers and avoided Henry's gaze. Sunlight shone through the bay window behind her, causing her to squint as the light radiated around her and the armchair she was in. There were some curtains she could close, but she didn't get up to pull them to, as if accepting the annoyance.

She wore a lace white top and classic denim jeans, purple and orange striped socks poked out the ends. She was as slim and lean as Maureen had been but had the looks of her father. The cleft chin, the blue eyes hidden behind thin-rimmed glasses, and the curly black hair that fell down over her shoulders.

The black-and-white cat on her lap stood up, arched its back in a stretch, and then sat down in a new position. Probably sensing Siobhan would be in need of more comforting.

"You're at Oxford?" Henry asked.

"Cambridge," she corrected.

"Doing a master's in mathematics?"

"Yes. I want to go into research after."

"What kind?"

"Not sure. Quantum computing." She shrugged. "Possibly robotics. I don't know yet."

"Very good." He sipped his coffee, feeling conscious about smacking his lips. "So, what I'd like to know is what you can remember about 2008."

Her eyes welled up, and she stroked the cat's head. "I thought you would."

"But I don't want to ask you about your mum."

She sniffed.

"What was school like?"

She wiped away a stray tear. "Fine. Well, hard after Mum disappeared. But" – she shrugged – "I think you have a choice between two things when something like that happens. Your mum disappearing. You either spiral out of control or you do the opposite."

"You did the opposite? You tried to regain control?"

She looked at him with renewed interest. Almost as if she felt he understood her plight a little. "Yes," she said, relaxing into the armchair.

"You focused on schoolwork?"

"Yes," she said, almost guiltily. Henry looked her up and down and realised he'd underestimated how lean she was. She was very thin. Too thin. The armchair's cushioning hid her condition as did her white lace top. But where her arms were visible, he could see the bone clearly.

"When did you become ill?" he asked.

"Bulimia isn't an illness."

"It's a medical condition. And it's how you tried to control what had happened to you."

She lowered her head. "It's a failure of character."

"Right. How so?"

Her blue eyes hardened. "It's inefficient for an organism to eat food and then expel it before it's consumed any of its nutrients."

"Yes. I'd agree with you there." He sipped his coffee. Then, as if struck with an idea, he said, "But what if that organism's been through what you have? Don't you think we could cut it some slack?"

The steeliness in her eyes eased up. She thought about it, and eventually said, "Possibly…"

"I mean. What you've been through, you and your brother, is exceptional–"

"I didn't choose to be exceptional."

"Aye. Neither do others in your situation. Though, there's not many who've been through what you have. I've investigated hundreds of murders, but your mother's was one of a kind. Why do you think I'm sat here now, fifteen years later? There's absolutely no shame in letting it get the better of you. You're only human, Siobhan. Like the rest of us. None of us are robots yet."

Siobhan sniffed. Her eyes were red, and she smeared a tear across her cheek.

Henry gave her a few minutes to regain her composure before asking, "Was school good before your mum went?"

She shrugged. "I was eight." Fresh tears dripped down her cheeks. "How good could it have been?"

He asked a more direct question. "I guess maths was your favourite subject?"

She nodded. "It's the only subject that's ever made sense."

"Why was that?"

She shrugged. "I like finding solutions to things that have them. You know where you are with maths. There's always an answer, you just need to find it. There aren't any mysteries."

Sensing he was stepping onto dangerous ground again, Henry asked another question. "Any other subjects you liked?"

"Erm… Subjects? PE."

"PE? That's good. Team sports?"

She nodded.

"Well, sports are good for you. They help clear your mind. Which ones are you into?"

"I don't play much now. I don't have the time. Plus" – she pointed at her thin frame – "I don't have the strength. I did do a lot of exercise when I could. Probably too much." She sniffed again. "I've played netball, badminton, tennis. I was on the regional team for netball through my A levels and during my degree."

Henry noted the tennis. "Excellent. What position did you play?"

"Goal attack. I have a good aim. Probably still do, but I need to practice." She smiled wistfully. "Yeah. Maybe I'll get back into it. When I'm better. But I was a good player. I enjoyed it."

Henry nodded as if he was impressed. She'd perked up, and he could continue asking her questions that she wanted to answer, but he only had a limited amount of time. And the answers he needed were to questions that she didn't want to be asked. He hated the idea of popping the bubble but had little choice. "You also played tennis? Like your mum did?"

"Yeah." Her tone changed. The bubble had burst.

"Did you go to the same club as her?"

Exasperated with him, she slouched back in her armchair and stared up at the ceiling. "Do you know what it's like to have your mum go missing?" she asked after a pause.

Henry wasn't sure if he should answer, but she was waiting for a response. "No. What is it like?"

"It's shite. No one cares about me or Paul. Dad, a little, as he's the sad abandoned husband. But us, the kids? Never. She's not been here for fifteen years yet she hangs over us all the bloody time." She straightened her thin legs, and the cat jumped off them, sensing the atmosphere had changed.

Henry took in what she'd said. "I know. And I'm sorry to do it, Siobhan. I really am. But I'm here to find out what happened to your mum, and if I can't find out, the police might go after your dad."

"Might? They already think he did it."

"Aye. I'm aware of that." He looked at her with renewed interest. Her anger had an element of righteousness to it. "What do you think?"

"What?" she asked, breathlessly.

"What's your view on your father?"

"I…" She couldn't speak. Too shocked at being asked to share very private thoughts about whether she believed her father killed her mother.

Henry waited for an answer.

She shook her head. Refusing to play the game. "No. I don't…"

Henry held up his hands in submission. "Alright. Let's move on."

"No. I don't want to answer any more of your questions."

"Let's get back to tennis," Henry said, trying to regain control. But she was already getting out of the armchair.

"You think that my mum was killed because I played tennis? Is that what you think?" She turned to look at the living-room door. "Or you do think my dad did it, and you're just playing a game? One or the other."

Henry shook his head. "I don't think anything yet. All I know are the facts, and I don't want to share all of them with you, as it wouldn't be appropriate."

"Why?" Her blue eyes were alive with self-righteous fury. All those years of pain and longing for her missing mother had fuelled a nasty mixture of anger and hate. "I deserve to know."

Henry stared back at her. "No, you don't. There are things you'd best not know. And why I'm asking you these questions is my business, not yours."

She gritted her teeth. Clearly, being refused what she felt she deserved was making her angrier.

"Listen, Siobhan. I can play it the easy way, which is what I'd prefer to do, or I can play it hard. I am an experienced detective. That nonsense your dad talked about. The Bloodhound. That's mostly beer-talk. But there's truth to it. I do put my nose to the ground and find the truth. And I've decided to do that with this case. I *will* find out what happened to your mum."

She blinked away some of her rage.

Henry carried on. "I am here to help you, even if it doesn't seem like that right now. I'm not the enemy. The enemy is the person who hit your mother over the back of the head and pushed her into Swinfeld. I'm looking for that person, and I need your help to do it. If you decide not to help me, that'll be your choice. But it'll take me longer if you don't.

"So, think about it. What would you prefer? Help me find the person who's done this to your life so they can face justice? Or let them get away with it? Because, honestly, I don't think we have much of a window to find them. I fear that if we don't get to the bottom of this soon, we never will."

She wrapped her thin arms around her torso as his words settled in her mind.

"So, what will it be?" he asked.

She lowered herself into the armchair. The cat jumped back into her lap a few seconds later and kneaded her skinny thigh muscles. Siobhan stroked the cat, and Henry heard it purr.

"What do you need to know?" she asked, her voice empty and brittle.

"Let's get to the bottom of this tennis business."

Chapter Twenty

Siobhan dug the tips of her slender fingers into the top of the cat's head. Her eyes flitted between the cat and the grey living-room carpet. Tim had returned to the room offering more coffee, which interrupted the conversation. But he had quickly got the message he wasn't welcome and left.

Siobhan opened up more about the sports she'd played as a child. The netball, the badminton, and the tennis. She explained how her mother had taken her to a kids' group at Heaton Tennis Club. Maureen had clearly liked the fact she could take her kids and drop them off at the club while she practiced with adults. And it was kids, plural, as Paul had gone with them.

"Was Paul any good?" Henry asked Siobhan.

"He hated it. He'd sneak off and walk around the building." She shook her head. "I don't know what he did."

Henry thought he already knew the answer to the next question but asked to get confirmation. "When did you stop going to Heaton Tennis Club?"

She looked up from the carpet. "When do you think?"

"You tell me."

She exhaled. "You need me to say it, don't you? It was after Mum died." The cat gave a short meow, and Siobhan rubbed its head.

"And you stopped playing then?"

"Apart from school, yes."

"When you went to the club, did you ever see your mother with anyone else?"

She shrugged. "She had a trainer, I think. Some guy. But she normally dropped us off in the kids' area. There were about… fifteen of us there?" she said, not sounding sure.

"You said you saw her with a man. Can you remember who?"

She shook her head. "The guy who trained her? I can't remember his name."

"Did your mother train alone?"

"There was another woman sometimes. Blonde hair, I think."

"What was she called?"

She shook her head. "I don't remember."

"What did she look like?"

Siobhan scrunched up her face as she tried to recall, but gave up, exhaling, like it was a job too much for her. "I can't remember. I was only seven or eight. It was just some woman. Blonde hair. I don't think I ever met her."

Blonde hair? Henry remembered Shelley Peters' short blonde hair. "Did this woman work with your mother?"

She shrugged. "I have no idea."

"Did you ever go into your mother's work or meet anyone from it?"

She shook her head again, looking frustrated that she couldn't answer his questions.

"Alright," Henry said, sensing he'd hit the bottom of the well. "Well, that's it for now. You've been a great help."

"Really?" she asked, sounding doubtful. "I hardly know anything."

"No. You've done a good job. Now, can you fetch your brother?"

She huffed. "I'd rather not. You know he won't talk to you."

Henry shrugged. "I'll let him try to tell me that. But I don't fancy his chances."

Siobhan seemed reluctant to get out of the armchair, but after collecting some effort, she pulled herself up. The cat scurried off through the door.

"Will you let me know if I can help any more?" she asked, standing in the centre of the room.

Henry's speech about needing her assistance had sunk in a little too deep. He nodded and tried to look kind. "You have done, lass. But I'll let you know if I need any more. Don't you worry."

She appeared slightly content with that and left him alone in the living room.

After a few moments, Tim slipped inside and closed the door behind him.

"So?" he asked.

Henry looked up at him from his chair. "She doesn't remember much. But has confirmed that Maureen played tennis and that she played with someone. A blonde woman. Can you tell me who that was?"

Tim's eyes narrowed. "A blonde woman? How would Siobhan know that?"

"She went to the tennis club as a kid with Maureen."

"Did she?" Tim was surprised by that.

"You didn't know?"

Tim put effort into working out if he did or not, then shook his head as if he was being stupid. "I did, yeah. Sorry, I usually worked twelve-hour shifts back then. Six till six. Nights and then days. And I often went out for a drink or two after the day shifts. What Maureen and the kids got up to during the week..." He stopped before fully admitting he had no idea what his wife and children had done with their lives.

Henry said, "Anyway, this blonde woman who played with Maureen could be Shelley Peters."

"Her boss?"

Henry nodded. "Could be. I've no idea how we can prove it." He thought of the thick wad of papers Jean was currently reading and hoped Shelley Peters' name would be among its pages. But it would take time before he could get the answers.

"You mean her boss played tennis with her?" Tim asked again.

"Could have."

The living room door opened, and Paul stepped in.

Tim looked at his son. Then, nodding as if he understood something unspoken, he said, "I'll let you two talk." He walked out, mulling over the news Henry had given him, looking even more confused.

Paul crossed the living room. If Siobhan took after her father, Paul took after his mother. Tall, lean, dark hair, and bright brown eyes that took in the room and Henry. Stubble covered his strong jawline, and Henry wondered if it was designer stubble or if he just couldn't be bothered to shave.

He slumped on the sofa in the same spot he'd taken earlier. His white T-shirt had some tech logo on it that Henry didn't recognise, and Paul patted his jeans pockets for his phone. Pulling it out, he placed it on the sofa as if expecting a call.

"Will this be long?" Paul asked.

"As long as it needs to be."

Paul looked at the armchair Siobhan had recently vacated. "Did she cry?"

Henry thought it an odd question. "What if she did?"

Paul looked down at his white socks. They were stained yellow around the toes. "She always cries. It gets to her, all of this."

"And it doesn't get to you?"

He sniffed but didn't answer.

"So, how was school?"

"If you want to know what school was like, then it was probably exactly the same as what she told you."

"Oh, right? What did she tell me?"

He looked at Henry. "That everything was normal until Mum went away… was killed… and then it all got messed up."

"What were your favourite subjects?" Henry asked.

Paul scoffed. "Who cares what they were? How does me liking science help you find out what happened to my mum?"

"It might help, or it might not. I won't know until you tell me."

Paul shook his head like the whole thing was stupid. "I liked science. Tech stuff. Which was shit back then, as there wasn't much at school like that. I messed around with computers at home."

"You work in IT now, don't you?"

He nodded. "Software development. I'm not some IT technician. I don't mess around with cables, so don't get the wrong idea."

"What did you do outside of school? Apart from messing around with computers?"

He exhaled. "Played football with my mates. Went to the park. I don't know, I was eleven or something."

"What about tennis?"

"Tennis?" Paul asked, as if Henry had said something he'd never heard of.

"Siobhan suggested you played it."

Paul considered it and said, "Oh, right. At Heaton? Yeah." He laughed at himself. "I'd forgotten about that. I didn't like tennis. Proper boring. I play ice hockey every now and then. I'm a pretty good goalie."

"Interesting choice. How did you get into that?"

He shrugged as if it was of little interest to him. "Dunno. At uni. I can't ice-skate that well, so I'm better staying near the goal."

Henry nodded as if that revelation intrigued him, and then he asked, "How long did you play tennis?"

Paul huffed. "I don't know. A couple of months. Siobhan did it longer, I think. But I got into trouble and Mum forced me to come along."

"Trouble?"

"My mates got caught smashing windows, and I was implicated." Paul shook his head like it all seemed stupid now. "Mum grounded me and forced me to come to tennis."

"Were you good?"

He shook his head. "Terrible. I snuck off and walked around the club."

"Right? Ever see your mum play?"

"Mum play?" he asked, confused.

"She played tennis at the same time?"

Paul thought about it. "Yeah, she did. But I don't think I ever saw her play."

"Ever see her at tournaments?"

He shook his head. "I don't think so. I mean, I hate playing it, so watching it is even worse. It wouldn't matter if my mum was playing or not."

Henry nodded as he considered what Paul had told him. "No more after-school clubs or anything?"

Paul shook his head. "None. Can I go now?"

Henry couldn't see any point in making him stay and talk more, but shook his head all the same. "Not yet. Did your mum ever take you to Swinfeld?"

The question stirred something in Paul. His blunt arrogance was unsettled, as if a thunder cloud had formed over his head, casting him in shadow. "Swinfeld? I think we went for a walk up there once or twice. But not around the time when she went missing."

"When was the last time you walked around it with your mother?"

He seemed stumped by the question. "I don't know…"

"Do you have any idea why she'd take the dog over there to meet someone?"

Paul shook his head, unwilling to answer.

"Did you like your dog?"

"Polly?" His voice broke with emotion, and he forcefully cleared it. "Yeah. She was a good dog."

"Who walked her?"

"I did, and Dad, sometimes. But mostly me. She was my dog. Siobhan likes cats. I can't stand the things."

"Did you have other pets back then?"

He shook his head. "Just Polly."

"Right."

Staring into the distance, Paul relived his memories. "She died when I was at uni, Polly. You know, every time I looked at her, I wished she could tell me what she saw that day. She must have been there when Mum was..." He sniffed. "Polly must have seen it happen. She must have tried to protect Mum. She was a big dog, scared of nothing. She wouldn't have let someone hurt my mum like that. They found Polly later that day. She didn't have any injuries or anything, but she was never the same. She lost a bit of her happiness; it was like she regretted what had happened and could never get over it."

Paul shook his head. "It's crazy to think it, but imagine if Polly could have talked. She'd tell us what happened to my mum. When the dog died while I was at uni, I realised we'd never know what had happened to her. The truth died with Polly."

"How do you feel about that?"

"Shite. But sometimes bad shit happens and there's no rhyme nor reason to it. It is what it is. End of."

"You don't think we'll ever find out what happened to your mother?"

Paul looked at Henry, took his time to think about it, and then shook his head.

Henry couldn't keep his gaze for long, it was like he was staring into the same pair of eyes from the missing-person poster.

"Can I go now?" Paul asked.

"Aye."

As he stood up, Henry asked, "What breed was Polly?"

Paul put a hand on his thin waist. "What? You don't know?"

Henry couldn't say that he did.

"She was a damn bloodhound."

Chapter Twenty-One

Henry went into the kitchen after allowing Paul to go back upstairs. He found Tim standing at a marble worktop, leaning his elbows on it. His mobile hung limply from his hand, as if he'd just ended a call in which he'd received bad news.

Seeing Henry approach, he straightened up and forced a smile, which seemed desperate and sad.

Henry noted Tim's face was grey and his eyes red. "What's happened?"

"It was Ellie." Tim's eyes dropped to the phone in his hand. "She says they're looking to press charges today."

"What have they found?"

"She couldn't tell me over the phone. Said to ask you." He raised his chin in the air, as if getting ready to face his fate. "So, what is it? What have they found?"

Henry realised Hargreaves must have meant the phone records that proved Tim had tried to call Maureen several times on the day she went missing. DS Emsley must have found them and brought them to Acton's attention.

Closing the kitchen door so the kids upstairs couldn't overhear, Henry turned to Tim, who stood with his head held high, as if preparing himself for a firing squad.

"They've found some phone records," Henry said. "It looks like you called Maureen a number of times the morning she died."

Tim's nose twitched. He stared into the distance while his brain processed the news. "I did. Aye."

"So, what I think they'll be doing – and it's what I'd be doing if I were them – is say you had an argument with Maureen at home that morning, possibly about the love letters, let's say–"

Tim went to defend himself, but Henry held up his hand to quieten him.

"Let me finish," he said. "Let's say you found the love letters at some point and went into a frenzy. You had an argument before leaving for work. At work, you called Maureen multiple times. Eventually, you got through and arranged to meet her at Swinfeld Reservoir. You sneaked out of work, leaving the police station, and headed up there in your police uniform.

"After confronting her, you lost your rag, and struck her across the back of the head with your police baton. Then, you weighed her down with some materials you'd brought with you and pushed her body into the water."

Tim leant on the marble top for support. His big chest took sharp breaths. "But that's not true."

"Isn't it?" Henry said, stepping towards him. "So, what is the truth?"

Tim gave him a sidewards glance.

"I interviewed you back in the day about leaving work. You were gone three hours in the middle of your shift. Why?"

Tim shook his head. "As I said, I went to the dentist."

"So you did, and we checked up on it. We found you went to get a filling done. But that appointment only accounts for one hour. So where were you for the other two? I mean, are you surprised they're coming after you? Because, in all fairness, you look to be in a very poor position."

Tim spun to face him. He was taller and wider than Henry and was using his physical strength to intimidate the older man. But Henry wasn't bothered. He stepped closer until their noses nearly touched.

Henry carried on. "Go on. Where were you? Because if you tell me the truth, I might be able to help you. If not" – he shook his head, wearing a dismissive expression – "then they'll get you. If the CPS go ahead with the prosecution, your career's finished, even if you get acquitted in court."

"I know!" Tim said, stepping away from Henry.

"They might even take your police pension. Your reputation will be shot to pieces. No one will want to hire you for private work. Emigrating might be your only solution. Even then, the murder charge will follow you."

Tim's big shoulders rounded over, and he stared down at the worktop.

"If you help me torpedo their evidence, it'll buy us some time to find out what really happened. But I need you to be honest."

"I was..." Tim started, but he couldn't finish.

"Was what?" Henry asked.

"I was meeting someone."

"Who?"

"I was having an affair."

Henry wasn't that surprised. He had thought it a possibility. "With whom?"

"With a colleague."

"Who?"

Tim shook his head as if he wasn't ever going to say. "I daren't tell you."

"In the police?"

He nodded.

"A woman?"

Tim glowered at him. "Of course, a woman. I'm not like that."

Henry observed him, wondering who this mystery woman was, while also feeling he didn't need a second secret lover to deal with. The Villers' marriage must have been a shambles if both husband and wife were seeing other people on the side. If Maureen hadn't been killed, Henry doubted the marriage would have lasted much longer. It would have ended eventually in a messy divorce.

Tim's fists were scrunched up, and he turned his back on Henry as if he couldn't bear to look at him.

"Go on, Villers," Henry said. "If you don't tell me, you won't be helping yourself. Those accusations that you've just called a lie will be levelled at you in court. You'll be in the dock for your wife's murder. The mother of your children. And if you make it that far, you'll have already lost your job and reputation."

Tim shook his head. "I can't tell you who it was."

"Why the hell not?"

"Because you'll go to her and ask for corroboration."

Henry nodded. "Aye. That's what you need."

"But she won't be able to give it to you. She was married at the time and still is."

"Her husband didn't know?"

Tim shook his head. "We stopped after Maureen died."

"Have you spoken to this woman since?"

"She got promoted."

"To what?"

Tim didn't answer. "She was a good copper. Good at leading people. I always said she'd go far."

"And she's still in the police?"

He nodded. "I can't tell you what position she has now."

Henry thought that was odd. She must be high up in the upper echelons of the West Yorkshire Police. "Right. So she's in the top brass?"

Tim eyed him up then shook his head. "I can't say any more."

Henry's mind ran through the senior officers in the police. He kept up to date with the goings-on in high command, only so he could assure himself that his old enemy Murphy never entered it. However, the command was fairly pale, male, and stale, as the insult went. There weren't many women, except for the chief constable, Mary Jones.

An icy feeling crawled down Henry's spine, and he looked at Tim leaning against his worktop, a man gripped with fear and shame.

Henry felt that same fear and shame latch onto him, as if it was contagious. "It's not Mary Jones, is it?"

Tim glanced up at him in shock, but tried to pretend it wasn't the truth. "No. It's not."

"Nonsense. I think I've hit the giant between the eyes." Henry shook his head. "So, your alibi for not murdering Maureen lies with our current chief constable? The operational head of West Yorkshire Police? And if we asked her about it, it could destroy her marriage and probably her reputation?"

"Shut up," Tim said, keeping his voice low. He glanced at the closed kitchen door, as if worried his kids upstairs would overhear.

Henry saw his quandary in a new light. Either he admitted to having an affair with the highest officer in the region, dragging her into this messy murder case, or faced being charged with his former wife's murder.

"Bloody hell," Henry said, exasperated. "What kind of mess have you dragged me into?"

"You can't tell anyone about this, Henry. No one."

"What? How am I supposed to help you if–" Henry's buzzing phone interrupted him. He looked at the number. It was Jean, his next-door neighbour.

"Hello," Henry answered gruffly.

"I've found the names," she said, sounding excited. She coughed before continuing. "All three were down for the same year. 2007."

"Which three names?" Henry asked, putting his half-finished cup on the worktop.

"Maureen, Shelley, and Arnold."

Shelley's ex-husband, Henry thought. He stared at Tim and said, "I think we have something."

Chapter Twenty-Two

Henry drove his Skoda towards Addingham. He wanted to double-check the names that Jean had found before he headed off back to Leeds to question Shelley Peters. Traffic was thankfully light on the roads in Ilkley, and the sun was hidden behind white fluffy clouds, so he didn't have to squint through the windscreen.

So, Maureen and Shelley had practiced together at Heaton Tennis Club, if Siobhan's memory could be trusted. And the two – plus Shelley's ex-husband – had competed in the Ilkley Tennis Cup.

He recalled the message on the Tennis Cup flyer that the secret lover had written: 'M, you should reconsider. I bet you'll win this time.'

Who had written that? Was it Shelley or Arnold?

As he drove out of Ilkley, he saw the tennis club in the valley below. The clouds covering the sun cast the club in shadows. Henry glanced at it and then looked straight ahead. Did this all start and end with a tennis club in Ilkley? He couldn't believe how that could be so, but at the moment, it seemed to be the case.

When he arrived in Addingham, he took a parking spot on Main Street further down from his cottage. He got out and headed to Jean's.

She answered the door wearing her blue surgical mask. The plastic gloves were back on and didn't fit very well. She kept having to pull them back over her hands.

"I'm not letting you in," she said. "I'll still be contagious."

"Nonsense," Henry said, climbing up her front steps. "I'm coming in."

"Henry!" she said, like a schoolteacher at the end of her tether. "You're not stepping inside this house!"

He took his foot off the front step. "Well, how the hell can I see these names?"

"Wait," she said.

She then disappeared behind the door, only to come back a minute later with three sheets of paper in her gloved hands. "Here. I kept my mask and gloves on while I touched them, so you should be safe."

Henry took the sheets from her and glanced at the names. He saw three were highlighted in yellow. Shelley Peters and Arnold Peters were next to each other. Maureen Villers was in the next column.

"Thanks for looking into these," Henry said.

Jean nodded. "Pleasure. What do you think it means?"

Henry frowned and tried to think of an answer. "I've no idea right now, to be honest. But it gives us the ammo to speak with Shelley Peters again."

Jean appeared to understand. "I looked her up online. She's some businesswoman in Leeds?"

Henry should have guessed that Jean would do some snooping on the names he'd given her. "Aye. What did you find out?"

"Not much, really. She runs some sports business. I couldn't understand what it does. Marketing or something?"

"You're not the only one," Henry concurred.

Jean covered her mouth, despite the mask, and coughed. "I tried looking up Arnold. Found his LinkedIn profile but couldn't look at it without an account. And I've no use for a thing like that. Is he the husband?"

"Aye. Ex."

Jean nodded. "I didn't get what he did either, to be fair. Does he work in finance or something?"

"Yes. In Dubai."

"He looked to be a bit smarmy. She seemed alright, though. Maybe a bit uptight."

Henry nodded as if he valued the opinions Jean had formed by looking at a few profiles online.

He folded the sheets of paper. "Well, thanks again for these."

"I can look through the rest and see if I can find anything else?"

Henry shook his head. "It's alright. But what you could do, actually, if you're interested…"

Jean raised an eyebrow.

"Could you look online for any pictures from the Ilkley Cup in 2007? People don't like seeing pictures of the truth when they're trying to lie. It tends to put them off."

* * *

Henry headed back to his cottage to check on Tessa. She was curled up on the sofa and opened one eye to check who he was before falling back asleep.

"Lazy toerag," Henry said, as he went into the kitchen.

He took a photo of the list of tennis players with his phone and then switched on the kettle. After sending the image of the highlighted names to Hargreaves with no explanation, he opened the back door.

The air inside his kitchen was musty. A mixture of the dog's empty food bowl that he'd not washed in a while and the bin that needed emptying.

He sat down at the round table, cup of tea in hand, and pored over his notes. Looking at the information linked to tennis and work, he picked up the black marker pen and drew a line between them. He then added: 'Shelley and Arnold Peters played tennis with Maureen. Ilkley Tennis Cup, 2007'.

Taking a sip of his tea, he considered scribbling down what he'd learnt from Tim about his alibi. But thought it best not to write that down. He almost wished it wasn't true. He would have preferred it if Tim was the main suspect, just as it made things simpler. But the truth was always more complicated than our expectations, he thought.

How the hell had Tim ended up having an affair with Mary Jones? he wondered, getting mildly annoyed. She must have worked in Otley back then, but Henry couldn't remember. He'd worked out of one of the bigger stations in Leeds and knew the network of CIDs in the area and the senior brass. But he hadn't bothered getting to know uniformed officers as much, unless their paths crossed during a case. And he couldn't recall ever running into Mary Jones.

He'd only met her for the first time recently via a video call, which had happened by mistake rather than design. He suspected Murphy was close to her, only because she was a source of power, and he was attracted to power like slugs were drawn to soggy leaves.

And this old affair with Tim would damage Mary Jones, Henry realised. Then a devious question arose out of his mind. Would bringing her down undermine Murphy? He must be dependent on her patronage. Would losing her as a boss unsettle his tangled web of influence? But then he refocused on the task at hand. Finding Maureen's murderer and bringing him or her to justice was the aim. If he didn't do it, Tim would be wrongfully charged and have his life ruined. And his kids' lives would get even more messed up.

Glancing over his notes on the table, he recalled the mysterious texter and the email they'd sent. Henry would have to get to the bottom of that, as well. How was it related to all of this?

If Arnold Peters was Maureen's secret lover and had killed her for some currently unknown reason, could he be the one who sent Henry the image of Hargreaves and Tim getting intimate? Or could it have been someone he hired? Arnold Peters worked in finance and flew around the world in business class. A man like that could easily afford a private eye, or someone more sinister.

The hairs on the back of Henry's neck quivered, and he got a chill, as if someone had stepped over his grave. He drained his cup of tea and stepped out into the backyard. The tall fences gave him privacy, but he still felt vulnerable.

Whichever way he went with this case, he'd be meddling with the powerful. A chief constable or a high-flying financier. People like them didn't appreciate being meddled with. And they often had the means to make sure no one did.

He went back inside his kitchen and closed the back door. But sometimes, it was necessary to poke our betters in the eye, he thought. Not only because from time to time they deserved it, but also because they needed reminding that power was fleeting.

"Look at me," Henry said, chuckling. "I'm turning into a Buddhist."

His phone rang, and he saw Hargreaves' name on its screen.

"Hello," he answered.

"I'm outside. You'd best come and tell me what's going on."

* * *

Henry closed the passenger door, and Hargreaves merged her Audi into the traffic on Main Street. She wore her designer sunglasses, despite the sun still being hidden behind fluffy clouds. Henry guessed she'd been inside her office for most of the afternoon, reading dusty papers.

"So what are these names you sent me?" she asked.

"They're names of people who competed in the Ilkley Tennis Cup in 2007."

Hargreaves kept her eyes on the traffic. "I saw little Miss Shelley Peters' name on it, along with her husband?"

"And Maureen Villers. The three of them must have signed up together. I doubt Maureen entered the competition without knowing her boss and her boss's husband were going to be playing."

"That bloody woman!" Hargreaves slammed the steering wheel with her palm. "Does she think we're that thick?"

"I don't know. Possibly."

"She even told us that tennis story. Which, by the way, was shite. Proper marketing pitch nonsense, that was. Bet she thinks it's a winning story."

"Aye, probably thinks it's as good as her tennis skills," Henry said. "However, as a rule, I try not to judge other people's anecdotes." He didn't tell her why, but he had been accused of telling tired and boring stories.

They headed into Ilkley in the direction of Leeds and came to a slow stop behind a queue of traffic waiting at lights that were generally always red.

Hargreaves sighed at having to go at a slow crawl. "So, I take it we should head back to Leeds to ruin Shelley's afternoon?"

"Aye. I should think so," Henry said. He then saw the time on the dashboard. Peak rush hour. The roads would be backed up from here to Leeds city centre. It would take over an hour for them to get to Shelley's office, assuming she'd still be there. "Are you sure we'll get there in time?"

Hargreaves nodded confidently. "Oh yeah. You're forgetting something, my old friend. I'm still a copper." She leant towards him to open the glovebox and pulled out a blue beacon light. Cables trailed after it. She lowered the window, and stuck it on the roof.

"Plug it in," she told Henry.

He found the plug at the end of the cable and put it into a USB socket in the console. Hargreaves clicked a button on the dashboard, and police sirens boomed out of the car.

"I had lights installed under the grille, as well. And a siren," Hargreaves said, speaking loudly over the noise. "We'll get there on time."

She pulled out of the line of traffic and steered her car over the centre line, causing everyone else to move onto the sides of the road.

Hargreaves kept a steady pace and then sped through some red lights.

"See, what did I say? We'll be there in no time," she said, chuckling to herself.

Chapter Twenty-Three

Henry and Hargreaves arrived at Shelley Peters' office tower quicker than Henry had expected. The cold air inside the lobby remained, chilling the sweat that had formed on his brow. This time, he welcomed the coolness, as he and Hargreaves had rushed from her Audi's parking spot.

A steady stream of office workers exited the lifts and strolled towards the doors, stepping outside to see what was left of the day. Henry guessed, from the number of them, that working from home was no longer a thing.

He and Hargreaves managed to get a lift to the third floor, which proved difficult as they were taken up with employees trying to descend through the building. While waiting to arrive at the third floor, Henry hoped Shelley Peters would still be in the office. But his level of hope was dropping with each floor they climbed. He didn't want to think they'd just rushed to Leeds for no reason. Glancing at Hargreaves, who wiped her forehead under a jet-black fringe, he guessed she was thinking the same.

They stepped out into the corridor lined with frosted glass on one side, and images of sports personalities on the other. The young woman remained at a reception desk, with the view of Leeds city centre and its docks behind her. She was talking to a colleague who had a large sports bag over her shoulder and looked to be on her way home. Henry and Hargreaves strode towards them.

"Is Shelley Peters here?" Hargreaves asked.

The receptionist turned away from her private conversation and said, "I'm afraid she's stepped out."

"Stepped out?" Henry asked. "Meaning she'll be back in the office?"

As the receptionist looked at them both, a glint of recognition filled her eyes. She must have remembered them from earlier, Henry thought.

"Shelley's at a meeting across town. Elland Road," the receptionist said.

"Leeds United's stadium?" Hargreaves asked, sounding flustered. "When's she back?"

"She can take a while over there. They usually wine and dine her."

Henry checked his watch. It was nearly 6 p.m. If they took Shelley out to dinner, she might not be back until late – if at all. He glanced at Hargreaves, who seemed to have come to the same conclusion.

"Where do they go for dinner?" Hargreaves asked.

The receptionist shrugged. "The latest fancy place, normally. I wouldn't know."

"But she won't be at the stadium for long?"

She shook her head. "Not usually." She shrugged as if she had nothing more to tell.

Henry looked at Hargreaves, who gestured for them to step away from the reception desk. The receptionist returned to her private conversation with her colleague, who had stood by and watched the exchange.

"What do we do?" Henry asked Hargreaves when they'd stepped far enough away to avoid their words travelling.

"We could head to Elland Road, I suppose. Though, I'd rather not. I support Bradford," she said, pulling a face that suggested she found the idea repulsive. "But if we go and she's not there" – she shrugged – "I don't fancy ringing every restaurant in town to see which one Leeds United are booked into."

"We've also lost the element of surprise," Henry said, nodding at the receptionist. "She's going to call Shelley and warn her as soon as we step outside."

Hargreaves bit her lower lip and mulled it over. "Well. We could stay around here and wait for her to turn up, if she does… But I don't fancy our chances."

"Hang about," Henry said, "I've got an idea."

He strode back to the desk and laid his hands on its top. "Would you tell Shelley Peters that we'll be back here tomorrow morning at 7 a.m. sharp?"

Hargreaves tilted her head to the side as if she had an issue with what he'd said.

The receptionist appeared confused and glanced at her colleague beside her, as if unsure she'd heard Henry correctly. "At seven? I'm not sure the building's open then."

"I'm sure Shelley can make it happen. We are investigating a murder, after all."

Henry thanked the receptionist and walked back to the lifts. Hargreaves came to his side. "I'm not waiting until tomorrow. Tim could be arrested tonight. Plus, I can't be bothered dragging my arse across Yorkshire at 7 a.m."

"I know. But I've thought of a way to maintain our element of surprise."

"What's that? You've told her we'll be back in the morning."

"Do you have Shelley's home address?"

Hargreaves realised what his plan was and nodded. "Aye, I do."

"Good. Let's go wait for Mrs Peters to get back home. She can tell us if that fancy restaurant was any good."

* * *

Shelley Peters lived in a mid-century bungalow in a secluded area of Alwoodley, an affluent leafy suburb of Leeds. Henry guessed Shelley's modernist house had been built in the late 1970s and costed a pretty penny. The sun set over the tops of the oaks and poplars that loomed over the squat building, streaking the sky with lines of gold and red.

Hargreaves drove her Audi along the drive, which was well-maintained and lined with trees. The house's many glass panels reflected the hues of the dying sun. Henry could see through them into the interior, and noted the rooms were all painted in neutral tones and had wooden furniture minimally arranged throughout.

"Nice place," Hargreaves said, as she pulled up next to the large front door.

Henry agreed. But then he realised the place didn't provide much privacy. Someone could watch you live your life without you knowing. He looked around at the green leaves on the trees and bushes surrounding the house. They provided cover now, but in winter, when they'd fallen to the ground, there'd be nothing but twigs shaking in the wind to protect you from prying eyes.

The clock on the dashboard said it was 8.30 p.m. They'd had dinner in Leeds city centre before coming over, with the idea that Shelley would take her time with the Leeds United management. Hargreaves insisted on a noodles place that had fluorescent neon signs outside and was as noisy as hell inside.

Henry hadn't been keen on it, as he thought the food would repeat on him. And he was right. He covered his mouth as a belch rose out of his gut. He tried to maintain as much dignity as he could as he let it out, but Hargreaves didn't seem to notice.

Headlights came down the long drive towards the house.

"It must be her," Henry said.

When the silver Mercedes came into view, it slowed to a stop. A moment passed where its driver seemed to consider reversing back down the drive.

As if sensing this, Hargreaves started her Audi's engine.

"Do you really want to chase her?" Henry asked.

Hargreaves didn't answer, but her determined expression did.

The Mercedes idled before them. Its interior was shrouded in darkness, with the declining twilight unable to penetrate its windscreen.

"Is that Shelley or not?" Henry asked.

Hargreaves leant forward. "I don't know."

The Mercedes made a decision. It reversed at speed away from them, back down the driveway towards the road.

"For fuck's sake!" Hargreaves said, turning on her blue lights. The siren disrupted the calm around them, and a flock of sparrows fluttered off the branches of an oak above. "Put your seatbelt on!"

Henry just managed to stick the buckle into the slot when Hargreaves sped forwards.

She quickly gained ground and was in front of the silver Mercedes, which was still reversing down the driveway.

The headlights of Hargreaves' Audi lit up the driver. A man in his fifties squinted at them. He had dark hair and a tanned face, which Henry remembered from an online profile picture.

"Who's that?" Hargreaves asked.

"It's Arnold Peters."

The Mercedes exited the driveway, spun around to face the opposite direction, and raced down a residential street. Wheels screeched, and engines roared.

Hargreaves chased after it. The Mercedes' silver rear end reflected the blue lights in the grille.

"Shit, shit," Hargreaves said.

"What?" Henry asked.

"I'll need to report this. But how the hell do I explain why you're in my car?"

"Tell them you were giving me a lift–"

"And say I thought it might be a good idea to stake out someone's house with you in my car?" She took a hard corner, which flung Henry into his door.

The seatbelt cut into his stomach and shoulder, and he doubly regretted eating those noodles.

"They're going to know you're helping me with this case," she said.

Henry understood her plight. "Well, what do you want me to do? Roll out of the car?"

She appeared to consider it but then shook her head as if it'd be a bad idea.

Henry was relieved.

"Shit," Hargreaves said, sounding mortified. "People will think I'm like Barnes. Always letting you hang around."

Henry rolled his eyes at her comment and focused on the road ahead.

They followed the Mercedes onto a main road, where it cut up the traffic and caused mayhem. A double-decker bus swerved out of its way and mounted the pavement. Henry glimpsed a cyclist being flung off his bike.

"We'd better get this bloke out of this built-up area," he said.

"What do you think I'm bloody doing?"

A sign for Leeds Inner Ring Road came towards them, and the Mercedes headed in its direction.

"Right, we'll cut him off there." Then Hargreaves shook her head. "Shit. I'm going to have to call this in. I've no bloody choice."

The Mercedes made some distance ahead of them before joining the Inner Ring Road. It remained in the left lane, undertaking the cars on the right, before weaving dangerously between them, jumping from lane to lane to make progress.

Hargreaves seemed numbed by indecision. Her face had gone pale, and she was slowing her vehicle down.

Henry snapped at her. "Don't bloody hang about! Do you want to catch him or not?!"

Determination returned to her eyes, and she pressed the screen on the dashboard, calling the police control room.

After presenting herself to an operator, she said, "I'm pursuing a suspect on Leeds Inner Ring Road. I need immediate backup – and possibly a helicopter if you have one."

The operator explained she'd see what she could do and asked Hargreaves to hold.

Hargreaves gripped the steering wheel, and with the sirens and lights going on her car, zipped between the other vehicles on the dual carriageway.

The Mercedes was ahead of them, but not by much.

Henry glanced at Hargreaves, who was snarling out the windscreen, channelling her rage to make the car go faster. And it appeared to be working.

The phone call clicked, and the operator said her call was being transferred to a senior officer.

After a moment, Superintendent Murphy's voice boomed through the car's speakers.

"Hargreaves? What's this I hear you're in a high-speed pursuit on Leeds Inner Ring Road?"

The noodles in Henry's stomach roiled at hearing his old partner/enemy's voice.

Hargreaves answered Murphy. "Sir, I'm chasing a person of interest for the murder of Maureen Villers."

"Who are you chasing, Hargreaves? A suspect has been cuffed and banged up. He's in a cell in Bradford."

Hargreaves gasped and lost her focus on the road. "Tim's been arrested?"

"Aye. He's behind bars. Acton's pressing charges. There's a final interview tomorrow morning before everything's sent to the CPS. He thought a night in a cell would wear down this bloke's resolve, and I agreed." Murphy paused. "So, again, Hargreaves, can you tell me who you're chasing on Leeds Inner Ring Road?"

Her blue eyes watered, and she gave Henry a quick look. "They've got it wrong, Murphy. It wasn't Tim who killed her."

"That's for this bloke to prove in court, Hargreaves, isn't it? We find evidence and pass it to the CPS. It's up to them to close it, not us."

"What if we've got it wrong?"

Murphy exhaled down the phone. "If we've got it wrong, we'll apologise in time. But you know what it's like. With our limited resources, we can't reinvestigate the same case over and over again."

Hargreaves bit her lower lip, slowing down her pursuit of the silver Mercedes – allowing it to get further and further away. "I know. But it's personal, this one."

"What have I told you about making things personal? It'll be your downfall."

"But it wasn't Tim Villers, Murphy. He didn't kill his wife."

"Well, if he can prove he didn't kill her in twelve hours, he won't be charged with her murder. If not, he's heading to a Crown Court. I need my detectives back on other cases. As I often say, the number of violent crimes has gone up, but my number of officers have gone down. I can't be sending my people in search of fifteen-year-old ghosts."

Hargreaves appeared to understand him but was torn by the reality of the situation. She appeared unable to argue, despite clearly wanting to.

So, Henry decided he'd chime in. He'd had enough of Murphy's pontificating and wanted to wind up his old partner.

"Tim Villers didn't kill Maureen, Murphy," Henry said loudly.

Hargreaves turned slowly to look at him – expression holding more shock than anger.

After a stilted silence, Murphy asked, "Henry Ward? Is that you? Have you died and come back to haunt me?"

"I'm not dead yet. And when I do shuffle off this mortal coil, I wish nothing more than to come back and terrorise you."

"Is that a threat?"

"Aye. A supernatural one."

Hargreaves shook her head, and Henry guessed she wasn't impressed with the two old men bickering.

"Hargreaves," Murphy asked, "why is that old git sat in your car during a high-speed pursuit?"

Henry chuckled at Murphy's insult. Murphy was basically the same age as him, but his smile dissipated when Hargreaves' Audi slowed into legal speeds.

Arnold Peter's Mercedes became a silver speck on the horizon.

"Hargreaves?" Murphy asked again, wanting a response. But Hargreaves seemed too shaken to think of an answer.

So, Henry said, "Getting back to Villers, Murphy. He didn't kill his wife, and if you were in any way a decent copper, you'd know that."

"Oh. Is a man who got kicked off the force for corruption calling *me* bad copper?"

"Aye, 'cause you focused on climbing the greasy pole instead of your job."

"Get away with you," Murphy said.

"Would you two shut it!" Hargreaves snapped, clearly at the end of her tether.

The shock of losing Tim was only just sinking in, Henry thought. "Tim Villers is innocent," he said.

Murphy replied, "Is he now? Says who?"

"I know someone who can corroborate his alibi."

"One of your supernatural friends, is it?"

Henry glanced at Hargreaves, who was staring at the road ahead lost in thought. He knew she wouldn't like what he had to say and wished he didn't have to say it, but it was the only card he had left to play.

He doubted Tim had used it, otherwise the man wouldn't be sitting in a police cell in Bradford.

"Your chief constable can confirm Tim's alibi," Henry said.

In a flash, Hargreaves was glaring at him. She looked wounded. Her eyes traced Henry's face, searching for signs of insincerity, but didn't find any.

"What do you mean?" Murphy said, his tone of voice suspicious. "The chief constable isn't involved in this."

"She is," Henry said. "She's well into this. Ask her yourself."

Henry looked at Hargreaves. Not only had he jeopardised the career of the most senior officer in the region but, by the looks of Hargreaves' thunderous expression, he'd also lost her as an ally.

"You can bloody bet I will ask Mary Jones," Murphy growled, before cutting off the call.

* * *

Henry and Hargreaves didn't share a word while she returned him to Addingham. In fact, the atmosphere grew so intense, Henry was prepared to ask her to let him out in the stretch of wilderness between Bramhope and Otley, so he could call a taxi. He didn't though, as he knew they had words that they ought to share.

"Listen," Henry said eventually, as they passed through Otley. His voice burst the bubble of tension that had built up between them. "I should have told you about the chief constable."

Hargreaves clenched her jaw and kept her eyes on the late-summer night through her windscreen.

Henry had hoped he'd have got a reaction from her, but knew he hadn't even scraped the surface. "I only found out today. And Tim made me promise not to tell a soul. Even you."

Her jaw moved as she ground her molars.

He glanced at the car's terminal. "I also probably shouldn't have spoken when Murphy was on the call." He exhaled, realising he'd put Hargreaves in a very bad position by speaking. There was no telling what hellish punishment Murphy was concocting for her. "Aye. Speaking up was a very silly thing to do–"

"Shut up," Hargreaves snapped, eyes still on the road, but full of fire. "We're through. You hear me. I don't know who you are. Have never met you. You're nothing to me."

Henry was taken aback. "Right. Because of Murphy or the thing with Tim?" he heard himself asking, and then regretted it when her fire-filled eyes glared at him.

"Don't you speak to me again," she said. "We're through."

Chapter Twenty-Four

Henry was sitting at his round table in his kitchen, poring over his notes while eating toast. He'd not slept well.

Hargreaves hadn't said a word to him before dropping him off outside his cottage at 10 p.m. She'd sped off without giving a cold goodbye, and that icy atmosphere still hung around him.

He could understand why she was hurt, as he'd kept the information about Tim's alibi from her. If she'd known about it, she could have done something with it earlier – gone to see the chief constable or, at least, passed on the information to Acton so he could deal with it officially.

Not that Acton would have acted on it for certain.

As Henry knew full well, the thing most detective chief inspectors feared most was discovering crucial evidence linked to a senior officer. Especially one who played a key role in deciding promotions.

Alone in his kitchen, slumped over his table and dressed in his shabby dressing gown, he wondered if anyone actually appreciated the work he'd done his whole life.

Of course they did, he reminded himself. If not the wider community, at least the families of the victims whose lives had been irreparably maimed by thoughtless violence.

People like Tim and his children.

All three were desperate to know what had happened to Maureen. But even if they found out, Henry wasn't sure what good it would do them. At least they would know for certain and would be sure that whoever was responsible faced justice.

Henry glanced at the clock on his kitchen wall. It was nearly 7 a.m. He remembered the warning he'd given Shelley Peters' receptionist the previous evening about returning at this time to question her.

Henry doubted Hargreaves would be on her way to Leeds at all, but he hadn't heard anything from her. He also didn't know what Murphy had done with the information Henry had given him last night. Would Tim still be having breakfast on a tray in his police cell while waiting to be interviewed? Or had Murphy spoken to the chief constable and confirmed his alibi?

Getting up, he went over to restart the kettle. Tessa padded into the kitchen from the living room and trundled to the back door. He let her out while the water boiled. It had rained overnight, and the flagstones in his backyard were damp. Water dripped off his browning plants, and the trays under the pots were overflowing.

Maybe the water company would repeal the hosepipe ban soon, he wondered. Then the drowned village at Swinfeld would return under the water, only to reappear in a few decades, when climate change eventually made droughts a yearly occurrence.

He heard his mobile phone ring inside, and left Tessa to find it. Picking it up from underneath his notes on the table, he saw it was an unknown number.

His heart pounded in his chest for a few beats. What if it was the chief constable calling him to give him a bollocking?

Then he remembered he was retired and that she couldn't fire him. He answered the call and recognised the young man's voice.

"Is that Henry Ward?" asked Paul Villers.

"Aye," Henry answered. "Are you alright?"

"You'd best come round. I need your help."

* * *

Henry rushed through his front yard after dressing quickly. Main Street was starting to get busy with the early rush-hour traffic. A double-decker bus on its way to Leeds motored past, kicking out diesel fumes. Henry was hurrying past Jean's front gate when he heard her call out to him.

"Where are you off to so early?" she asked.

Stopping, he saw her standing on her front doorstep, dressed in a pink hoodie and matching tracksuit bottoms. A fresh blue surgical mask covered the lower part of her face.

Henry rolled his eyes, knowing better than to pretend he'd not seen her, and side-stepped into her yard.

"Where are you going at this time of the morning?" she asked again.

Another bus rolled past on Main Street, heading in the opposite direction, and Henry waited until it'd travelled down the street before answering. "There's a crisis at Tim Villers' house."

"Crisis?"

"Aye. The daughter. Siobhan. She's not in good shape."

Jean's eyes widened. "What do you mean?"

"She's locked herself in her room and threatened to kill herself."

"Well, they ought to call the police!"

"They have done. But it's the police who've caused all this." He realised he was wasting precious time explaining things to Jean. "Look. I'd best go."

"Is she Maureen's daughter? The dead woman's?" Jean asked, as if she were a close friend of the deceased.

"Aye. She's clever, Siobhan. She's at Cambridge doing maths."

"I'll fetch my coat," Jean said.

Henry tried to protest, but she'd already closed her front door and disappeared. In a moment, she returned and slipped a white PVC raincoat over her shoulders.

"What are you doing?" Henry asked. "What about your COVID?"

"I feel better now, and I've got my mask. Besides, have you ever talked a young girl out of trying to kill herself?"

Henry shook his head. Of course, he hadn't. "Have you?"

The sadness in Jean's eyes answered his question, and they both headed to his Skoda.

Chapter Twenty-Five

Paul Villers opened the front door dressed in a NASA hoodie and blue chequered pyjama bottoms. His dark hair was dishevelled as if he'd just dragged himself out of bed, and his brown eyes glanced anxiously at Henry.

Paul appeared puzzled when he saw Jean step into the house, but quickly forgot about her as he spoke to Henry. "A mate rang early this morning to tell me Siobhan put something weird on social media late last night–"

"How weird?" Henry asked, following Paul down the hallway.

"Sounded like she was suicidal. 'The world's just too cruel for some people, and I've had enough of it.' She even used the hashtag '#End_it_all'."

Henry shared a pained look with Jean. Then she asked, "Have you spoken to your sister?"

They'd reached the foot of the staircase, and Paul turned to her. "Sorry, but who are you?"

Henry started to explain, "This is my neighbour–"

"I'm Jean Whitehead," she said. "Former teacher and Ofsted inspector. I've completed the Mental Health First Aid course and ASIST, the suicide intervention training. So, I'm more than qualified to talk your sister out of harming herself, if it's come to that. You should be talking to me, not Henry – bless him, he's only a retired detective."

Henry felt the barb, but knew she was right, so he conceded with a shrug.

"Have you heard anything from your sister?" Jean asked again.

Paul shook his head and looked up the staircase. "After the police took Dad away last night, she just cried and went upstairs. I didn't know she'd locked herself in her room until I tried talking to her this morning after my mate called."

Paul chewed on a fingernail, and Henry noticed his pale hand was shaking. Presumably, the realisation that he'd lost his mother, father, and potentially his sister was sinking in.

Jean placed her hand on Paul's shoulder and attempted a smile through her blue face mask. "Don't worry, chuck. Let's go speak to her and see that she's alright."

Paul rallied some strength and nodded. He went up the stairs, and Jean gave Henry a look that suggested she was being optimistic.

Henry concurred. If Siobhan had been suicidal the previous night, and hadn't made a sound since, then they might already be too late.

They followed Paul to the first floor. There were doors leading to four bedrooms and a bathroom. All of them were open except for one. Henry felt a slight chill as he approached it. His adrenaline kicked in and iced the contents of his stomach. He watched Jean stride down the carpeted hallway towards Siobhan's locked door. Paul remained a few metres away, as if he daren't get any closer.

Jean knocked delicately on the door. "Hello, Siobhan. This is Jean Whitehead. I'm the neighbour of Henry Ward."

There was no sound from inside the room.

She continued, "I suppose you met Henry yesterday? No doubt he asked you loads of questions. He is a bit nosy like that, but you get used to it."

Henry huffed. Jean Whitehead calling someone else nosy was a bit rich, he thought. Pots and kettles, and all that.

Jean brushed her curly blonde hair behind her ear and pressed it against the door. She narrowed her eyes a moment. "Siobhan? Can you hear me?"

Jean's eyes became more resolved. "So, you're in there? Are you okay?"

Henry couldn't hear a thing and glanced at Paul, who stood with his arms folded across his chest and his head bent low.

By the look of Jean's face, she'd heard something inside the room. "Siobhan, love. Can you open the door? We just want to come in and see you're okay? You understand that, don't you? We just want to make sure you're alright because we all care about you and your well-being. Paul's here, and he wants to see you."

Jean narrowed her eyes, her ear still pressed to the door.

"What's that?" she asked.

After a moment, she got a reply, and Henry could just about hear it. A faint murmur from the other side of the door.

"Is she alright?" he asked Jean.

Jean glanced at him and shook her head. Speaking quietly, so her voice didn't travel, she said, "I think she's barricaded the door." Jean looked at Paul. "Have you tried opening it?"

He chewed his thumbnail and nodded. "I couldn't get through."

"I think she's attempted something, but it's not worked," Jean said, stepping towards Henry. "Best get an ambulance."

Henry exhaled. He couldn't believe things were getting worse for the Villers family so soon after Maureen had been found.

"I'll go call one," Henry said.

Paul shook his head with his phone already in hand. "I'll do it." He pushed past Henry and rushed down the hallway, descending the steps two at a time. Henry thought the kid couldn't get away fast enough.

"I'll keep talking to her," Jean said. "Make sure she stays conscious."

Henry watched her turn back to the locked door. If Siobhan had attempted something, she was already in danger. And if their only hope was waiting for an ambulance to arrive in time, then they really were in a pickle.

But he felt useless in the situation.

All he could do was stand and watch Jean talk through a bedroom door. And what would the ambulance crew do when they arrived and couldn't get past the barricade. They'd have to call the fire brigade to knock it down with axes, and how long would that take?

Then he had an idea. The back of the Villers' house had an extension that stuck out into the back garden. Henry thought perhaps the parents' bedroom and Siobhan's looked out over it. The roof of the extension was flat and wide, and he thought it was more than sturdy enough to hold his weight.

As he entered the parents' bedroom, Jean interrupted her stream of calming words to ask him, "Where are you going?"

"I'm off to find another way around," Henry said, not stopping to explain.

Chapter Twenty-Six

The bedroom Tim Villers shared with his new wife had grey walls and a matching-coloured duvet over the double bed. The large window was half-open, and a warm summer's breeze blew into the room.

There were a few signs of Tim's new wife around the room. Perfume and cosmetics were lined up on a modern dressing table, with a few pieces of women's clothing hanging over its chair. Henry wondered where this new wife was, and assumed she'd elected to stay away from the crisis.

Jean shouted at him from the hallway, and he headed to the window before she could begin to talk sense into him.

Sliding the window open, he realised he could easily fit through the gap. He peered outside and saw the double camber clay tiles on the extension roof. They appeared sturdy enough and, if he kept away from the edge, he should avoid falling into the back garden and breaking his neck. After moving the chair by the dressing table, he stepped onto the new Mrs Villers' garments and crawled out of the window. He eased himself onto the roof. The pleasant breeze blew over him, and the sun shone through white clouds.

Keeping his body close to the brick wall, he shimmied along to Siobhan's bedroom window. He realised it was open, but the curtains were fully drawn, blocking his view in. Henry positioned himself in front of the window and opened it as far as it would go. Realising it'd be more difficult to climb through without a chair to help him, he pressed his boot on the brick wall and pushed himself up.

He managed to fit his head and shoulders through the gap, but the curtain wrapped around him and stopped his progress. Losing momentum, he fell backwards out of the window and onto the roof, landing on his back. The tiles underneath seemed to struggle with his weight. He felt winded, and, suddenly, started to slide headfirst down the clay tiles towards the edge.

He was about to shout for help when he dug his fingers into the gaps between the tiles to stop the descent. The back of his head hung over the three-metre drop – the wind gently caressing his scalp through thinning hair.

"Bloody close call there, Henry," he said, scolding himself.

Getting up carefully, he pressed himself up against the wall and tried to get inside Siobhan's bedroom again. He pulled open the curtains this time and saw Siobhan lying on her bed.

She didn't appear to know he was there.

Henry spotted what was blocking her bedroom door: a chair, a cabinet, and a pile of clothes. Three medicine packets rested on the bedside table, alongside a half-finished glass of water.

Henry didn't give himself the time to think what that meant. Pressing his boot against the bricks under the window, he made another attempt to jump into the room. He lifted himself upwards and rolled his head forwards through the opening, landing on the carpet with a thud.

Blood rushed to his head, as he looked around the room from upside down.

He knocked over a flimsy desk as he righted himself. Getting his boots tied up in a laptop's cable, he eventually brought it down from a cabinet with a crash, smashing the thing beyond repair.

"What in the name of all that's holy is going on?" shouted Jean from the other side of the door.

Henry ignored her and hauled himself up. Apart from his wounded head and feeling like he'd taken a few tumbles, he was fine.

He staggered towards the bed where Siobhan lay.

Her eyes flickered to life, and her pupils rolled to the side to take in Henry.

"What do you want?" she asked through cracked lips.

"I'm here to help," Henry said, putting his hand on her forehead. "What did you take?" Her skin was boiling to the touch.

"I don't know…" she said, closing her eyes again and slipping back into the comforting place she'd been.

"Henry! What the bloody hell are you doing?" Jean demanded to know from the other side of the barricade.

"I'm opening the door," he said, leaving Siobhan's side.

He pushed the cabinet of drawers out of the way, then kicked away the pile of clothes from around the chair's legs and managed to dislodge it from underneath the door's handle. He pulled the door open and found Jean scowling at him.

"What the hell are you playing at?" she asked. "You're not a bloody action hero, you know! You had your hip replaced not so long ago."

"No thanks, then?" he asked, but she'd already pushed past him and rushed to Siobhan's aide.

"That ambulance best hurry itself," she said, looking at the medicine packets on the bedside table. "She might not have long."

She delicately tapped Siobhan's cheek, raising her out of her stupor.

Siobhan peered at Jean. "Are you the angel I was talking to?" she asked weakly.

Jean grabbed hold of Siobhan's hand. "I'm no angel, love."

Siobhan smiled as if she thought the opposite. "I think you are. Thanks for bringing me back. I shouldn't have done what I did…"

"Now now, love. I'm just glad you're alright," Jean said.

Henry heard sirens heading towards them through the open window. "Sounds like help's arriving."

But Jean didn't answer him. She just patted Siobhan's hand and told her she'd be okay.

* * *

Siobhan was wheeled into the back of the ambulance on a stretcher. Jean wrapped her arm around Paul, who remained on the driveway standing next to his dad's car. He'd got changed out of his pyjamas and looked slightly more presentable in jeans. He stared mournfully at his sister as the ambulance crew fastened her into the back of the vehicle and hung an IV drip to the hook on the wall.

One of them jumped out and asked, "Is anyone coming with her?"

Paul turned to Henry. "What about my dad? He might need me to go to the station – if they let him out."

"Go with your sister, lad," Henry said. "I'll see to it they let your dad out soon. Don't you worry."

Paul narrowed his eyes as if he struggled to understand something Henry had said.

Jean patted Paul's shoulder. "I can go with her if you like? But it'll be best there's someone she recognises there when she wakes up."

And she would wake up, Henry thought. The paramedics had quickly clocked on to the fact that Siobhan hadn't consumed all of the pills she'd planned to. And once they'd administered a drug to protect her liver, they checked her vitals and said she'd make a full recovery. She would most likely be sectioned, however, Henry realised, but he kept the information from Paul as the lad had been through enough.

Paul seemed to have made up his mind. "You're right, Jean. I'll go with her." He fished a pair of keys out of his pocket and chucked them at Henry. "Lock up the house when you leave, please." His brown eyes locked onto Henry's. "And thanks. I didn't know who else to call. I phoned the police, but they didn't bother coming, did they?"

No patrol car had turned up, and Henry doubted one would roll up later that day to see if they could be of any assistance.

"It's alright, lad," he said.

Paul grabbed Jean's arm, nearly shaking her. His eyes bore into hers and went misty. "Thanks… I'll never forget what you did for my sister."

Jean smiled through her mask. "I didn't do much, love." She cleared her throat. "Go on, then… They need to set off."

Henry came to stand next to Jean as the ambulance rushed off towards Airedale Hospital. "You did a good job in there," he said. "Where did you learn all those mental health emergency skills?"

She exhaled like she didn't want to think about it. "I was a teacher for a long while in secondary schools. And then I got involved in community groups in the village, and one of my granddaughters has problems… And she's still with us. Thank God."

Henry sensed not to ask her any further questions.

"What do we have to do now?" she asked. Her shoulders slumped under her white raincoat, and she looked more tired than Henry had ever seen her.

"Worn yourself out?"

"What do you think?" She coughed.

"Come on, I think Tim has one of those fancy espresso machines. If I can figure out how to use it, I'll make you one."

She nodded and wrapped her arms around herself. "I'm probably due more paracetamol, too."

"So you *are* still sick?" Henry said, leading her back into the house.

"I'm better than I was–" she coughed again "–and what about you, thinking you're a bloody action hero? Climbing through windows? You're sixty-four and have dodgy hips."

Henry batted away her question with a shrug and a cheeky grin. "It worked out alright in the end."

He managed to get the coffee machine working, and Jean sat down at the kitchen table with a glass of water in hand. She peeled off her face mask and warned Henry for the fourth time to keep his distance.

He rolled his eyes and made her a coffee by pressing the button on the machine, which was easier than he'd thought.

Then the call came through to his phone.

Pulling it out of his pocket, he realised it was another number he didn't recognise, from a mobile.

"Hello?" he asked loudly over the sounds of coffee beans being ground.

There was no answer at first, and he wondered if it was the chief constable or Shelley Peters. Or, perhaps, the mysterious texter whom he'd almost forgotten about.

"Ward," Murphy said, sounding furious.

"Superintendent Murphy?" Henry asked, feeling his heart beat double time. "What do I owe the–"

"We need to talk. Where are you?"

The coffee machine finished brewing, and Henry passed the cup to Jean, who quickly covered her mouth with her mask as he got closer. "I'm at Villers' house," Henry said to Murphy.

"You're…?"

"I'm in Tim's kitchen if you must know."

"Why is it every bloody time there's a case that's a complete pain in the backside, you're smack bang in the middle of it?"

"What is it you want, Murphy?"

Murphy exhaled down the line. "I need to talk… about that business."

Henry guessed he meant the information about the chief constable. "Is Tim still in a police cell in Bradford?"

"No. He's currently being questioned." Murphy snorted. "Not over the phone, idiot. Can't you remember the rules?"

Henry reminded himself of the regulations about discussing active cases over mobile phones, and then wondered if Murphy was calling him from his personal phone or the work one. Was he on official business or not?

"So, are you coming over to speak to me?" Henry asked. "It's just that, I've got quite a lot going on at the moment."

"Aye. I'll be there in twenty minutes."

When Henry hung up, he wondered where Murphy was if he was only twenty minutes away.

Jean spat her black coffee over the kitchen worktop. "Bloody hell! That's strong," she said, wiping up the liquid with a tissue. "Is there no milk to put in it? It'll blow my head off."

Henry shook his head. "I've already checked the fridge and there isn't any. Besides, it'll give you a new lease of life."

She picked up her cup again. "I'll have a go, but don't blame me if it sends me doolally."

"I think we're beyond worrying about that," Henry said, chuckling to himself.

Chapter Twenty-Seven

The last time Henry had seen Detective Superintendent Murphy in a car, the senior officer had been sitting in the back, as if he was a senior politician being chauffeured around. But on that late morning, Murphy was driving the modern version of a panda – a small electric buggy marked with West Yorkshire Police's florescent yellow and blue colours.

The vehicle whirred to a stop on Tim Villers' drive, and Murphy stepped out wearing his dark-blue superintendent uniform. A string of colourful squares lined the top of his lapel, and his epaulettes were emblazoned with crowns and diamond-shaped pips. Murphy cradled his hat under his arm, and his bulldog-like face peered around the quiet residential street, squinting in the sun. His beady eyes alighted on Henry, who was standing in the living-room window, watching.

Henry gave him a weak wave, and Murphy strode towards the house.

He wouldn't offer him coffee, Henry thought, as Jean had been right, it was rocket fuel. He'd left her in the kitchen where she was listening to *Woman's Hour* on the radio while trying to clean up and do a crossword puzzle at the same time.

Murphy didn't bother knocking at the door and entered the house as if he owned it.

Henry waited for him in the hallway. "In here," he said, gesturing to the living room.

Murphy took a seat on the sofa, his hat resting on his lap, and peered around the living room, as if mildly impressed. Then, as though remembering why he was there, he took a deep breath.

"It was a very serious allegation you laid on me last night," he said, eyeballing Henry.

"I wouldn't call it an allegation," Henry said. "It's evidence in a murder investigation."

Murphy scoffed. "Murder investigation? You talk like you're still in the game. But you're not. You're a has-been, Henry."

"Right, and what does that make you? A never-will-be?"

Murphy's expression soured. "I've been talking to people up at Otley station. Delicately, like. To see if there's any legs to this… allegation."

"I thought you might have. It must be a shock to the system for you, having to get out of your office and do some police work. Though, sniffing around for gossip seems like your type of thing."

Murphy wasn't amused. "Right? Is it? And what's yours? Just look at you. You're a bottom feeder. A crank. A nosy parker. I mean, what do you actually do now? A proud police career, if you ignore what happened at the end, has been laid to waste. All you do now is walk around and hassle people, while getting in our way – slowing us down. How many cases have you now prevented us from completing?"

"Excuse me?" Henry said, taking the bait. "I think you'll find I've closed these cases far quicker than you lot. Often without your help."

"And sometimes with," Murphy said, his eyes measuring Henry's response.

Henry avoided going down that route, as he knew Murphy wanted to talk about DI Barnes and DS Hargreaves. "I do my level best to help people, most of whom ask me to get involved because your lot have messed everything up."

"Really? And what's this business with Tim Villers? Who asked you to stick your nose into that? I mean" – Murphy looked around the living room as if it made his point for him – "how is it that I find you in his lounge?"

"His daughter took ill this morning, and the son called me to come and help. They're both at Airedale as we speak. She's fine, by the way. Your concern has been noted."

"What was wrong with her? A bad cold? A funny stomach?"

"Aye. Overdoses can upset stomachs."

Murphy ground his jaw shut, seemingly displeased he'd not seen that coming.

Henry continued, not wanting to give his old adversary any ground. "And do you know why she took all those pills? She watched her father get dragged out of this house, accused of murdering her long-lost mother. An allegation that we all know to be false."

Murphy leant forwards, as if sensing an opportunity. "*Do* we know it's false?"

"Well, I doubt you'd be talking to me if you thought it wasn't. You would have fobbed me off already."

Murphy's saggy cheek twitched.

"Which makes me think you've found something," Henry added.

"Your perceptive skills haven't declined over the years," Murphy said, leaning back into the sofa.

"I'm practicing them more now than I ever have."

Murphy nodded like he was listening to something he half-agreed with, but Henry doubted he was listening.

Murphy brooded for a moment, and then came to life as if following a new train of thought. "I've done some investigating, and I've stumbled across a few things that might help Tim Villers."

"Oh, aye?"

Murphy fixed his eyes on Henry. "A few colleagues who worked with Mary Jones and Tim noticed they were very… 'pally'."

"Only pally? Not more?"

Murphy shrugged. "That's to be determined. But looking at the facts, I'd say they were an item."

"You've no hard evidence?"

"It'll be near impossible to find anything concrete on an illicit relationship that took place over fifteen years ago. All I have to go on is what people saw at the time."

"And what did people see?"

Murphy studied the rim of his hat, which rested on his lap. "I spoke to a couple of officers who'd been there back in the day. They remembered hearing things about the two being more than friendly. And apparently one of them walked in on them."

"Walked in on…?"

Murphy shook his head. "I'd best not say, I wouldn't want to give your heart a shock. But put it like this, I have enough information to confirm suspicions."

Henry watched Murphy rotate his hat around in his hands, turning it as though he were winding in an invisible rope. Enough to hang the chief constable's career with, Henry thought.

"You want to bring her down?" Henry asked.

Murphy became aware he was being watched and tossed his hat onto the cushion beside him. "What I want is not a factor in this."

Henry chuckled. "I've heard some bollocks drop out of your mouth before–"

"She's a good chief constable. On the ball. Knows how to manage. A good technocrat."

Henry waited a moment, before saying, "But?"

"She's not a leader. She's a pen-pusher. Always has been. She's never been on the streets, well, not for a long time. She's never followed a case through and brought down criminals."

"Have *you*?"

Veiled anger flitted across Murphy's eyes. "You know I have. For nearly ten years we did it together."

Henry nodded to accept they'd been partners once, but didn't share his views on Murphy's detective skills. "So, why is it you're here? If you have enough evidence to torpedo her career, why not go ahead and do it?"

Murphy stretched out his legs, crossing one polished loafer over the other. "I have enough to confirm suspicion, but if one of the people within the affair admitted to it… That would really speed things along." He raised an eyebrow. "It'd be worth its weight in gold. That's why Tim needs to open his mouth."

"Hasn't he already?"

Murphy shook his head. "He's not been asked to. I've kept this very close to my chest, Henry. Only a select few officers have been told – officers I trust."

Henry wondered if Murphy counted Hargreaves as one of those officers. The two had been close before. However, after the past few days, he wondered if that was still the case.

He then considered what Murphy was driving at. "So, DCI Acton is, as we speak, questioning Tim about his involvement in his ex-wife's murder, completely unaware that he has the wrong person?"

Murphy huffed through his nostrils. "Yes. At the moment. And if Villers' alibi can be corroborated, I'll make sure no further action is taken against him."

"And then you'll look for Maureen's real killer?"

Murphy narrowed his eyes as if he didn't know who Maureen was.

Henry snapped. "The dead wife! The poor woman who had her skull caved in and was pushed into Swinfeld Reservoir. The woman we found not two days ago."

Murphy nodded as if he remembered. "Aye. We'll look into it. But Henry, I think you're missing the point here."

"No, all things considered, I think *you're* missing it. I'm here to find out who killed Maureen Villers. To find out who tore her away from her husband and kids."

Murphy stood up and walked around the room like he couldn't contain the energy within him. "No. You're missing the point entirely. In this country, we have thousands of sexual and violent offences, including nearly seven hundred murders, every bloody year. And the numbers are rising.

"Seven hundred murders, Henry. That's seven hundred Maureens. People who've had their lives cut short by thuggery and violence." He gritted his teeth, clearly disgusted by what he was about to say. "Do you know how many of those murders we solve?"

"Not enough."

"Not nearly enough, no. And that's not to mention the hundreds of thousands of other offences. Crime costs, and it costs the victims of all crimes equally. No matter if it's murder or not.

"Imagine this family multiplied by hundreds of thousands every year. It's a sodding disgrace, Henry. How are we, as police officers, supposed to hold our heads high with numbers like that? Violent crime has essentially been legalized." He shook his head as he heard his own words. "We're stumbling through a category-seven hurricane of shit, with only a cocktail umbrella to protect us."

"Alright," Henry said, gesturing for Murphy to sit down. "You can get off your podium. I get you want to bring down Mary Jones so you can replace her."

"Aye. I do," Murphy said, remaining standing. "This is my chance to clean up shop. Sack the layabouts, hire lean hard-nosed coppers, like we had back in our day. And put this region right again."

Henry didn't seem enthralled with the speech, so Murphy stepped closer to him, keeping his eyes on his. "Listen, man. Can you really say that this is a desirable situation? I mean, did you really think you'd be investigating cases in your retirement because the police service had broken down beyond repair?"

"If it's stuffed beyond repair, how do you think a mere mortal like you can fix it?"

Murphy's eyes bulged, and Henry wondered if the man was having a religious experience. "Zero tolerance."

Henry had heard enough. "Right, yeah. Banging up kids for smashing windows will really sort things out."

Murphy looked slighted. "Well, what's *your* bright plan?"

"As you frequently point out, I'm retired, so I've no need for one."

"Nonsense. You've had more than eleven years to think about it."

"Alright, you really want to know? I'd say it's community policing. Get officers back into neighbourhoods and out of those central offices. Yes, data and computers are important and all that, but so's the community that they serve."

Murphy wasn't impressed. "Very quaint. It could be a good idea, if we had the money. But do you know how much a bobby on the beat costs these days? Way too bloody much."

"Aye, but what about the costs of 'zero tolerance'? You'll only bang up people who'll go on to become hardened criminals. You know the repeat-offending rate."

"The problems of the prison service are theirs to sort out. I've got enough of my own to be getting on with."

Henry rested back in his armchair, observing Murphy as he stalked towards the bay window to look at the front lawn.

"So, what is it you want me to do? Why are you here?" Henry asked.

"I want you to persuade Tim Villers to come forward with what happened between him and Mary Jones."

"So she can be toppled while you can ascend?"

Murphy kept his back to him and didn't answer.

"Alright, and what do *I* get out of this?" asked Henry.

"I don't crush you for interfering in police business these past few years." Murphy straightened his neck. "How many cases have you done privately now?"

Henry didn't reply.

"Don't worry, I'll be able to find out. I'll just look up my detectives' communications. It's DI Barnes and DS Hargreaves who've been illegally feeding you information, isn't it?"

That was it, Henry realised. The thing Murphy was going to use in order to get what he wanted. Namely, the end of Mary Jones's career and his own ascension as West Yorkshire Police's chief constable. Bringing down the force's first female chief constable so he could implement his tired and useless policy. One that did nothing but create more hardened criminals and clog up the already broken justice system.

"So, need I look at Barnes's and Hargreaves' communications? Or will you get me what I want?" Murphy's expression suggested he knew which way Henry was going to go.

Henry couldn't see Barnes and Hargreaves chucked out on their ears. If Murphy was going to turn the region into a hellish police state, the force would do better with hard-working detectives like them in it.

"I'll see what I can do," Henry said, staring down at the beige carpet.

Murphy slapped his shoulder. "Good man."

But Henry didn't feel 'good'. Far from it. He felt like throwing up.

Chapter Twenty-Eight

Tim Villers was released half an hour later. The official reason was that the investigating officers needed more time to put together their case against him. The real reason, or the one Henry had learnt from Murphy, was that the detective superintendent had called Acton and ordered him to release him.

Henry watched a taxi from Bradford roll down the residential street. It parked outside Tim's house, and after a moment, he stepped out through the front passenger door. Tim appeared very frail. A broken man, he thought. His head was bent low, his shoulders sagged, and his dark curly hair was oily and messy, as if he'd slept rough the previous night. His blue hoodie was creased, and as he got closer to Henry, he had the taint of holding cells on him – a mixture of prison door grease and excrement.

Tim squinted in the daylight as he looked at Henry and Jean standing on his drive. "Have I got you to thank for this?"

Henry tried a smile, but then saw Tim wasn't being grateful – a slow-boiled rage was barely hidden behind his eyes.

"Aye," Henry said. "I managed to get you released."

Tim walked past them and headed towards his front door. "I heard Detective Superintendent Murphy had me released," he said gruffly, talking loudly into the breeze.

Jean gave Henry a worried look that said something was amiss.

"I spoke to Murphy," Henry admitted. He didn't want to say what they'd spoken about, but by the way Tim was behaving, he reckoned he'd already figured it out.

Tim shuffled up the front steps and into his house. At the threshold, he turned to Henry. "I told you I didn't want anyone knowing. I wanted it kept quiet," he said. He then looked at Jean, suggesting he wasn't going to continue discussing a private matter in front of a stranger.

"Here, Villers," Henry said. "I know what you said, but you were looking at a murder charge and all the hell that comes with it – being locked up until the court date, facing life behind bars for something you didn't do."

"I asked you not to tell anyone," Tim said, leaning on his door frame as if he was too weak to stand. "And what did you do? Within twenty-four hours, I'm released and the whole bloody world knows."

"I only mentioned it to Murphy," Henry said, holding his head high. "I'm not ashamed of freeing an innocent man."

"But I told you not to," Tim said. His rage made the blue in his eyes glow. "If I chose to go down rather than speak about it, then that's my decision. Not yours."

"I don't care what you choose, Villers. You didn't kill your wife and you have an alibi that can prove it. If you go down for it, we may never find out who really killed her."

Henry noticed Jean was looking at him with a confused expression on her face. She was struggling to follow the conversation, but he wasn't going to annoy Tim even more by explaining it to her.

Tim ground his teeth and struck the door frame with his hand, but his weakness meant he only slapped the wood. "I said not to tell anyone! Not until I'd figured out what–"

"Shut up. Your kids need you," Henry said, stepping towards him.

The rage slipped from Tim's eyes, and he looked into his house. "Where are they?"

Jean patted Henry's arm and answered for him. "Mr Villers, there's been an incident."

Tim frowned at her. "And who the hell are you?" he asked, as though the question had been annoying him for some time.

"I'm Henry's neighbour. I came here because your daughter needed emergency help–"

Leaving them on the drive, Tim ran into the house with renewed vigour. Henry heard him shouting his kids' names as he bounded up the stairs, and when he came back outside, panic and fear were etched into his face.

"Where are my kids?!"

* * *

Henry and Jean asked a harried nurse for directions to Siobhan's bed, but Tim didn't stay to listen and rushed off into A & E. Henry followed after him, leaving Jean with the nurse.

Airedale General Hospital was busier than Henry had ever seen it. There were people everywhere. What few seats they had were all taken, and people leant against a nearby wall; even a woman with a cast on her leg hadn't managed to get a seat.

Henry walked the tatty vinyl floors past a row of beds. Pale-green privacy curtains were drawn around some, while others were open, letting the whole world see the patient in their bed.

Henry had flashbacks of when he was last here. He couldn't remember much of it – as it'd happened during his drinking days – but he'd fallen badly outside a pub after closing. Flashes of memories plagued his mind: of shouting at nurses and paramedics to leave him be, of the pain in his leg sustained in the fall, and of the mind-numbing headache as he sobered up in hospital.

Hoping none of the nurses or doctors would recognise him, he kept his head down. And if any did, he could at least persuade them he was back in the temperance brigade.

Siobhan was on a bed at the far end of the row. Thankfully, her privacy curtain hadn't been closed, allowing Tim to see her. She had an IV drip on a pole next to her, with a tube running into the top of her hand. She'd pulled the baby-blue blanket up to her chest, but it was too short, and her purple and orange striped socks stuck out the end. A NASA hoodie, presumably her brother's, lay by her feet. That was the only sign that Paul had been there, as Henry realised he wasn't with her now.

When Tim ran to Siobhan's side, she visibly shrunk into her blanket – too ashamed to face him.

Tim pulled her unwilling head to his chest, gasping air as if he'd been starved of it. Tears dripped from his eyes, and he let them fall down his cheeks.

Henry felt awkward watching the intensely private scene and turned his back to them, as though he was guarding their privacy from the rest of the patients.

Jean headed towards him, making sure her face mask was securely on. She'd stayed longer with the nurse, probably getting more information about Siobhan's status, Henry thought.

"The nurse thinks she'll be fine," Jean told Henry. "There shouldn't be any liver damage, as they reckon they intervened in time."

Jean watched the scene between Tim and his daughter unfold behind Henry, and her eyes got misty. Looking away, she waited a moment before asking a question Henry had been expecting.

"What did you tell that horrible Murphy to free Tim?" she asked.

Henry shook his head. He wasn't going to discuss it there and then.

But Jean didn't accept his silence. "No. Go on. Tell me what you said?"

He glanced quickly behind him at Tim and Siobhan – who'd given into her father's embrace and was sobbing into his chest.

"I know that Tim didn't kill his wife," Henry said. "He has an alibi that can be corroborated."

"By whom?"

Henry considered his words wisely. "Someone… high-up."

"That's good, isn't it?" she asked, clearly not understanding Tim's outburst earlier.

"To some. But definitely not for the person who can corroborate it."

Jean tried to think why it would be a problem for the other person, then her eyes widened in surprise. "It's a woman, isn't it? Was it an affair?"

Henry grunted. "Nothing much gets past you, does it?"

Jean glanced over Henry's shoulder at the father-and-daughter moment. "So, his mistress has to confirm she was having an affair with him?"

"Yep. And I've got to persuade him to make it all official."

Jean tilted her head. "Why you? You've nothing to do with that, have you?"

Henry wanted to agree with her but couldn't. He wanted to tell her the truth, that if he didn't convince Tim to come clean about his relationship with Mary Jones, Murphy would come for him.

But she got there before Henry could say anything. "Ah, that horrible fella's bribing you, isn't he? If you do this, he won't get you into trouble?"

He couldn't bring himself to tell her that Murphy would also get *her* into trouble. He didn't wish to stress her out. Not while they were standing in the middle of a busy emergency ward.

Instead he said, "I'll need to persuade Tim that it's the best thing for him to do. I mean, do you think him going away for life would be good for the kids? And what about Maureen? We'll never find out who really killed her, would we?" He shook his head and grunted to himself. "Especially when the real killer's out there, running around scot-free."

"But can't you work that out yourself?"

"What? Figure out who the killer is in a fifteen-year-old cold case?" He huffed, and then he genuinely considered her question. Could he figure it out?

"I don't know," he said. "Possibly. Though, it would be easier if I had the backing of the police. If they think it's Tim and press charges, they won't dare help me – in case I prove them wrong."

Jean reflected on it a moment and nodded. "We'll have to have a word with him, then," she said, looking at Tim and Siobhan.

"No. *I'll* have a word with him. He hardly knows you."

"He'll listen to me," she said, seeming very sure of her herself.

"How do you know he will?"

"Well, he's a lady's man," she said.

Henry nearly burst out laughing, but when he saw she was being deadly serious, he wondered if she had a point.

* * *

Paul Villers found his father still holding his sister and forced himself not to let the emotion get to him. He remained standing at a distance near Henry and Jean, trying not to look at the rest of his family. He had been in another part of the hospital, trying to get phone reception to call his dad. Unfortunately, it turned out Tim's battery had died while he was locked up the night before, and his phone hadn't been charged since.

Tim spotted his son standing next to Jean and called him over. He then wrapped his big arms around him and wept again, making Paul even more overwhelmed.

After quietly discussing their plan, Henry and Jean managed to get Tim away from his children when a nurse came to change Siobhan's IV bag and check her vitals. Paul took the opportunity to get some fresh air outside, and Henry suspected he might take a taxi back to Ilkley.

Henry led Tim down a corridor towards a coffee machine with Jean following behind, as if she was shepherding a pair of sheep. A green-clothed hospital porter pushed a bed past them, and Henry glimpsed the shrivelled-up old man lying in it. The man appeared to be halfway between life and death, and Henry felt a chill as he made eye contact with him.

It was as if he was witnessing a future not that far off.

Keeping his mind off his own mortality, Henry selected a cappuccino from the machine and wondered if it'd be made with fresh milk or not. He asked Tim what drink he wanted, but the big man looked worn out and hugged himself as though he were cold. His bleary eyes looked up and down the corridor, searching for potential threats that could emerge at any time. Eventually, after staring at the machine for a moment, he decided not to drink anything. Henry chose for him, thinking some caffeine and sugar would do him good, and then Jean approached from behind.

After nodding at Henry to say she was ready, she cleared her throat. "So, what do you think you'll do about all this police business?" she asked Tim.

Tim appeared to find the question inappropriate and scowled.

Henry jumped in. "Aye. If you don't pull something out of a hat soon, Acton will have you back in a police cell."

Tim clenched his jaw, and Henry wasn't sure if he was angry with them for bringing it up or angry with Acton.

Tim accepted the cappuccino Henry offered him and took a big gulp of the scolding liquid. Wiping his lips, he said, "You want me to come clean about Mary, don't you?"

"I want you to be free and with your kids. I also want to find out who really killed Maureen," Henry said, carefully sipping his own boiling hot drink.

"I'm not oblivious to what you've done for Siobhan." He glanced at Jean. "She speaks very highly of you."

Jean's cheeks above her mask reddened. "Oh. I barely did anything."

"But…" Tim said, with his eyes fixed on his half-finished paper cup. "I can't do that to Mary. It'll destroy her career."

Jean shook her head as though she'd misheard him. "So, you'd rather destroy your life and your kids' lives for some woman's career?"

"No. It's nothing like that," he said.

"Well, what is it like?"

When he didn't answer, she said, "I think you've done a great job with your kids."

Tim seemed surprised. "Really?" He shook his head. "Then why the bloody hell did one of them try to top herself?"

"Because she saw her father get dragged out of her house in handcuffs," Jean continued. "They've lost their mum, those kids. Don't let them lose their father, too."

Tim scrunched up his lips and considered what she'd said.

Henry blew the steam off his own drink and watched. He sensed Tim was reluctant to come clean but could be worn down and persuaded to talk. He doubted he would be the one to do it. If anyone could whittle down a man's resolve, it was Jean.

"Imagine how it'll be when Siobhan sees you in the dock," Jean said, shaking her head at the idea of it. "Charged with murdering her mother, when we all know you didn't–"

"It might not get that far," Tim said, looking to Henry for agreement. "The Bloodhound here might find something."

Henry shrugged. "My investigation has been stalled due to what's happened to you and…" He gestured in the direction of Siobhan's bed.

"But I want you to stay focused on this. If you find the real killer, I won't have to out Mary, and I'll be free."

Henry shook his head in disbelief. "Here, Villers. In all fairness, that's doubtful right now. I mean, if I find out who did it, I'd need a hell of a lot of proof for Acton to drop his case against you."

"Well, can't you find out who it was?" Tim looked at him with admiration, but Henry could see he was beginning to have doubts.

"I…" – Henry held out his hands – "I don't know." He remembered staking out Shelley Peters' house and then chasing her ex-husband down Leeds Inner Ring Road with Hargreaves at the wheel. "There's a new line of inquiry, I suppose."

"Are you sure, Henry?" Jean asked, clearly worried that their game plan was quickly disintegrating. "Are you sure you can find out what happened to Maureen? You said it yourself, it's been fifteen years. And if Tim comes clean now about this woman, he'll be safe, and the kids will have their father back."

Henry sipped his cappuccino and thought about it. If he could find the real killer, and prove it was them, then Tim would be released, Mary Jones would remain in post, and Murphy would be left dangling in the wind.

A smile spread across his lips, and he nodded at Jean. "Aye, I think I can give it a go." He checked his watch, and it was nearly eleven. So much had happened that morning, he was surprised it wasn't later. He turned to Tim. "Listen," he said, "let's make a deal. Give me until 7 p.m. this evening to make progress, and if I don't, you'll have to come clean about Mary Jones."

Tim didn't seem moved to agree.

"If you don't, Murphy and Acton will have you back inside, and they *will* press charges," Henry added.

Tim drained his paper cup of coffee. "Eight o'clock. And you've got a deal. But, Henry, she's not a bad copper is Mary. She's doing her best. I can't let her be kicked out because of me. Besides, there's the chance she'll deny the whole thing. It could get messy." He stared down the corridor when another hospital bed was pushed down it. "Plus, the kids won't be happy when they find out I cheated on their mum."

"What's worse? Them knowing you cheated on her or thinking you killed her?" asked Henry.

Tim looked at him, and, for an instant, he looked like the self-pitying blue-eyed boy he really was inside.

Henry took that as his answer. "Listen, I think I might have a plan. But either way, you best get the idea into your head that you'll need to disappoint those kids one way or another."

Tim nodded, lost in his own thoughts. "If they can be disappointed any more."

Chapter Twenty-Nine

Jean questioned Harry about his plan to solve the fifteen-year-old case on their way back to Addingham. Henry drove his Skoda along the quiet late-morning bypass away from Airedale Hospital, with Jean needling him for answers.

The sun was high, and the azure skies were dotted by lamb-like fluffy clouds – the kind Henry had seen on adverts for boxes of chocolates, though he couldn't remember the name of the brand. He wished he was sitting up on one of those clouds – as far away as he could possibly get from Jean, while she kept harassing him for a response.

She'd make a good investigative journalist, he thought, or interrogator for a terrifying authoritarian regime.

Jean continued talking, mostly to herself. Her mask was still on, and Henry wondered when she was going to take it off.

"I mean," she said, "we had a plan, didn't we? I was going to get him to agree to come clean about what's-her-name and saving himself – and you…" Jean shook her head. "Why the bloody hell did you change tack halfway through?"

She got annoyed with his lack of answers and threw her hands in the air. "Well, that's the last time I bloody try to help. I could have talked him round, you know? He was wanting me to do it. I could see it in his eyes" – she shook her head again as rage flickered inside her – "but no. Just as I had him in the palm of my hand, you go and bloody agree with him. And then you go and say you've got a plan. What bloody plan, I ask? You've not got one. If you had, you wouldn't be in this–"

"Alright, Jean! Give it a bloody rest, will you?!" Henry said, losing his patience. He'd had twenty minutes of it and couldn't handle any more.

"Finally. He speaks."

"Listen, I think Tim has a point. If I can find out who killed Maureen, then Acton will leave him be and Murphy won't bring down West Yorkshire Police's first female chief constable."

Jean folded her arms and stared out the passenger window. "Well, you could have told me instead of making me look like an idiot."

"I don't think you looked like an idiot at all." He exhaled. "Look, it's mostly my fault. I let Murphy get into my head and forgot I could have carried on with the case. I still have some time to find out what happened to Maureen." He shook his head. "I mean, that's the whole bloody reason I got involved in this. I've been trying to get to the bottom of Maureen's disappearance for fifteen years."

"Aye, and you've now given yourself nine hours to solve it." Jean rolled her eyes. "Which I very much doubt you'll do."

"Well, if I don't, Tim can make a statement about Mary Jones, throw her under the bus, and Murphy can become the new chief constable. But if all that happens, the chance of us finding out who really killed Maureen will pretty much disappear."

"Why?"

"Do you really think Murphy will let me carry on looking into it when he's in charge?" Henry chuckled at the idea of it. He gripped his leather steering wheel and ground his teeth together. "He's always been jealous."

"Jealous?"

"They called me 'The Bloodhound'."

"Right… and what's that when it's at home?"

"It was a nickname the rank and file gave me, as I 'always got my man', which wasn't true. Anyway, Murphy hated it. Hated me, really. He was jealous because I usually closed the case, while he was always two steps behind. I mean, he wasn't such a bad detective. Middling, I suppose I'd call him, but not terrible or incompetent."

"Well, I can see why he didn't like you – if you thought he was 'middling'."

"It's just… this is what I'm good at. I'm good at solving cases, getting into the details, listening to people. He wasn't. He was good at climbing that greasy pole. Which is probably why I got kicked out of the force, and why he's still in it – still trying to reach the top of that bloody pole. Whatever there is up there on top, I doubt it's worth all the hassle. Speaking for myself, I've never been minded to find out."

Jean went quiet and watched the grass in the fields over the drystone walls and the houses beyond. "So, let me understand this. You want to solve an old case, that you've not been able to solve in fifteen years, by teatime?"

Henry took a few moments to consider her question. "Yes. That's pretty much it."

* * *

Henry let a nerve-stricken Jean return to her cottage while he went into his own. He needed a few moments to think through what he had to do. As for the plan he'd mentioned earlier, he didn't have more than a few wisps of an idea.

Tessa was waiting for him behind the front door and barked her annoyance at having missed her morning walk.

"I don't have time now," Henry said, shooing her away.

He went into his kitchen and opened the back door so she could run around the yard. Switching on the kettle, he pulled out the chair from underneath the round table.

His notes lay on his tablecloth.

Sitting down, he pulled the sheet of paper towards him and picked up his marker pen. The nib squeaked as he jotted down his account of seeing Arnold Peters the previous night and chasing him around Leeds.

Why had he been there? Henry wondered, putting the lid back on his pen and tossing it onto the tablecloth.

The kettle clicked to finish, and he got up to make himself a cup of tea. While it was brewing, he went out to look at Tessa, who was sniffing the far corner of the yard with the midday sun shining down on her.

As he squinted into the backyard, he attempted to think of reasons why Arnold Peters had arrived at his ex-wife's house the previous night. What did Arnold want to talk to her about? Had he known Henry and Hargreaves were onto them? Was Arnold there to warn Shelley? And if that was the case, how had Arnold learnt about it? Was Henry being followed? Was his phone tapped?

Not that he or Hargreaves had much on Shelley and Arnold Peters, Henry thought. All they had linking them to Maureen were the records from the Ilkley Tennis Cup and the fact they used to work together.

But Shelley had claimed she was unaware that Maureen had played tennis in the past, which was clearly a lie, as she was in a tournament with her. And when there was a lie, there was something to cover up.

Then there were those love letters, with the secret lover also having written on a flyer for the Ilkley Tennis Cup addressed to Maureen Villers. 'M, you should reconsider. I bet you'll win this time.'

"I bet you'll win this time," Henry said out loud.

Tessa stopped sniffing some weeds that grew between cracks in the paving stones to stare at him.

"Win *this time*?" Henry staggered back to the table as if in a dream.

He leant over the piece of paper, where he'd drawn the three circles that contained the words: 'husband', 'work', and 'tennis'. A line already linked work and tennis together, now Henry drew another one that linked all three.

"Husband, work, and tennis," he said to his kitchen table, as if he knew what he was getting at but wasn't quite sure.

Tim must have known his wife was competing in tennis matches, especially a tennis tournament, he thought, his mind working overtime. It was Hargreaves who told Henry to look into tennis in the first place, as Tim had told her it was worth looking at. But there was something else there, Henry could feel it. Something that linked all three.

"Husband, work, and tennis," he said again, as though repeating the mantra would make things clearer in his mind.

But in his mind's eye, whatever that linked them together was covered in a thick mist, with only parts of its outline visible.

It was an object. Something hard and real.

He knew he had to speak to Shelley and Arnold Peters to find out what they had to say for themselves. Then he had to talk to Tim to find out what linked them all.

Henry shook his head. He couldn't see how Tim was involved. Look at all the trouble he'd gone to prove his innocence. But Henry then realised Tim was reluctant to make his alibi public.

The words Tim had said came to mind. "Besides, there's the chance she'd deny the whole thing."

What if Mary Jones did deny the whole thing – because it wasn't true, Henry wondered. Maybe she'd had an affair with Tim, but it had petered out by the time Maureen died.

Henry's eyes skimmed over the details of Maureen's cause of death. A narrow, blunt implement had caused forceful trauma, resulting in hairline fractures in her skull. Then she'd been wrapped in tarpaulin, tied up and weighted down, and pushed into the cold waters of Swinfeld Reservoir. With any hope, she'd have been dead before she went into that dank water; and if she wasn't, she'd have died quickly as the waters swilled through that coarse covering.

"Is there something that links all three?" he asked, certain of his answer.

He remembered his cup of tea with the tea bag still left in it. Now it'd be too bitter to drink. He sipped it anyway, while fishing his phone from his pocket.

There was that damned silver Mercedes he and Hargreaves had chased the previous night. If Hargreaves hadn't let Murphy get into her head, they might've caught up with Arnold Peters. Then Henry might be able to link those three things: 'husband', 'work', and 'tennis'.

All he had to do was find Arnold.

He hesitated before making the call, as he didn't think she'd want to hear from him. Especially not when he was going to ask her for a favour. But he dialled regardless. He was onto something, and over the past two years, he'd found Barnes to be his best source of information.

"I can't talk long. I'm busy," Barnes said as she picked up.

Henry heard the beeping of a pedestrian crossing and the engines of traffic rattling by. She must be in the centre of Leeds, he guessed.

"Listen, Barnes," he said, not feeling proud of himself. "I need some help with this Maureen Villers case."

"I was taken off that, remember?"

"Aye. I know. But… There's something about it that's really getting to me."

Barnes didn't seem moved to help. "I've got less than ten minutes to grab a sandwich and eat it before I interview a ten-year-old boy who saw his sister murdered. So, if you don't mind, Henry–"

"There's a silver Mercedes I'm looking for."

"Then call a car dealership."

"Hargreaves and I chased it last night through Leeds, but it gave us the slip. Surely officers have been told to be on the lookout for it?"

"I've no idea, Henry. As I've mentioned, there's a little boy and a social worker waiting for me back at the office."

Henry knew he was dangerously close to destroying any goodwill between him and Barnes, as he could also tell she was too overloaded to help. But he couldn't help himself.

"Listen, Barnes, there's something about this case that's gotten into my bones. I can't explain it. It's like the answer's staring me in the face."

Barnes huffed down the phone.

"Please."

"Are you alright, Henry?" she asked, sounding slightly concerned for him.

"I can't put the pieces together. It's driving me half-bloody-mad."

He heard her move the phone from one hand to the other. "A silver Mercedes, was it?"

"Aye. Hargreaves must have reported its registration number last night, but I can send it to you again. I wrote it down last night."

Barnes let out a groan that filled Henry with dread. He'd pushed her too far.

"Fine," she said, "I'll have a look later, but I really need to go."

"Before you do, why else would a man kill his wife?"

Barnes was silent for a moment. "What do you mean?"

"This Tim Villers, if he did kill Maureen, then why? It can't have been out of jealousy. I mean, he had the morals of a tomcat."

"I've known fellas like that before. They're allowed to play around but their partners can't."

"Hmm," Henry mumbled, unsure if that was the answer.

"But if it's not jealousy, look at the other deadly sins. What about greed?"

"Greed?" Then the mistiness in his mind cleared, and the object that linked 'husband', 'work', and 'tennis' suddenly became visible.

Placed before a cool, grey expanse of water, a silver object glinted, and Henry could almost taste copper from a coin.

Then he knew what linked the three: money.

Chapter Thirty

Henry went upstairs to his office to read through the case files, taking his lukewarm bitter tea with him. He'd left Tessa curled up next to the potted fern in the backyard, dead to the world.

Henry seated himself at his desk and slurped some tea, grimacing at its taste. He wiped a layer of dust from the varnished surface of the desk while waiting for his computer to stir itself to life.

When the screen announced it was ready for his commands, he clicked his way through Maureen Villers' case files with no clear intent of what he was looking for.

His mind repeated the mantra he'd started downstairs: husband, work, and tennis.

He knew the three were related, and that money could be the factor that bound them. All he had to do was prove that and find Maureen Villers' killer.

"Greed," Henry mumbled to himself, as he clicked on another document to skim it. "Or money."

If greed had been the motive, he'd best look at the work documents, he thought. Maureen had been the head of finance for Leeds Luxe. She oversaw the money, giving her ample chance to succumb to greed. And Henry had come across a few cases in the past where finance directors had given into temptation and lined their own pockets. But Henry didn't get a sense that Maureen was embezzling money. By all accounts, she had a good reputation and was considered reliable and hard-working. Would she have thrown all that away so she could enrich herself? Plus, there hadn't been any signs of secret bank accounts. The family had been comfortable, living off the salary Maureen took home, which was higher than Tim's police wage.

"Greed?" Henry asked himself, sounding less sure of himself.

He then came across an old photograph of Arnold Peters. His smirking face filled Henry's screen, with its pointed features and well-coiffed dark hair. Arnold's suit and shirt looked expensive and tailored. A self-made man who was secure in his position, but who had a glint in his eye that suggested he wanted more.

"Now, if there was ever an image that epitomizes greed," Henry said, raising up his bitter tea to take a sip.

Then an idea struck him; he started clicking with more intent, and turned on his printer.

Glancing at his phone, he wished Barnes would call him with an update on the silver Mercedes Arnold had been driving the previous night. But he doubted she'd ring him at all. She'd be in the middle of that terrible interview, gently coaxing information out of a traumatized child.

Well, all clues pointed to Arnold Peters, thought Henry. He wasn't sure he could make much progress without first speaking to him. And the international businessman could have already fled to Dubai, unless he was still in the country, laying low – which Henry guessed was more likely.

Henry had one other option to find him but had been putting it off. He knew for certain Hargreaves wouldn't take his call, especially after what she'd said to him the previous night.

But he had no choice. He had until dinner time that evening to find out what happened to Maureen all those years ago, or Tim Villers would be forced to bring down the force's first female chief constable allowing that swine Murphy to claim her job.

Henry couldn't let that happen.

He dialled Hargreaves' number, and, unsurprisingly, she didn't answer. He tried again and again, hoping he'd wind her up so much she'd be compelled to pick up and give him a bollocking.

His fourth call was answered, but not by Hargreaves.

A man answered; his voice triggering half-remembered memories.

"DS Emsley speaking. This is DS Hargreaves' mobile phone, but she's not at her desk." He sounded mildly pissed off. The constant ringing must have provoked him to answer her phone. "Can I take a message? As she's not here right now."

Henry's mind raced through his options. Should he come clean about who he was, claim to be someone else, or even just hang up?

Henry was half-minded to end the call, but instead he said, "Emsley. It's been a long time."

DS Emsley went silent.

"It's Henry Ward here." An introduction Henry realised wasn't needed. "I was calling Hargreaves to have a word."

"DCI Ward? Still can't keep out of this case," Emsley said in a half-joking way. "How are you doing? How's retirement?"

"I can't complain. The real trick, I've learnt, is to keep yourself busy."

"Aye."

"You mustn't be far off from it yourself?"

"Oh," Emsley said, laughing with more force. "A few years of grind left for me. Especially after they changed the pension rules."

"Oh aye. I'd forgotten all about that. How many years do you have left, then?"

"More than I care to think about. You got out just in time." Despite his pleasant tone, there was an element of malice in Emsley's voice.

Henry chuckled, pretending it was a joke. "Well, is she about? Hargreaves?"

"She's been in and out of the office all morning. I think she might be ill. Upset tummy or something."

"Right," Henry said. "That's unfortunate."

Emsley grunted. "Well, if you don't mind, DCI Ward. I'd best get on. I'll tell Hargreaves you called. Though, if you ask me, she might be off the rest of the day. She doesn't look too good."

"I see. Do you know why?"

"No idea. You know me, sir, no one tells me anything." Emsley gave a self-deprecating laugh.

Henry noted the old habitual 'sir'.

Emsley continued, "Though, I did hear she was chasing some car around Leeds last night."

"Oh aye?"

"Pursuing a BMW or something around the Inner Ring Road, I believe she was."

"It was a silver Mercedes," Henry corrected, before biting his tongue to stop himself from saying any more.

"Was it?" Emsley asked, picking up on it. "Did she tell you that, sir?"

"Possibly."

"Ah… that's odd. I wonder what that's all about."

"Any news about the fella driving it?" Henry asked, hoping he hadn't crossed the line.

Emsley didn't sound suspicious. "I believe they picked up the fella last night."

"Right, I see. Well, that's good," Henry said, trying his hardest not to betray his excitement. "We can't have madmen speeding on our streets."

"I completely agree, sir."

"Is she speaking to the driver now?"

"Hargreaves? Oh no. As I said, I think she must have a dicky tummy or something. In and out the office all the time."

"I suppose he's still in custody, this driver?"

"Well…" Emsley sounded stumped at the question. "I'm not sure. I heard they had him in a cell across Leeds."

Henry assumed Arnold Peters was being held at the police station closest to where he and Hargreaves had given up the chase. He wanted to ask Emsley to double-check but knew that'd only arouse suspicion.

"Is that everything, sir? Only, I'd best get on."

"No, Emsley. That's been very enlightening. It was nice to speak to you again."

"Aye, sir. The feeling's mutual."

* * *

As Henry drove into Leeds, he found the early afternoon traffic lighter than he'd expected. The sun broke through the fluffy clouds, shining down on the grey-stone houses on the outskirts of Leeds. He squinted at its rays and focused on the double-decker bus he was stuck behind.

He'd dismissed the idea of just turning up at a police station and demanding to speak to a detainee. The desk sergeant would have him booted out of the building. So,

Henry had considered asking Barnes or Hargreaves to get him permission to speak to Arnold, but neither of them would answer his calls.

So, he decided on the next best thing – wait outside the police station until Arnold Peters was released, and then make his move.

He hoped Arnold was still being held when he arrived at Morley police station. It was an oddly shaped box-like building that had been constructed in the 1960s and hadn't aged gracefully. The tired brickwork, altered over the years, bore the pockmarks of cement where builders had succeeded in keeping the station from falling down.

He didn't bother driving into the car park when he saw the CCTV cameras on the side of the building. Instead, he found a spot on the opposite side of the road.

He sat and waited. What did he hope to learn from Arnold Peters? At the very least he hoped he'd find out why the man was back in the region. Surely, he'd been provoked to return after Maureen's body had been found. Which peaked Henry's suspicion.

Half an hour went by, and Henry regretted not bringing a bottle of water with him. There was a Co-op shop further down the road, and he was considering going to get refreshments when he recognised the man exiting the police station.

Arnold Peters blinked at the daylight. His double-chin was unshaven, and his suit jacket hung over his shoulder. His creased shirt failed to hide the paunch that had developed over the years. All that jet-setting and fine dining must play havoc on the waistline, Henry thought.

Arnold was about to cross the road, when Henry pulled up his Skoda in front of him.

He called out through the open window, "Arnold Peters, it's been a while."

Arnold lowered his head to peer through Henry's window. He looked even more confused until he realised who he was. "What the hell do you want?"

"Want a lift somewhere?"

"I've got a taxi coming."

"Get in," Henry said, keeping his eyes on the road as if he wasn't bothered what Arnold decided to do.

Arnold didn't move from the pavement. "Who are you?"

Henry eyeballed him. "Don't play games with me. You know exactly who I am. I was the lead investigator into Maureen Villers' murder. Former DCI Henry Ward."

"Former? Then what the hell do you want with me?"

"Get in, and I'll tell you."

Arnold shook his head. "Nah. If you have something to say to me, I'll call my solicitor back here and you can talk to him."

Henry chuckled. "That just shows me you've got something to hide."

Arnold looked minded to end the discussion, knowing that was what his solicitor would advise him to do.

"I saw you at Shelley's last night," Henry called out. "I want to know why you wanted to talk to her."

Arnold narrowed his eyes. "That's personal."

"Right. So *personal* you had to speed across Leeds to get away from us?"

Arnold seemed alarmed at this – wondering how Henry knew about the car chase.

Henry spotted a taxi approaching. "You can get your taxi, but I'll only follow you. And I doubt the driver fancies losing his licence to shake me off."

Arnold poked his head through Henry's window. "This is harassment."

"If you tell me what I want to hear, I'll leave you be."

"And what's that?"

"The truth."

Arnold lifted his head to watch his taxi park further down the street. He was visibly torn between getting into it or speaking to Henry.

"Mr Peters, I know more than you think," Henry called out to him, hoping to force his hand.

Arnold chuckled. "I'm not worried about a retired copper. I've got bigger fish to fry."

"Well, get in then – if I'm such a lightweight. What have you got to lose?"

The taxi beeped its horn again.

Arnold swore, and then threw open Henry's car door. "You can give me a ride to the train station. And I'll speak only if I want to."

"Alright, deal," Henry said, knowing full well he wasn't going to keep to it.

Arnold put his seatbelt on. He seemed appalled at the state of Henry's aged Skoda, with the coating of black and white dog hair on everything. Which was rich, Henry thought, considering the man had spent the night in a police cell.

Indicating, Henry merged into traffic and drove past the abandoned taxi.

Now he had a key player involved in Maureen's death in his car, his mind raced through the questions he wanted ask. And then he alighted on the most important. "Actually, would you mind me taking a detour?"

"Where to?"

"Oh, I think you'll know it. It's Swinfeld Reservoir," Henry said, watching Arnold's expression. "Where else were you thinking?"

Chapter Thirty-One

"Why the bloody hell are you bringing me here?" Arnold asked again, getting even more frustrated with Henry for not answering.

Henry kept his eyes on the country lane ahead. They were almost there; he'd kept schtum the whole time, with the intention of driving Arnold into a frenzy.

And it was working.

Whenever Henry glanced at the overweight businessman, he saw sweat marks above the rolls of fat in his creased shirt. Henry had made sure the heating was on full blast and kept the windows rolled up despite it being a warm afternoon.

Make them sweat and then squeeze them for info, Henry thought.

They were nearly at the car park for Swinfeld Reservoir, and as Henry slowed the car to a crawl so he could turn into it, Arnold tried the door handle.

It was locked.

"For God's sake! What is this? A kidnapping? Are you not getting enough money from your police pension, so you fancied getting cash out of me? Well, it's not going to work."

As Arnold shouted in Henry's face, Henry tried his best not to inhale his bad breath. Spending a night in the cells with no toothbrush gave interviewees terrible halitosis.

Henry turned into the half-empty car park and pulled into an empty bay. He spotted a young couple preparing a pushchair for their newborn at a nearby car.

"Why the fuck are we here?" Arnold shouted. He turned on Henry, as if ready to strike him.

Henry held up his finger to his lips with one hand and lifted his phone in the other. "I'm recording all of this, so please be careful what you say."

Then Henry continued, talking as politely as he could. "Also, should anything happen to me, several people, including active police detectives, know I've just picked you up." He smiled, hoping that it'd mask his lies. "So, you'll only have a limited amount of time to get out of the country before you're arrested."

Arnold shook his head, offended. "You think I'm the killer? Is that it? That I killed Maureen fifteen years ago?"

"And did you?"

Arnold stared out the passenger window at some grass blowing in the breeze.

"I've never killed anyone," he said quietly.

"Then, do you know what happened to Maureen? Do you know why she was killed?"

Arnold huffed. He looked dog-tired. His complexion was red as if he was close to having heart complaints. "It was a terrible thing that happened… But I didn't really know the lass – to be honest."

"Oh, you didn't?"

Arnold made eye contact. "Alright. I knew her from Shelley's company, but that was all. I didn't know her outside of work. And I barely had anything to do with that company."

"Oh right. Weren't you the lead investor?"

He shrugged. "I invest in hundreds of companies. It doesn't mean I know their heads of finance on a personal basis."

"So, you never spoke to Maureen outside of her work?"

Arnold shook his head and glanced around the car again, growing frustrated.

"Would you mind looking at those papers on the back seat," Henry said.

Arnold looked into the back for a moment, as if sensing a trap, and when he spotted the sheets of paper, he picked them up gingerly.

Quickly skimming through them, he asked, "Why've you given me a list of names?"

"Ever played tennis?"

Arnold grunted a laugh. "Look at me. Do I look like I get enough exercise? I have a personal trainer and only see him twice a year. After my jollies and on January the first."

"Ah. So, you've never played a tennis tournament then?"

Arnold stopped leafing through the papers, quickly realising what they were. "I might've done…"

"You played in the Ilkley Tennis Cup with your wife and Maureen Villers back in 2007. You might have played in more with her before then."

Arnold stared at his highlighted name on the same page as Maureen's.

His red complexion went a deathly grey. He slammed the papers onto the dashboard and looked through the windscreen, undoing his shirt collar button.

It was incredibly hot in the car, so much that even Henry's head was spinning. "Fancy a walk around the reservoir?" he asked.

Arnold glanced out the window. "This is where she died, isn't it?"

"Ever been?"

He shook his head. "Never." He scoffed. "Looks like a dump."

"Nah, it's alright actually. Though, whoever killed poor Maureen thought it was a dump. She was bound up in tarpaulin and dropped into the water." Henry shook his head. "Imagine that. Poor woman."

Arnold shifted in his seat. "Alright, you can stop this. I didn't kill her. I didn't even know her that well."

"Apart from the tennis tournament you played together."

Arnold glared at him. "So, I played tennis with her. So what?"

"Why lie about it, Mr Peters?"

Arnold waved hot air in his face. "It's boiling in here. I can't sodding breathe." He pressed the button to roll down the window, but the engine wasn't on. "Get this open, will you?"

"We'll get out and have a walk around, shall we? I'll show you the spot where she was dumped?"

Arnold sucked in sharp breaths. "No. I'm alright."

"There's no water in there now. It's just the basin, and all the stuff people have chucked in over the years. Who knows what else we'll find."

Arnold tried the door handle again, but it was locked. "Let me out, for God's sake. This is abduction."

Henry held up his hands in self-defence. "I'll let you out, but first I want something from you."

"What? A written confession? I didn't bloody kill Maureen!"

"I know. I believe you." Henry produced a biro pen from his pocket. "All I want is for you to write a statement claiming you didn't know Maureen personally. Apart from this tennis business."

Arnold eyed him suspiciously. "Is that all?"

Henry nodded. He leant back and retrieved more paper from under Tessa's tartan blanket on the back seat.

"Here, write on this. You only have to say that you didn't know Maureen in any way – outside of work and tennis."

Arnold took the pen, keeping his eyes on Henry. "Then you'll let me go?"

"I'll drop you off at the train station, and then we're done. You'll never hear from me again."

Huffing again, Arnold said, "I'd rather get a damn taxi. If any will pick me up here." He leant forward and used the dashboard to rest on as he started writing. "How many words?"

"Just a few," Henry said. He peered over Arnold's large shoulder to watch him compose his statement. After a few scribbled words, Henry knew it was a match.

"Interesting handwriting you have."

Arnold leant back to admire his penmanship. "Well… it's alright. I hardly write with a pen these days, it's all keyboards–"

"Would you mind turning over that sheet of paper you're writing on?"

The suspicion returned to Arnold's face. He flipped the paper to find something printed on the back.

A handwritten letter.

Maureen's love letter.

"Do you recognise that?" Henry asked, not needing him to answer.

Arnold's face went paler still. Panic spread from his eyes to his jaw, which nearly fell open. "No… I…" His lower lip quivered. Then, regaining control, he said, "I didn't kill her."

"But you were having a relationship with her?"

He turned slowly to Henry. His face expressing how broken he was inside. "I did… I did. You've bloody got me there."

* * *

"Tell me everything," Henry said, shifting himself in the driving seat so he could watch Arnold's confession.

The large businessman, sweating and exhausted, appeared ready to tell all. He heaved his hefty chest, lined with sweat marks, and exhaled his bad breath.

"We didn't mean for it to happen. It just did. I mean… I wasn't always a womaniser, though people thought I was. I largely kept it away from Shelley. She knew what I could be like – but she never knew the full extent of it." He scrunched up his face. "It didn't go on for that long with Maureen."

"How did it start?"

"A Christmas do in Leeds. 2006. I'd spoken to her beforehand but thought she was boring. You know, not my type."

"You prefer flashier women?"

Arnold looked at him, gauging if it was an insult. "Kind of," he said, defensively.

"So, you got talking at a Christmas party?"

"Aye. We got talking, and she seemed to have more about her. She'd let her hair down a bit."

"How long did it go on for, the affair? Until 2008?"

Arnold took a moment to answer. "I think you know how long it went on for. You've bloody found my letters."

"Talking of those letters, you called Tim an 'undeserving husband'." Henry cocked an eyebrow to express the irony.

Arnold looked at him. "I might have done. If Maureen cheated on him, it was because he pushed her to it. She wanted companionship. Someone there for her."

"Isn't it a bit 'kettle calling the pot'?"

"It wasn't a constant thing. It was on and off. I had to be careful around Shelley, as I didn't want her to find out. And Maureen, bless her, was guilt-ridden by the whole thing." He huffed. "To be honest, it wasn't very sexual. It was mostly flirting, weekends away whenever she could, which wasn't often. But eventually it became more."

"Love?"

Arnold smirked. "If there is such a thing. No. More… mutual respect. She was bloody good at what she did. Hard-working, knew how to handle money, could run businesses far bigger than Leeds Luxe ever was. Shelley, bless her, is alright at what she does, but she's better at talking the talk. It was Maureen who kept that business going. I tried poaching her a number of times for my other concerns. We discussed it a lot."

"Oh, right. Does this explain Canada?"

Arnold shook his head, as if he was confused. "No."

"You never heard her talk about a life in Toronto?"

"It *was* a silly dream she had. Fly over there and get set up. She'd always wanted to live there. She'd watched that TV show, *Due South*, was it? She really fancied doing it. But I just thought it was that – a fancy."

"And why didn't you both fly over there?"

"Well… I had the cash to do it, but I'm not a fan of the cold. Why do you think I got away from here? And for her, it was the kids. She couldn't leave them with him."

He seemed momentarily upset and gripped his cheeks under his red eyes. "That's why I didn't understand her suddenly swanning off over there? As that's what we all thought at the time. Eventually, I reconciled it, thinking she'd had enough of everything here and thought 'sod it'." He shrugged. "You know, I flew over a few times."

"To Toronto?"

Arnold nodded. "I braved the cold to see if I could find her, when all the while she was dead and dumped in that bloody water." He cleared his throat, swallowing the emotion he'd released.

Henry peered out his windscreen, allowing Arnold a moment. "What I don't get is why you and Shelley have been so cagey about all this."

Arnold suddenly became alert.

Henry noticed and asked, "What was it? Was it Leeds Luxe?"

Arnold nodded and then averted Henry's eyes by looking out the passenger window. "There was a black hole in its finances."

"From what? Debt?"

Arnold glanced suspiciously at Henry. "How much do you know?"

"Enough…" Henry said, pretending he knew more than he did. But he was quickly forming ideas: someone had been embezzling money. This is how the greed element came in. 'Husband', 'work', and 'tennis' were all united by greed, Henry thought.

Arnold waited for him to reveal his hand. But Henry had no cards to play.

Looking at his choices, Henry knew he had three. Either Arnold himself was embezzling money, which Henry doubted, or Maureen was, which was also not credible.

"Shelley was committing fraud," Henry said with authority, as if he had a stash of evidence hidden away to prove it.

Arnold, presumably still shocked by Henry's reveal of the tennis tournament list and the love letters, only nodded. "How did you find that out?"

"Fraud squad are doing a thorough look into Shelley's books," Henry lied.

Arnold raised an eyebrow. "But she had them all destroyed."

"Not Leeds Luxe's, but her current business. That sports thing."

Arnold rolled his eyes. "Right. I suspected she'd be up to it again, but I hoped she wouldn't be so bloody stupid."

"If you knew she was embezzling money, why did you invest in Leeds Luxe?" Henry asked, after a few moments' reflection.

"I gave her the seed capital to set it up, and then I maintained a limited exposure. I don't think she set out to commit fraud… she just got a taste for the finer things in life and used the company's cash to pay for them. Then it got out of hand. If you saw the shithole where she grew up, you might understand."

Henry's mind raced through what he'd just learnt. Shelley was embezzling money at Leeds Luxe, and her husband was having an affair with its head of finance. What a messy situation that company was in.

Henry looked beyond the stretch of grass that extended to the embankment of the empty reservoir. "You don't think Shelley…?"

Arnold shifted in his seat. "What? Killed Maureen?" he asked, incredulously. "Never. She's a self-serving swine at times, but she'd never kill a human being. She's vegetarian for starters."

Henry recalled establishing an alibi for Shelley Peters but couldn't remember what it was.

"Don't bother considering it," Arnold said, waving warm air into his face. "She didn't do it. I can see you thinking it through. She was in meetings the whole day that Maureen died."

"Ah, so you considered it enough yourself to look into it?"

Arnold's sidewards glance gave him away.

Henry asked, "Tell me what happened leading up to the 10th of April, 2008."

"What can I say?"

"Did you see Maureen?"

He shook his head. "She'd been keeping her head down. Didn't want anything to do with me. Even when I called in at the office on the 8th, she turned me away. Threatened to tell Shelley."

"Why was that?"

Arnold shrugged. "Like I said, she'd always felt terrible about us. That's the problem with having affairs with good people – they can't handle the guilt. But I did think she seemed a bit off. She wasn't her usual self."

"Do you know why? Had something happened?" Henry asked.

"Well…" Arnold's eyes drifted off into the distance as if his mind was shovelling through forgotten memories. "There was something bothering her, aye… She wouldn't go into detail. Shelley might've been aware of it."

"Was it the embezzling?"

"I don't know. It could have been, but Maureen normally pretended to know nothing about that, and Shelley was daft enough to believe her."

Henry raised an eyebrow. "Then what was it?"

Gripping his chin, Arnold peered thoughtfully into the distance. "I'm not sure… I mean, it was years ago."

"You said 'she'd not been her usual self'. In what way hadn't she?"

Arnold made another attempt to remember, straining his face as he put in the effort. "If I recall correctly… It was something to do with her phone. She'd never answer the bloody thing – like she was afraid of it."

"Why did she do that?"

"No idea. When I asked her about it… she just said something silly, like she was receiving too many sales calls."

"When did this happen?" asked Henry.

"A few months before she disappeared, just before she…"

Henry let Arnold drift off into his own personal despair while he reflected on why Maureen wouldn't answer her phone. Well, because she was avoiding someone, he realised.

"Was she only ignoring your calls?"

Arnold shrugged. "Perhaps, but she didn't answer other people's, either. Such as Shelley's."

Odd, thought Henry. "And why didn't you mention this at the time?"

"I've only just remembered it myself. It didn't seem that important back then."

An idea struck Henry. "Could it have been a disliked friend?"

Arnold gave an unconvinced shrug.

"Or an unwanted admirer of some sort?" Henry asked.

Arnold appeared offended by the idea. "Admirer? Well, I don't know."

However, Henry thought he was onto something. Then the recollection of sitting in Gary Steele's horrid flat in Shipley came to mind. The failed tennis star whose career had cratered, who found himself training amateur tennis players in Bradford. Gary even admitted to trying it on with Maureen, and his shame was still fresh as he'd relived her rejection.

Henry asked, "Was it her tennis coach who was trying to contact her?"

Arnold cocked an eyebrow. "Tennis? No. Nothing like that… I don't think." Biting his thumbnail, he focused on the distance as if searching for the answer to a tough quiz question. "No… it might have been something else… I don't know. I never thought it'd be important."

"Any little detail could help us find her killer."

Arnold gave up trying to remember. "Shelley might have known more about it."

"Shelley?"

Arnold nodded. "She and Maureen were close, which complicated things with me and Maureen."

"Talking of Shelley, why were you at hers last night?"

Arnold's defences went back up. He fingered the empty buttonhole on his shirt collar. "I needed to see she was alright after Maureen had been found."

"Right," Henry said, not quite buying it.

"And seeing as you've got your claws into her current business dealings, she probably needs my help. But that's all I have to say on the matter."

Henry remembered he'd pretended there was a fraud investigation going on into Shelley's current business. He wondered if he should come clean about his lie, when an idea struck him. "Here, let's say we made a deal?"

"What's this?" Arnold said, sounding interested.

"I might be able to extinguish that fraud investigation if Shelley tells me what I need to know."

Arnold's stare nearly bore through Henry's forehead. "You're retired. How can you influence a fraud investigation?"

Henry knew full well he couldn't influence any kind of police investigation. But he was sure his powers of persuasion could stretch to ending an inquiry that didn't exist.

"Get her on the phone and ask her who this unwanted admirer was that Maureen was avoiding," he said. "If Shelley tells me, you have my word that the fraud investigation into her sports business will disappear."

Arnold appeared tempted by the offer, but he lifted his phone in the air. "The batteries are dead. I was in a police cell all night, remember?"

Henry rooted around near the gearbox and presented Arnold with a charging cable. "Stick this in, and then call her."

Arnold snatched the cable from him. "Right. I will. Then will you let me out of this sodding car?"

"I'll take you wherever you need to go."

Chapter Thirty-Two

Arnold Peters held up to his end of the deal. Once he eventually got his ex-wife on the phone, who hadn't answered his first few calls, he explained the agreement he and Henry had reached.

Shelley claimed she was completely innocent of fraud, which Henry suspected might be true for her current business.

Arnold told her to calm down and explained that the ongoing – and fictional – investigation would be wrapped up if she told Henry the name of the unwanted admirer who'd been bothering Maureen.

"Which admirer?" Shelley asked, her voice coming through the loudspeaker.

Arnold glanced at Henry and back at his mobile phone. "Well, I don't know. She was being funny with her phone before she disappeared. Not answering it and whatnot."

"What do you mean?" she asked, as if a new understanding had struck her. "Wait. How did *you* know she was having issues with her phone?"

Henry could see from Arnold's flushed face that he'd never come clean to his ex-wife about his relationship with Maureen.

"Never mind that," Arnold said, after clearing his throat. "Just bloody tell us if you know who she was avoiding." He glanced at Henry again. "Remember – this detective could make a lot of trouble for you go away."

"There's nothing to investigate, so if the police wish to waste their time–"

"Shelley, this is about Maureen," Henry said, losing his patience and speaking before Arnold. "Finding out what happened to her is what's important. Not which funds you've been stashing in which account."

Shelley's side of the line fell silent.

"Shelley?" Arnold asked. "Can you remember a day or two before she went missing. Maureen… she'd been ignoring our calls. Yours and mine."

"Again… how do you know so much about Maureen? I thought you hardly knew her."

Arnold shook his head. "Shelley, focus, would you? Someone had been bothering her. Who was it?"

Shelley huffed. "It was fifteen years ago, Arnold. I barely know what's upsetting my PA today, let alone what was annoying my head of finance all those years ago."

"Shelley. You two were close."

The line went silent again – for too long.

"Shelley? Are you there?" Arnold asked.

No answer.

Henry and Arnold shared a look, wondering if she'd hung up.

"Shelley?!"

"I'm here! Christ. I'm trying to remember."

"Right," Arnold said.

They gave her time to think. Henry looked out across the grass towards the empty reservoir and saw the young couple from earlier returning with the pushchair. They must have done the full walk already, and then he realised they had been parked there for over an hour.

"She might've been ignoring calls, yes. Perhaps… I think I asked her about it, and she said she was receiving loads of sales calls."

Arnold gave Henry a look which said, 'Didn't I tell you?'.

Henry leant closer to the phone. "Listen, Shelley. Can you remember if she'd ever had issues with her tennis coach?"

"Her coach?" Shelley asked, sounding bewildered.

"Aye. Did she ever mention him?"

"No, never."

Henry tried to hide his dissatisfaction. "Right, was there ever any mention of an unwanted admirer or someone she was avoiding?"

Shelley let out a sharp laugh. "Maureen? She was too strait-laced for anything like that. Or so I'd thought."

Henry noticed Arnold's cheeks flush at Shelley's barb.

Henry continued, "Did anyone strange try to contact her before she died?"

"No, she never mentioned anything."

"What about a month or two before then? Do you know if anyone approached her or anything?" Henry asked, fearing he was hitting a brick wall.

"I don't know…" Then Shelley gasped. "Oh, hang on!" She sounded excited. "There was something."

Henry and Arnold looked at each other.

"What was it?" asked Henry.

"It was in January… No. Maybe February of that year. She said someone was leaving her odd notes."

"You what?"

"Post-it notes. She'd find them in the morning stuck to her car windscreen. They were from some fella who reckoned he fancied her."

Henry frowned and mouthed a question to Arnold, asking if he ever knew about this. Arnold responded with a confounded shake of the head.

"What can you tell me about these notes?" Henry asked Shelley.

"Well, Maureen thought they were stupid and found them annoying. She even showed me one, and I thought it was juvenile."

"Did she know the person who was leaving them?"

"Erm…" Shelley went quiet on the line. "I think it was someone she knew through her husband."

"A copper?" Henry asked.

"Erm… Yes, I suppose he might've been."

"Did she ever tell you his name?"

Shelley moaned as if in slight pain. "Possibly. Did she tell me his name?" she asked herself.

Henry wondered who this copper could be. It had to be someone who worked with Tim. Henry had the names of the officers stationed at Otley on his computer at home, but that wouldn't help him at that moment.

"There was a name… yes," Shelley said. "Something like Gensley? Fenbury?"

Henry frowned as if the names were made up. "You sure?"

"Maureen only said his name a few times."

"And why didn't you tell us this back in 2008?" Henry asked, trying his best to swallow his frustration. A lead like this would have changed the whole investigation.

"I recall asking her about it a week or so after she'd told me, but she said the fella had stopped doing it. So I forgot all about it. Anyway, I thought she'd fled to Canada, like everyone else did."

"Leaving her husband and kids?" Henry asked.

Shelley laughed. "Husband? Tim was a lousy one of those. Almost as lousy as my own."

Arnold bristled.

Shelley continued, "I thought she'd met someone else and was getting ready to go off with them and divorce Tim – she had just cause. I expected her to send for the kids afterwards."

"But she never did," Henry said.

"No. She didn't. Perhaps now I can see why, as that's not *your* style, is it, Arnold? You're not the type who starts new lives – especially when kids are involved."

Arnold gripped his phone tightly and eyed it with spite. "I don't know what you're–"

"Save it. Are we done here? Can I assume this fraud investigation has gone away?"

"Hang about…" Henry said. "You've not given me the name of this copper who was leaving creepy notes."

"Yes, I have. Gellery… or something."

Henry's mind raced through all the officers he could recall working at Otley station. None were called *Gellery*. "Are you sure?"

"Aye," Arnold concurred. "That doesn't sound like a real name."

"Gellery? Well… no. Maybe you're right. Hang on. What are those steam trains up near Skipton called?"

Henry and Arnold shared a perplexed look.

"Embsay?" Henry asked.

"That's it. Embsay," Shelley said, sounding proud of herself.

Henry didn't know a single officer in West Yorkshire called Embsay.

But he did know one called… "Emsley?"

"No. I'm sure it was Embsay…" But she sounded doubtful. "Or Emsley… I suppose."

By then, Henry had already thought it through and couldn't shake that shocked feeling.

"Jesus H Christ…" he whispered to himself and then picked up his phone to call Hargreaves.

* * *

Henry asked Arnold to get out of his car before reversing at speed out of the parking bay. Arnold seemed to enjoy getting some fresh air and wished Henry well in finding out who'd killed Maureen.

Speeding around the sharp turns in the country lanes, Henry redialled Hargreaves' phone over and over. But she didn't answer. Looking at the clock on the dashboard, he saw it was nearly dinner time. Acton and Emsley would soon be pressing charges against Tim Villers, meaning they'd be getting him into Leeds Central police station so they could charge him officially for his former wife's murder.

When all the while, it was a serving detective who'd murdered her. One that was inside the investigation, steering it towards Tim – the most obvious culprit.

"Most murders are committed by a family member," Henry said under his breath, shaking his head. DCI Acton had believed that so much, he'd also missed the signs.

Henry couldn't believe the killer had been involved in the investigation. How had Emsley ended up on the original MIT?

Come to think of it, Henry couldn't remember. When it came to detective constables, sometimes it came down to who was available and not who you preferred. Henry couldn't remember how Emsley had snuck onto his team.

And he'd done it again with the second inquiry. Conniving his way onto the investigation a second time, now that they knew Maureen had been murdered.

The murder weapon had been a police baton. Henry shook his head. Emsley could have easily laid his hands on one of those. The murder had been premeditated, with the equipment being placed there beforehand. Was Emsley the type to plan something like that? Henry didn't know, but suspected the man was up to date with investigative procedures and would know how to cover his tracks.

But why had Maureen gone up to Swinfeld? She wasn't known for going up there and she'd taken the time off work in which to do it. Henry could only think that she'd been contacted by her stalker, who asked to meet her up there.

Why would she go willingly? Unless she wanted to have a confrontation with him, telling him to leave her alone. She did take her large dog with her for backup.

"But Emsley?" Henry said to himself, almost laughing. The man was an idiot. A harmless one at that. The 'wouldn't hurt a fly' sort.

Why would he kill Tim Villers' wife?

Henry had no idea. But there must be a reason. Tim slept around. Maybe he'd slept with someone Emsley was after or even his own girlfriend. That was assuming Emsley had ever had one. Maybe he hadn't.

Had Emsley worked at Otley station? Henry didn't have an answer for that. Emsley was a detective constable at the time, working not only out of Wakefield, but loads of stations in the area. He could have ended up at Otley at some point and come into contact with Tim and his wife.

Henry's car flew off a bump in the road and touched air for an instant before landing.

Slowing down, Henry decided to drive more carefully. He didn't want to die before he'd told someone who'd killed Maureen.

"But Emsley?" he asked again, glancing at his own eyes in the rear-view mirror. "Are you sure?"

He was. Certain. Emsley appeared affable and soft, but Henry had always thought it was a front – that something harder and darker lurked behind. And it seemed that, at some point, Maureen had provoked him.

All Henry had to do was prove it, before Acton, under the influence of Emsley, pressed charges against Tim Villers.

Chapter Thirty-Three

Henry arrived at Leeds Central police station. The imposing recently built office building looked like it homed marketing companies similar to Shelley Peters'. The two indicators that it was a police station were the Union flag on a pole and the West Yorkshire Police's sign by the front door.

Henry stepped through that automatic doorway and strode towards the front desk, manned by a police officer. On his way over, he'd formulated two plans and hoped he'd have the chance to use the second.

"I need to see DS Hargreaves or DCI Acton as soon as possible," he said, before realising he'd interrupted a conversation between the desk officer and an elderly woman in front of whom Henry had barged.

"In a moment, please," the officer said, glaring at him.

Not having that moment to spare, Henry stepped into the foyer and peered up the staircase to the offices upstairs. Hargreaves must be up there somewhere, he thought. Taking out his phone, he tried her number for the twentieth time.

He then noticed the double doors on the ground floor that led to the holding cells. He'd been through there recently on another case and wondered if Acton and Hargreaves were already in an interrogation room with Tim – detailing the charges of murder against him.

"Sir?" asked the desk officer. "Who was it you wanted to talk to?"

Henry noticed the elderly lady making her way out the automatic doors and approached the desk. "DS Hargreaves or DCI Acton. They're investigating a murder."

The office picked up the desk phone. "And *you* are?"

"I'm former DCI Henry Ward. I need to talk to them urgently."

"Ward?" the officer said for confirmation. Henry guessed she'd be too young to remember him. "I'll call their office."

Henry waited.

The desk officer smiled. "Oh, hello, it's the front desk. I have a Henry Ward here for a DCI Acton or DS Hargreaves?" The officer nodded. "Great." She hung up the phone and transferred her smile to Henry. "Someone's on their way."

Henry nodded his thanks and made his way to the foot of the staircase. After a few moments, he spotted DS Emsley walking down them, wearing his green tweed jacket.

Henry felt his pulse quicken at the sight of him, and did his best to calm his nerves. He couldn't give away what he knew already.

Emsley descended the steps towards him. "Oh, hello, sir. You wanted a word?"

Walking halfway up the flight of steps, Henry nodded. "Afternoon, Emsley. DS now, aren't you?"

Emsley smiled proudly, displaying crooked teeth. "I am, sir. After all these years. My presence has been noted." His smile faded. "Now, you wanted to speak to Hargreaves? I'll take you up to her."

"Aye," Henry said, realising he had the chance to go for his second plan. "Listen. Could we speak somewhere privately, just us two?"

Emsley's cow-like eyes widened with surprise. "Just us, sir? Are you sure?"

Henry shook his head. "There's something I wanted to ask you?"

Emsley stepped out of the way of a uniformed officer wearing a bulky bulletproof vest. Glancing back, Emsley gave a half-hearted laugh, as if the idea that Henry needed to talk to him was crazy. "What is it you want to know?"

"I want to ask you about Maureen Villers."

"Oh. Well, that's where we'll have issues, sir. As I can't discuss an active case with a former–"

"I know about you stalking her."

Emsley's eyes fluttered. The telltale sign of cheeks reddening gave him away instantly. But he was a smooth operator. The amiable persona returned, and he covered his mouth to cough. "What's this, sir? Stalking?"

"Aye. Let's find a room to talk in," Henry said, walking up the stairs.

Emsley remained on the flight of stairs, but when Henry had reached the top, he quickly followed. As Henry knew he would.

Emsley gestured to the first door in a long corridor and Henry followed him inside a store cupboard. Shelves of cleaning products lined the walls, giving off a citrusy chemical smell. A large floor-cleaning machine was parked in the corner next to boxes of printing paper, neatly stacked.

Henry had been expecting an office, not a storeroom, but thought any place would do.

Emsley bit his lower lip, deep in thought. "So, you've heard some nonsense about me 'stalking'?"

"Cut the crap," Henry said. "I know everything."

Emsley's eyes widened in surprise.

"I've heard you were pestering Maureen Villers."

Emsley jutted out his chin. "I don't know–"

"How did you meet her? That's what I want to know, but I suppose the truth will come out."

Emsley shook his head. He dug his fingernails into his thinning brown hair and scratched. "I've no idea where you've heard these lies–"

"Where did you get the police baton, Emsley? Was it Tim's you used or did you use someone else's? Because I know damn well that we detectives weren't issued them."

Emsley's eyes widened again, and he stopped scratching his scalp. "Well, I… Are you accusing me…?"

Henry continued, "I have one witness who says you were stalking Maureen, we have a murder weapon that you easily could have accessed, and I'm sure a deep delve into Maureen's phone records will prove you'd been contacting her continuously. Plus, there are her emails."

Emsley was doing his best impression of a wronged suspect. "I can't believe what I'm hearing, sir. Are you…? You're really saying I killed Maureen Villers?"

"Well, did you?" Henry leaned in, growing angrier. Emsley's insipid reaction was grating on him.

Emsley shook his head slowly. "I used to really respect you, sir, but maybe… I don't know." He suddenly looked concerned. "Perhaps, you're ill in the head? Possibly you've got dementia, on account of all that drinking you used to do."

Henry stepped closer to him. "What did you say?"

"We all knew you liked a drink or two, sir. On the original investigation, you used to slip out throughout the day and go to the pub. You'd come back with drink on your breath."

Henry had never heard anything so stupid. "I never drunk while on duty. Even when it was still legal."

Emsley wiped his mouth with a shaking hand. "I'm sure the time sheets from back then could corroborate you going missing during the day."

"Time sheets?! What are you playing at?"

"I'm just talking about your heavy drinking and your possible dementia."

"I'm sixty-four, you stupid sod. I don't have dementia. You're not that much younger than me, anyway…" Then Henry realised he was falling into Emsley's trap. Emsley had wanted him to change subjects.

"I'm perfectly fine upstairs," Henry said, tapping his own thinning head. "It's *you* we ought to be afraid of."

"Me?" Emsley half-laughed again. "But I'm just me… A nobody. I haven't murdered anyone."

"No? Never?" Henry watched Emsley's unchanged expression. "How about the stalking? Do you admit to that?"

He shook his head. "I've never stalked anyone, either. I've never done anything like that. I'm a detective. I uphold the law, not break it."

Henry heard his words attempting to mask the fear in his voice.

"So, you wouldn't mind us looking at all your communications?"

Emsley shrugged. "I always assume my correspondence is being analysed by someone, anyway."

What an odd attitude to have, Henry thought. "Good. Then you also won't mind me speaking with DS Hargreaves and DCI Acton."

"Well…" Emsley scrunched up his upper lip. "I don't believe they're available to you anymore."

Henry went to the door. "I'll make them available–"

Emsley grabbed Henry's shoulder. There was violence in his eyes. "I wouldn't. They're busy."

"Doing what?" Henry asked.

"Pressing charges against Tim Villers." Emsley then smiled. Not his usual insipid one, but a cunning one, like a wolf that had trapped its prey. "You're too late, Ward. Fifteen years too late."

Chapter Thirty-Four

Henry leant his forehead against the storeroom door. He was too late. DCI Acton wouldn't consider dropping the charges now, unless Henry brought him conclusive evidence that Emsley had murdered Maureen, and there was little hope of him doing that any time soon. But then Henry remembered another factor that gave him hope. Tim Villers had an alibi. Had he revealed it yet, as he'd agreed to do earlier?

It would bring down the force's chief constable and allow Detective Superintendent Murphy to ascend to the head of the force. But at least Tim would go free, forcing Acton to look for an alternative suspect.

That was if Murphy, as the new chief of police, continued the investigation, which, as the man had suggested himself, was unlikely.

Emsley stepped behind Henry, appearing to enjoy his despair. "Well. Nice try, old man. To be honest, I hadn't expected you to get as far as you did."

Henry turned to look at him. "I beg your pardon?"

Emsley continued with a new air about him – a dark, seething confidence. "You got very close. The only issue is, you had no evidence. And you'll find there's none against me, but plenty against Tim. That's why we're pressing charges against him as we speak."

"Unless he has an alibi," Henry said, smirking.

Emsley narrowed his eyes, unsure if Henry was toying with him. "But he doesn't have one," he said, losing confidence in himself. "He had that dentist appointment, but then where was he for the rest of those three hours?"

"Would you like to know? I'm sure Tim is letting DCI Acton know all about it. Like you said – as we speak." Henry watched Emsley's worried expression before continuing. "His alibi will need some corroboration, but it's a bloody good one." Henry stood back from the door, holding his head high. "What I'd like to know, is if *you* have an alibi?"

Emsley's confidence completely deserted him. "What?"

"Can you account for your whereabouts on the 10th of April, 2008 between 10 a.m. and 1 p.m.?"

Emsley blinked. He couldn't, Henry could tell.

"And can you tell me what car you were driving back then?"

"This is ridiculous," Emsley said, returning to his meek demeanour. "You can't possibly think I–"

"You know damn well what I think."

And an idea then struck Henry. "And what about that Canada nonsense? How does that factor into all of this?" Henry gripped his chin and scowled at Emsley. That whole line of inquiry came from the receipt for the plane ticket that'd been found. It'd forced people to believe that Maureen had run away. But where did it…?

Henry took a breath. "You had something to do with the receipt, didn't you?"

Emsley scoffed as if the idea was crazy.

But Henry continued, sure he was onto something. "Aye… I bet if I check my files, I'll find the detective who found that receipt was you." Another recollection struck Henry and he shook his head in shame. "And who did I send to talk to that travel agency…?" He scoffed at his own stupidity. "You again."

Henry gripped his forehead. How had he let himself be duped by one of his own? A fellow detective who'd committed murder and used his access to cover his tracks – ensuring the truth was never discovered.

Emsley was leaning on the stack of boxed printing paper with his arms crossed. "I literally have no idea what you're–"

"Oh, drop it. Acton and Hargreaves will uncover enough on you once they start looking. And when they do, what else will they find? Was Maureen the only person you've ever stalked?"

Henry let his question hang in the air, and then he recalled his own feelings of being followed these past few days. Even while he stood in his own backyard, he'd felt like someone was watching his every move.

And then there was that odd email with the photo of Tim Villers and Hargreaves in the front seat of a car, embracing each other.

"Ah, I see," Henry said, nodding as he realised. "You've made a habit of following people. You've been following me, and you've been keeping your eyes on Tim all these years. Why send me that old photo of Hargreaves?"

Emsley's eyelashes fluttered.

"What good did that do to anyone? So what if she had a relationship with him?"

Emsley's eye twitched. "I literally don't know what you're talking about."

"Save your breath." Henry stepped closer. "You can answer me this, though. How many other people have you followed?"

"None."

"How many other people have you killed?"

"None at all."

"Bollocks! Don't lie to me. I know it was you, Emsley. And you know they'll find enough proof to convict you. Fifteen years isn't that long ago. Hargreaves has found the CCTV footage from back then." Henry noted the flicker of terror in Emsley's eyes – and enjoyed it. "They'll track down whatever car it was you were driving back then and search the footage for it. And they've found Maureen's phone records…"

Henry stopped.

Hargreaves had said the phone records were missing pages. Who had been in charge of handling them?

Emsley.

Henry glared at him, his eyes narrowed by disdain. "You doctored them…"

The darkness glinted in Emsley's eyes.

"Shit," Henry said under his breath.

Emsley would've already destroyed the evidence of him contacting Maureen. And the phone companies wouldn't have the records anymore, they would have been deleted ages ago. The only hope of getting any hard evidence was the CCTV footage Hargreaves had found. Hopefully, Emsley wouldn't get the chance to destroy it once IT had loaded it onto the system.

But Emsley, appearing to be satisfied with Henry's silence, wore that wolfish grin. His unnerving confidence returned as he strode to the door.

Opening it, he turned to Henry. "You've got nothing. So, if you tell anyone about this, I'll push the dementia thing. I'll push it hard. And the drinking. We can both throw accusations around, *sir*. So don't bother trying."

Emsley slipped out of the door, leaving Henry alone.

Henry sighed. Defeated. What was he to do? Emsley had destroyed any proof of him being involved. And he might even be off to destroy any further evidence. He'd been planning this cover-up for years and had been getting away with it…

Until now.

Henry took out his mobile phone and checked it was still recording. Clicking 'stop', he sent the whole fifteen-minute exchange to Hargreaves before allowing himself a wicked grin.

* * *

Henry made it to the bottom step and walked into the foyer. He recognised the tall man entering through the automatic doors. Tim Villers stooped his head, and his curly hair looked unkempt. He slunk towards the front desk to announce himself, but Henry intercepted him.

"Don't say a bloody thing," Henry said, leading him by the wrist to the corner of the foyer. "I suppose you've only just turned up?"

Tim appeared confused at seeing Henry there. He nodded after a moment – his mouth slightly agape.

Henry shook his head. "Another bloody lie from that snake. He said you'd already been charged."

Tim appeared confused. "Acton called me half an hour ago. I've been trying to call you."

"I've been busy. Look, I know who killed Maureen."

Tim's mouth gaped again. "What? Who?"

"You ever heard of a detective called Emsley?"

"Shit Stick?" Tim asked, sounding at a loss.

"Come again?"

"Emsley? Looks like a sack of wet lettuce?" On Henry's nod, Tim said, "The fellas played a joke on him when we were training together years back. The joke involved putting a stick covered in – well, you can probably guess – in his locker..." The realisation eventually hit Tim, and he stopped babbling. "Shit Stick killed Maureen?"

"Do you know if they ever met?"

"Maureen and Shit...?" Tim seemed confounded by the question. "Well, yeah... they knew each other for years. I trained with him, you know. But they couldn't ever have been...?" Tim couldn't bear to ask, his face recoiling in disgust.

"No, they weren't an item. It was more of a stalker-stalked situation than an affair."

"I don't..." Tim gripped his brow. "I'm supposed to go in there and tell them all about Mary. What should I do?"

Henry shrugged. He didn't know. He'd done his bit, and he was hoping Hargreaves would swoop in with some more insights. But he hadn't heard a peep from her.

Then again, his phone was on silent.

He took it out and saw he'd received several calls from her. He was about to call her back but saw DCI Acton walking down the steps, followed by DS Emsley.

Emsley was wearing his deferential mask again and following Acton as a loyal deputy should.

Tim Villers, who was still recovering from the shock of finding out what had happened to his wife, spotted Emsley and instinctively launched himself at the stairs. Jumping up them, he shoved Acton's large frame to one side, making him fall down half the flight of stairs. Tim then pounced on Emsley, pushing him backwards.

Henry only processed what was going on when Tim started throttling Emsley. "Villers! Get off him," he shouted.

The foyer filled with shouts and gasps. Uniformed officers sprinted up the steps to save Emsley.

"Tell me why you killed her!" Tim shrieked, over and over.

Acton got himself up, dusted off his suit, and then eyeballed Henry. Shaking his head with disdain, he helped two uniforms drag Tim off Emsley.

Once they'd brought Tim into the foyer, Acton rounded on him. "What the bloody hell is wrong with you?"

Tim had spent most his rage but was still worked up. Two bulky officers remained behind him in case he went off again. "He killed Maureen!"

Emsley was on the staircase receiving first aid from a constable. Henry reckoned he enjoyed playing the victim.

Acton shook his head. "What? Emsley killed Maureen? Have you lost the plot?"

"It's true," Henry said, approaching Acton.

"I bloody warned you, didn't I?" the large man said, pointing at Henry. "I said to stay away from this, or I'll come down on you like a sack of shit."

"Emsley did it, not Villers. Tim has an alibi."

"Tim doesn't have an alibi," Acton said, glaring at Tim.

"He does," Henry said, standing his ground.

Acton looked around the disrupted foyer. "Would someone please tell me what is going on? Have I stepped into some kind of–"

"Sir!"

It was Hargreaves. She rushed down the stairs, stepping over Emsley without showing much concern. Holding a folder, she handed it to Acton when she reached him.

He took it suspiciously and opened it. "What is it?"

"The audit trails from the police database," she said, sounding slightly guilty.

Acton glared at her. A detective sergeant had no right to access these records, Henry knew. She must have used a log-in Murphy had given her.

Deciding to worry about that later, Acton flicked through the sheets of paper. "So? What am I looking at?"

"He's been deleting all sorts. Only a few minutes ago, he deleted a huge chunk of that CCTV footage that I found yesterday."

For the first time, Henry could see Acton was growing suspicious of Emsley. The large man flipped through the sheets or paper, reading it intently, then raised his eyes to peer at Emsley.

"I thought he'd go off and delete that CCTV footage," said Henry. "I bet you a tenner it's his car on it. Placing him near Swinfeld Reservoir on the day Maureen died." Henry glanced over at Emsley.

Acton looked up from the papers in his hand. "Have you asked IT to get that footage back?" he asked Hargreaves.

She nodded. "Already done, sir."

Acton leafed through the sheets of paper. "What else is there?"

"He's been deleting loads, sir. Not just stuff relating to the Villers case but other cases, too. Mostly stalking complaints."

Acton eyeballed Henry again, taking long deep breaths through his nostrils, making him look like a bull about to charge. "Is this your doing?"

"Mine?" Henry asked.

"I had this case nicely tied up…" He shook his head, as if he knew he was getting out of line. "Right."

Swearing under his breath, Acton pointed at Tim Villers. "Officers, get him in a cell. If all this stuff with Emsley turns out to be true, I might be able to overlook the fact you've kicked the shit out of one of my detectives – but until then, you're under arrest for assaulting a police officer."

Tim went to defend himself, but Henry shook his head. Letting himself be led away, Tim was taken into the holding cells.

Acton turned to the staircase. "DS Emsley. Some very serious accusations have been made against you, and they need to be fully investigated. I'd appreciate it if you could join me in interview room one."

The constable helped Emsley down the steps. He leaned heavily on the banister, and a lapel on his green tweed jacket was ripped. He held a tissue over his busted lip. "Sir, you can't possibly think–"

"Do as the man says, you bloody snake!" Henry said, losing his patience.

Emsley glared at Henry and slowly reached the bottom step. He walked unsteadily across the foyer towards him. And when he was only a few paces away, he lunged at him.

Henry tried batting him away, but Emsley quickly overwhelmed him and wrapped his hands around his neck.

Both men fell backwards onto the floor tiles, with Emsley on top.

The foyer filled with more screams while Henry stared up at Emsley's eyes, which had darkened so much they were almost black.

His fingers gripped Henry's neck, his thumbs pressing into Henry's Adam's apple so he couldn't make a noise or suck in a breath.

Everyone seemed too stunned to help.

Apart from Hargreaves, who was unmoved by the drama as she strolled over, pinched an ASP baton off a nearby uniformed officer, and struck Emsley's forearm.

Henry heard the bone crack, and Emsley screeched out in pain, releasing Henry so he could nurse his wound.

"Get him out of here," Acton said, coming to his senses.

Two uniforms dragged Emsley towards the holding cells where Tim had just been taken.

"Keep them in different cells," Acton ordered as an afterthought. "I can't have them killing each other."

Hargreaves helped Henry up, who rubbed his throat.

"Alright?" she asked.

He tried to talk but it was too painful, so he just nodded.

More uniforms belatedly rushed into the foyer, but the commotion was over and things were returning to normal.

Acton stepped towards Henry, glaring at him. "So, is this what normally happens when you get involved in cases?"

Henry coughed a response and then shrugged.

Hargreaves answered for him. "Aye. It's usually worse, to be fair. At least there's been no shooting this time." She then added, "Plus, after he's caused all this chaos, the old sod expects the bloody credit."

Henry glowered at her.

Acton shook his head as he stared at the holding-cell door. "Why the bloody hell did Emsley do it?"

Henry pointed at Acton's large chest and mumbled something.

"What was that?" Acton asked.

Hargreaves, like an interpreter, spoke for Henry again. "I think he says that's your job to find out."

Acton scrunched up his face – not liking the answer. He regarded Henry with an odd mixture of respect and rivalry. "Alright, give me an hour with Emsley, and I'll find out. Mind you, that's probably how long I'll have with him before the IOPC turn up."

"Good luck," Henry muttered. "When you find out why he did it, let me know."

Chapter Thirty-Five

Two days later, Henry was sitting in Jean's living room. The sun streamed in through the lace curtains and lit up the carpet, where her grey cat was sprawled on its back.

Henry's throat was barely any better. He'd seen a doctor, who told him to keep ice on it and let it heal. Henry was relieved Hargreaves had kept her cool about her and had broken Emsley's arm when she had. Otherwise, Henry was worried his neck would've been permanently damaged – or worse.

Thinking of Emsley, Henry was pleased the snake had quickly given into Acton's questioning.

It appeared Emsley's deference to authority was real, as he quickly confessed to stalking Maureen Villers and other women while under interrogation.

He had to be pushed further on whether he'd killed her, and only admitted it once Hargreaves and IT support found the footage Emsley had tried to consign to history.

It showed a brown Vauxhall estate car driving near Swinfeld Reservoir on 10 April. A car registered to Emsley's address.

Then more information came to light when they'd searched Emsley's home. Oddly, for a man who was so keen on destroying evidence, they'd uncovered his old passport in a drawer. It'd been stamped by Canadian Immigration a few weeks after Maureen had been murdered, and the dates corresponded with the payments made on her credit card.

Emsley's three-day trip had taken place during the original investigation, and Henry couldn't remember him being off work. But the time sheets from the original investigation showed he'd missed four days' work. It just went to show how much Emsley disappeared into the background – or how little attention Henry paid his lower-ranking officers.

Emsley had gone to considerable effort and expense to cover up his tracks. But why had he done it? What had forced him to murder Maureen Villers?

Acton had prised that out of Emsley through questioning, and Henry wished he'd been in the interview room to witness the confession. He'd had to settle for a second-hand recounting of it from Acton, who'd called him later that day.

Emsley had met Maureen Villers in a pub in 1997, long before she'd started seeing Tim Villers. He'd become infatuated with her, and this infatuation lasted even after she met Tim and got engaged. Emsley lost touch with her when he moved to Wakefield to work in CID. Then, in 2007, he was invited to a social event at Otley station and bumped into Maureen and Tim. Tim, whom he'd known from training, was the ringleader of the group that'd bullied him mercilessly.

It was around then that the stalking started, a hobby Emsley had been practicing in the intervening years with various women he'd come across.

By the end of February 2008, after months of being followed and messaged, Maureen became sick of Emsley. She sent him a warning: stop contacting her or she'd tell the police and provide them with all of his messages.

The following morning, she found an envelope taped to her car. Inside was a photo of her being intimate with Arnold Peters. A message was written on the back explaining that if she spoke out against Emsley, copies of the photo would be sent to Shelley Peters and Tim, destroying both Maureen's job and her marriage in one fell swoop.

It was in April, when Maureen was at her wit's end, that she contacted Emsley, asking to meet him.

Emsley guessed she was going to beg him to stop harassing her, and while she was pleading with him to leave her alone, he thought he might take advantage of her weakness. Something he admitted to doing with other women.

He'd intended to admit his undying love for her, to see if pity would get him anywhere, before becoming more forceful and dangerous.

So they arranged to meet at Swinfeld Reservoir, a private place with which Emsley was familiar.

Emsley claimed he'd gone with the intention of expressing his undying love, but Henry suspected that wasn't true, considering he must have prepared to kill her beforehand.

Her death wasn't frantic or emotional, but planned and intentional.

It was Maureen's laugh that had provoked Emsley to kill her; she 'cackled' after he'd been brave enough to share his feelings for her.

Poor thing, Henry thought, shaking his head at Emsley's homicidal idiocy.

After she'd told him she was going to out him to the police and her husband, Emsley struck her around the back of the head.

That was all it took for a police detective to commit murder.

Rejection.

The harsh words of a woman who wanted to be left alone.

What a sorry state of affairs, Henry thought to himself.

"Christ, they'll be here soon," Jean said, flapping into the living room and disturbing the cat. She was COVID-free and had binned all her face masks. Her blonde curly hair had been coiffed, and she was back to wearing make-up.

"The quiches are ready, and I've done two cakes, a lemon sponge and a chocolate one. I don't know what they like. Do you?"

Henry shook his head. He was still saving his voice.

"We'll sit in the backyard. It's still nice out, but they've said rain's due later." She stood in front of the mirror on the wall and flicked blonde curls out of her face. "Hopefully, they'll stop that bloody hosepipe ban now."

"Aye," Henry croaked. "Soon Swinfeld will fill up again."

"That'll take a while," she said. "But aye, it will."

The knock on the door drove Jean into higher levels of stress. "They're here!"

Henry hauled himself off the sofa and stepped over the cat to greet Tim Villers and his two children.

Hargreaves followed behind them. Looking around Jean's living room, she said, "This is nicer than your hovel, Henry."

Henry ignored her and welcomed Paul and Siobhan, who both received hugs from Jean. Siobhan had more colour to her face and had been out of hospital for a day.

As they followed Jean through the kitchen and into the backyard, Henry pulled Tim to one side. "So, how are things?"

Tim watched Jean point out places to Paul and Siobhan around the outside table. "Alright. I still feel stupid about what I did." He scratched his neck above his blue polo shirt. "I shouldn't have attacked Emsley like that. Even if he is a piece of–"

"Acton's dropped the charges, though? He says you were emotionally distressed?"

"Aye," Tim said, still looking disappointed with himself.

Hargreaves stopped stroking the cat and approached them to listen.

"Here, I just want to thank both of you," Tim said, his cheeks reddening. "I really was in a mess. They were gunning for me. Well, Emsley was, primarily. But they were this close to locking me up, while that twat was going to get away with Maureen's murder." Tim nodded his appreciation again. "I can't thank you enough."

"No need to thank us," Henry said, glancing at Hargreaves. "I always thought you were too obvious a suspect."

Hargreaves raised an eyebrow. "That's not what you said earlier. You were sure it was him most of the time."

Henry cleared his throat and didn't answer.

"Anyway, I was the one who worked it out," Hargreaves continued, cockily. "I said it must have been a copper who did it, and you said I was being stupid."

Henry frowned. "That's odd. I can't remember that discussion, and about Mary Jones? I've been keeping my eyes on the news but haven't seen anything about her resigning."

Tim shook his head. "I've not had to say anything about it, so I haven't."

Henry nodded, satisfied that the coronation of Detective Superintendent Murphy had been stalled… for now. "Well, that's good then."

"Are you coming, you lot?" Jean demanded from outside.

"Aye," Tim said, joining his children at the table.

Hargreaves sidled up next to Henry in the kitchen. "Still. Not bad, though; for an old codger. That recording you sent me was what made things click. Who taught you how to do that?"

Henry looked at her. "I'm not that old, you know. I'm only sixty-four."

She chuckled, but then suddenly looked serious. "Solving a fifteen-year-old case and getting Tim out of trouble… that's some good going."

"Well, your appreciation's noted. Though, it serves me right for not solving it in the first place."

"Well, you did have a traitor on the team. So don't be too harsh on yourself." Hargreaves nodded slowly to herself. "Anyway, I can see why they called you that nickname."

"Which one?"

"The Bloodhound. I thought it was stupid at first… but now? You sniffed out the truth eventually, even if you did steal my idea." She was grinning, but for the first time, Henry saw some admiration in her expression.

"Henry!" Jean shouted from outside. "Are you coming?"

"On my way," he said. "Well, Hargreaves. Let's celebrate finding the right man."

"Aye, Ward. Let's."

The End

If you enjoyed this book, please let others know by leaving a quick review on Amazon. Also, if you spot anything untoward in the paperback, get in touch. We strive for the best quality and appreciate reader feedback.

editor@thebookfolks.com

www.thebookfolks.com

Also in this series

MURDER ON A YORKSHIRE MOOR (Book 1)

Ex-detective Henry Ward is settling awkwardly into retirement in a quiet corner of Yorkshire when during a walk on the moor he stumbles upon the body of a young man. Suspecting foul play and somewhat relishing the return to a bit of detective work, he resolves to find out who killed him. But will the local force appreciate him sticking his nose in?

BUTCHER ON THE MOOR (Book 2)

Ex-DCI Henry Ward is woken in the middle of the night when a distressed woman calls him, demanding he arrest her son. After reluctantly heading over to her house, he makes a gruesome discovery before being attacked. With the police stretched, they reluctantly lean on Ward's local knowledge to track down a man with blood on his hands.

MISSING ON ILKLEY MOOR (Book 3)

Retired cop Henry Ward is taking a walk on the Yorkshire moors when he comes across a child's woolly hat. He quickly connects it with the apparent abduction of an eight-year-old girl from a local town. But when the child's mother acts like she doesn't care, he realises something is seriously wrong and takes it upon himself to investigate.

DETECTIVE ON THE MOOR (Book 4)

Henry Ward is considering rejoining the police when he is asked to investigate a lockdown party murder. A well-to-do local woman's son has been accused of the crime and she wants to clear the family's name. But when Henry starts private inquiries, he meets a wall of silence and will need to use all of his skills to get to the truth.

CRIMINAL JUSTICE
by Ian Robinson

An undercover cop starts walking a thin line when he infiltrates a criminal gang. He sees an opportunity to make some money and take down a pretty nasty felon, but his own boss DCI Klara Winter is on to him. Can he get out of a very sticky situation before his identity and intentions are revealed?

FREE with Kindle Unlimited and available in paperback!

THE BOOK FOLKS

Sign up to our mailing list to find out about new releases and special offers!

www.thebookfolks.com

Printed in Great Britain
by Amazon

44008662R00138